An Inconvenient Grand Tour

VICTORIAN GRAND TOUR SERIES
BOOK ONE

LISA H. CATMULL

SALTAIR PRESS

To Dr. Lucinda Bateman
at the Bateman-Horne Institute,
who helps me manage my pain enough to write,
and for anyone in pain of any kind

Let's travel together to the world of yesteryear.

ACKNOWLEDGMENTS

Thank you to my family for their unquestioning support, their love of pancakes, and the many times they ask, "Mom, can we write, too?" My husband is my sounding board and de facto writing partner, with an unerring sense of story.

Thank you to my editors, Michele Paige Holmes, Lorie Humpherys, and Heather Clark, for their insightful and intelligent guidance. I couldn't do this without your skills, wisdom, and eyes as sharp as eagles. Truly.

Thank you to my beta readers and reviewers for spending your time inside this made-up world as well as cheerleading for me and championing my books.

Thanks to Melinda Looman, who first recommended Georgette Heyer's books to me. Look what you started.

Thank you to Sarah Bell, Rob Hall, and Dave Skousen, my first screenwriting partners, and the many LDS independent filmmakers. You helped to shape and hone my storytelling skills.

Thanks to Allison Lane, Nancy Mayer, Karen Pierotti, and Mindy Burbidge Strunk for help with titles, peerage, and precedence.

And a special thank you to the writing conferences that helped a one-time screenwriter figure out how to write novels. Robert McKee, J Scott Savage, Dave Farland, Heather B. Moore, LTUE, Storymakers, WIFYR, the Writing Gals, SMIAH, and the Beau Monde—you've all had a profound impact on my writing, marketing, and launching as a new author. Thank you.

HISTORICAL NOTE

Historical Note

Dear Reader,

I am going to lie to you. It's true. This book is totally made up. Some of the events, artwork, and people are real, but mostly it's all fake. And hopefully, it's fun.

The Taddei Tondo is an amazing piece of art, actually owned by the Royal Academy, and the only Michelangelo owned by the United Kingdom still today.

However.

I lied. Sir George Beaumont donated it years and years before my characters buy it.

Lady Eleanor's father is based both on Sir George Beaumont and a little bit of Joseph Mallord William Turner. Sir George Beaumont donated several important works by the Old Masters to help establish the National Gallery in England. He detested J. M. W. Turner's style of painting, so it's ironic to combine traits of both in one man. But there you have it.

J. M. W. Turner actually owned the painting *Calais Pier* and donated it to the National Gallery. Percy would not have been able to buy it, but I thought he needed to show Eleanor his devotion. So he got it.

Galignani's bookstore and library in Paris was called "that old pirate's den" by Sir Walter Scott in 1826. It's still open today. But it was actually open when Papa and Mama went on their Grand Tour, too. I fudged. They would have seen it before. But let's pretend like they didn't.

At least two completely different paintings depict the St. Bernard Pass between Switzerland and Italy. Our characters encounter both paintings as well as the pass, which is as accurate as I've been able to portray. Only a little cheating. Just because I haven't actually been there. Yet.

And the duet from La Bohème? It's from 1896. Not 1854. But it's so beautiful.

The Royal Italian Opera, known today as Covent Garden, actually burned down in March of 1856. It would have been in ashes in April when our characters attend their performance.

"Still, Still, Still" wasn't published until 1865.

Schubert's 1825 version of "Ave Maria" is meant for a mezzo soprano, but I have a high soprano singing it. That would be Bach's version of "Ave Maria," in truth, but, again, we're going to fudge a little bit here. They're in Vienna. Of course they would sing Schubert's version instead of Bach's, but Eleanor is a high soprano.

My most egregious departure from history is the selection of Charles Stuart as the British ambassador to France. I originally set the story in the Regency era. When I realized that our characters would prefer to ride the train around Europe and moved the book into the Victorian Era, I retained the same man because he would understand Percy better.

Please enjoy the journey. I apologize for any other historical inaccuracies or blatant anachronisms. I love to hear what you know that I don't. And to find out more historical tidbits or meet other readers, follow me on Instagram @lisa_h_catmull and Facebook or sign up for my newsletter on www.lisacatmull.com. Enjoy the ride!

CHARACTER LIST

Lord Thomas Barrington, Earl of Barrington
Lady Anne Blake Barrington, Countess of Barrington
Lord Dunmore, Matthew Barrington (as oldest son, he uses the viscount courtesy title from his father.)
Lady Georgiana Dunmore, wife of Matthew Barrington
Mr. John Barrington, second son of Lord and Lady Barrington
Lady Eleanor Barrington
Lady Adeline Barrington, daughter of Matthew and Georgiana

Mr. Percy Hauxton, second son of the Earl of Shelford
Lady Arabella Shelford, his mother
Lady Octavia, his sister

The Duke of Woodford, Guy Claybury
Lady Jane Woodford, the dowager duchess, his mother

Miss Lucy Maldon
Mr. Arthur Maldon, Lucy's father
Mrs. Ellen Palmer, Lucy's widowed aunt

Miss Rachel Wickford
Mrs. Edith Wickford, Rachel's mother

Lord Walter Chelmsford, the Viscount Chelmsford
Lady Julia Chelmsford, the dowager viscountess
Mr. Peter Chelmsford, second son of Lady Chelmsford
Mr. Arthur Chelmsford, third son of Lady Chelmsford
Mr. Benjamin Chelmsford, fourth son of Lady Chelmsford

Miss Charlotte Harwich
Mrs. Catherine Harwich, Charlotte's mother

Miss Cecelia Duxford
Mr. Albert Duxford

Mr. James Felsted, prestigious orchestra and choir conductor

Colonel Curtis Loughton
Mr. Frederick Kempton

Mrs. Elizabeth Barrett Browning
Mr. Robert Browning
"Pen" Browning, their son

Sims, butler at Barrington Hall
Joseph, footman at Barrington Hall
Mr. Morrow, physician with whom Rachel works

George, groom at Lucy's stables
Finch, butler for Lucy
Jane, Lucy's maid

Sibley, lady's maid to Lady Eleanor
Parker, butler and valet for John in Vienna
Jones, butler for Percy in London

CHAPTER 1

May 1854

I'd been reduced to hiding in my own home. My sister-in-law, Georgiana, slept in the chamber nearest the stairs, where all the sound floated up from below.

I tiptoed down the hallway, past Matthew and Georgiana's adjoining bedrooms. How much longer would the renovation of the Dunmore estate last? Past John's empty bedchamber. It would be strange to have him return home from Cambridge today.

I was used to having Mama and Papa all to myself. Suddenly, Barrington Hall would be filled with family. I should love it.

But I wanted to find somewhere to be alone before facing so many people. Early morning was my best opportunity.

The candle flickered in the dim light as I crept down the winding marble staircase to the main floor of the house. Once I safely reached the entrance hall, I began to hum to myself.

A sleepy footman rested on a settee beneath the Rubens painting, his greying head drooping onto his chin. I nudged his foot gently and he startled awake.

"Could I get some candles in the music room?" I asked.

"Oh, it's you, Lady Eleanor. I thought it was Sims, gonna chop me head off for sleeping."

"No, no, just light me a few lamps or candles, please," I said. "No French Revolution today."

"Back soon." Joseph wandered off groggily.

I began preparing a list of scales and songs. Which pieces should I rehearse for the dinner party? I preferred to sing in private, so I desperately needed to practice a piece until I felt comfortable enough to sing in front of so many other people. Walter, now Lord Chelmsford, was finally out of mourning. Mama must have invited him. We'd missed two Seasons, and opportunities for me to meet eligible men were rare.

What would my friends be least likely to sing? What could I sing that he might like? I hummed a lively tune from *The Magic Flute*. Once I thought of Papageno's duet with Papagena, it was hard to get it out of my head.

"Warm and light now." Joseph returned to his spot by the settee. "I suppose this means you'll be wanting some hot rolls or scones from Cook."

"Thanks. You are my favorite footman. Don't tell the others. Bring a few rolls for yourself." I moved across the entrance hall toward the music room, now warm with the glow of oil lamps and candles in sconces.

I checked the light outside the window. Still pitch dark. I should have at least two hours to practice. *If Georgiana doesn't complain again.* I rubbed my hands to warm my fingers and began to play scales. After scales, I began singing a country air to warm up my voice. Quietly. Nothing that would carry upstairs.

I lost track of time and must have begun to sing louder than I realized. It was probably the Queen of the Night aria that did it. High notes require a great deal of power behind them, which I realized only after I heard shouting.

"Eleanor! Eleanor!" Mama's voice rang through the entrance hall. I put my head down on the keyboard.

Mama marched into the music room. "Eleanor!" she demanded. "Georgiana was sleeping! We discussed this yesterday. And the day before. And last week. You simply cannot practice this early."

"But—"

"Matthew came storming into my chambers again," Mama said. "Georgiana woke up early, so he woke up early, and now I'm awake. And you know how I feel about mornings."

"I am sorry. But she sleeps so late. Why can't they go back to Dunmore?" I said. "How long do renovations take?"

"Can't you take a day off? Practice less?" She picked up my music and began putting it away. "Just until they're gone. You rise so early."

"Who is in charge here—Matthew or Papa?" I said. Matthew always took Georgiana's side of every argument, and Papa had let Matthew make all the decisions since they moved in.

"I am. And I asked you to practice at a civilized hour," Mama said. She ran a hand through her straw-colored hair.

"Seven o'clock is civilized for some people. But the dinner tonight!" I pleaded. "I'm not ready. Every time I try to play, Georgiana gets a headache. It's been months since I could play. Stay and practice with me."

Mama paused. I knew she couldn't resist the chance to sing a duet with me.

"Eleanor Jane, I am serious," she said, but her eyes flitted to the music scattered on top of the piano. She loved *The Marriage of Figaro*.

"Just one?" I could see her softening.

"I expect you ready to leave for the Maldons' after breakfast." Mama sighed. She ran her hands over my chestnut colored hair, so different from her own, and put her hand on my cheek. "Your singing will be fine enough for Mr. Hauxton. I wish we could sing together. I miss that, too."

"My singing needs to be more than fine tonight, if the Chelmsfords are coming." I paused. "The Maldons'?" Mama was trying to bribe me. To distract me. To soften the blow. I loved talking to Lucy and Rachel more than anything in the world, but I knew what would happen if I went. "I always talk so long when we go there. I lose track of time. Can we stay home, just this once?" I begged.

Mama glared at me. "No. You know how sensitive they are about slights. I can't even serve a mushroom gravy when they eat with us, or they think I'm calling them cits. Ridiculous. Mushrooms are the finest addition to a gravy there is."

Lucy and I had become friends when she had money and Papa was a humble vicar, so I had never thought of her as an upstart or a mere "citizen" instead of a member of the gentry. Others in our neighborhood viewed her father with disdain for purchasing so much land and trying to establish himself as a gentleman.

Joseph entered the room with a tray. A rush of warm bread smell filled the room. A small dish of jam rested next to clotted cream. "Breakfast for you, Lady Eleanor," he said.

"And you've been bothering Cook again?" Mama asked. She paused. "What is that smell?"

"Strawberry jam, Lady Barrington. First of the summer," Joseph said.

"No, no. Is there a hint of lemon? Is it in the scones or in the jam?" she asked.

"I wouldn't know," Joseph replied with a straight face.

I could tell he was trying not to laugh. We both knew what was coming next. Mama could never stay mad for long, if we could distract her.

"I must ask Cook. Enjoy the rolls and scones. Yes, Joseph, you may have my portion," Mama said as she lifted the cloth and sniffed at the scones.

"Me?" Joseph put on an air of confusion. "That wouldn't be proper."

Mama replaced the cloth. "Pish. I know that you eat with Lady Eleanor in the mornings. I'll be in the kitchen." Mama hurried out of the room, muttering to herself. "Lemon. When did the strawberries ripen?"

Joseph set down the tray and broke a scone in two. He slathered fresh strawberry jam, still slightly runny, on the scone and put a dollop of cream on it. He offered me the first half.

I took a bite. The flaky scone melted in my mouth as I tasted the sweet and tangy jam.

"Help me. I need to practice, but the staircase takes this sound right up to Georgiana's bedroom," I said.

Joseph paused as he buttered a roll.

"There is another piano in your home. The maids complain about dusting somethin' that never gets any use," Joseph said.

"Where?" I picked up a knife and began to twirl it. If I could convince Mama to leave Lucy's home a little earlier than usual, perhaps I could have an hour to practice after all.

"The ballroom. Sits there collectin' dust." Joseph gathered up the tray and cloths. "If you was to be so far away when your brother and his friend arrived, I might not be able to find you."

I dropped the knife. Of course. How had I forgotten? Far away. I could close the doors, and no one would hear. If only Mama could be distracted.

"Perfect! But Mama will not cease until I am found," I said. "We have heard so much about Mr. Hauxton, and she is anxious to meet him before he leaves for Europe with John. She only has one week to interrogate him, and she will expect me to assist her. I need a diversion."

"It's your father's day to practice fencing. Still bothers him that he can't win against a man so much older than him." Joseph grinned.

"So, if you were to almost let him win today?" I asked. "Nearly, but not quite?"

"That might take a bit of time," Joseph said, "and I wouldn't be around to know where you might be hiding." He grinned.

I loved his crooked smile. "And Mama would be far more embarrassed that Papa was missing when our guest arrives. Joseph, you are a genius. Please tell Cook to give you as many scones as you wish."

"She already does," Joseph said, and winked as he left the room.

CHAPTER 2

I pulled the needle through the linen fabric. Lucy and Rachel pulled their needles through as well. I pushed my needle through again.

Lucy broke the silence. "Is he coming?" She glanced over toward her aunt, who ran the household for her father. Mama and Rachel's mother were still engrossed in conversation with Aunt Ellen, who chattered freely. Lucy set down her embroidery.

"Who?" I asked, although I was certain I knew who she meant.

Lucy pushed the linen out of Rachel's hand. "Walter! Who else?" She leaned forward. "What do you know?"

"John is bringing his friend, Mr. Percy Hauxton, but I believe Peter Chelmsford is traveling with them, too."

Rachel giggled.

Lucy shot her a look. "They're all just second sons. What about Walter? Is their mother's mourning over?" Lucy asked.

I glanced over. Mama wasn't paying attention to us, so I set my embroidery down and leaned forward. "I mentioned it this morning and she did not contradict me. That's as good as a confirmation from Mama. Cook's planning for fifteen, which leaves room for three extra guests."

Lucy bounced her heels. "It's got to be Walter and Peter and their mother. I mean Lord Chelmsford."

"I still feel like I'm talking about his father when I call Walter that," Rachel said.

Lucy patted her skirt. "Oh, I've got the perfect dress for tonight. Papa let me order a few new ones. Do you need to borrow one, Rachel?"

Rachel picked up her embroidery again, looking down at her worn dress. "No, I probably have something the Chelmsfords haven't seen for a while. But thank you, Lucy."

I hated to see Rachel so embarrassed. We all knew Lucy had five times as much money as Rachel's widowed mother. I tried to think of a way to change the topic of conversation. "It's time for True Confessions," I said.

"True Confessions," their voices answered in unison.

"You start, Eleanor," Lucy said.

"Fine," I whispered, "True Confession. I do not like my brother's wife."

Lucy and Rachel groaned.

"We already know that," Lucy complained. "But we like her. Something else."

"I ate breakfast in the music room with a footman today," I whispered. "Before everyone else was awake. True Confession." I left out his age and hoped they would assume he was one of the younger, more handsome ones.

Their eyes widened. "Oooh! That's better," Rachel said.

"My turn!" Lucy said. "I tried riding my horse astride, instead of side saddle."

"Which groom helped you?" Rachel asked hopefully.

"George." Lucy grinned. "And I was very clumsy. He needed to help me a lot. True Confession."

I wondered whether her father had any idea why Lucy spent so much time riding. She genuinely loved the exercise, but she also enjoyed the attention from the stablehands.

"Rachel?" I asked.

Rachel watched the ladies on the other side of the room as she whispered to us. "True Confession. I've been staying late at the doctor's to assist him after my mother's appointments. He lent me another book. My mother thinks it's Sir Walter Scott, but it's anatomy."

We gasped. That drew Mama's attention. She examined us closely from her position nearest to us. The other ladies stopped talking momentarily.

I knew better than to invite scrutiny from Mama. This conversation was not meant to be overheard.

I picked up my embroidery and began sewing again. "Anatomy! Does it have diagrams?" I asked under my breath. Proper ladies did not know about things like this. Naturally, that meant Lucy and I wanted Rachel to teach us everything.

Rachel nodded. "True Confession. Full page drawings. We need to have a 'poetry reading' at my house soon. I can show you all the diagrams."

"Anything else?" Lucy prodded, glancing at her Aunt Ellen.

"We are all dying for the Chelmsfords to re-enter Society!" Rachel said. "If none of you will state the obvious, I will."

"Lord Chelmsford," Lucy sighed.

"No one is as attractive as a Chelmsford man," Rachel said. "That thick, dark hair."

"The broad shoulders," Lucy said.

"The boxer's stance," Rachel continued. "And those strong legs."

"Deep brown eyes and dimpled chins," Lucy added.

Rachel sighed. Lucy sighed. I did not. I supposed they were handsome, but none had ever set my heart racing.

"There are four of them," I said. That was the best I could come up with. "One for each of us, since I will never have a London Season."

Lucy reached across and took my hands. "Poor thing. Neither will I. Even with Papa's wealth, I couldn't get an invitation to an event without you."

Rachel picked at a thread on her dress. "None of us will go to London, so I hope Arthur and Benjamin come home from Eton," Rachel said. "I love to see them riding about together. We must ride horses more often."

Lucy nodded her head and sighed. "Beginning tomorrow. No more walking anywhere. Meet at my stables, so George can help us."

I preferred to stay home and practice piano, but the house would be overrun. Riding with Lucy would be a welcome escape, and perhaps I would see Lord Chelmsford.

"The Chelmsfords are indeed perfection," Rachel said.

I studied Lucy and Rachel. What about my brother John? He didn't look much like a Chelmsford. He was tall, like me, not broad. Blue eyes, not brown. Blond curly hair. I was the only one with dark hair in the family, and none of us had a dimpled chin. Didn't either of them think my brother was perfection?

I had thought they had tender feelings for him at some point as we grew up together, and they hadn't seen him in two years. The Chelmsford brothers had only been in mourning for six months. But neither of my friends seemed to care that they would see John soon.

"Maybe one of Walter's brothers will come to dinner." Rachel twirled her needle and thread. "I hope it's Peter."

"Or better yet, all four of them. Maybe your cook was wrong," Lucy said.

Across the room, the ladies stood. Evidently, they had exhausted their store of gossip. We packed our embroidery baskets. My linen was a mess of unfinished patterns and half-completed rows of stitches. Much like my life felt right now. Scattered and frustrated. But I had a plan laid out and I just needed time to see it through.

I peered out the window of the coach at the manicured hedges framing the drive leading away from Lucy's home. I couldn't help but compare it with Barrington Hall. What would Lord Chelmsford see when he came to dinner tonight? As an earl, Papa managed a larger estate than anyone in the area. Would he be impressed? Did it matter to him? He had grown up next to us and must be accustomed to it.

The carriage wound its way down the lane and along the path toward home. I knotted my hands together in the strings of my reticule.

Would I have to compete with Lucy and Rachel for Lord Chelmsford's attention? I loved them dearly. We'd been through so much together: the death of Lucy's mother, Rachel's father, and my uncle. Lucy's rise from middle-class to wealth. Rachel's gradual descent from wealth to poverty. My father's ascendancy from a vicar to the earldom when his brother died unexpectedly. His retreat from London when a satirical cartoon mocking him was published. Through it all, Lucy and Rachel and I supported each other. We felt as close as sisters. How could I compete with them?

And yet, this was my only chance to marry. Despite what they said, they had other options. They could go to London or attend house parties. I could not.

But Lucy and Rachel were younger and more beautiful. And I could never compete with them if they truly loved Walter. Now Lord Chelmsford. I realized I was crushing my new reticule. I unclenched my grasp and began playing with the tassel at the end instead.

No, he would have eyes only for me. He had to. They could marry the younger brothers.

Lord Chelmsford is only a viscount, I thought. *Is that enough?*

It has to be. He's the only unmarried peer in the neighborhood. If someone challenged Papa's fitness to hold the title and it came before the House of Lords—

I shoved the thought away. Perhaps tonight after dinner we would sit alone on a small sofa by a fireplace. Far away from the others. He would realize how much he had missed me. How he had yearned for me all these months. How he could not live without me.

My mother's voice interrupted pleasant daydreams of Lord Chelmsford proclaiming his undying love. "What were the True Confessions today?" Mama smiled at me. She loved to know every detail about every family, whether they lived on our lands or not. She'd never truly stopped being a vicar's wife.

I shook my head. "You know I never tell."

"You always do. I'll tell if you tell. There's some good news this week." She raised her eyebrows at me enticingly.

"It's probably the same as mine," I said.

My mother clapped her hands. She loved this game. "I'll go first. Wink if I'm right." She thought for a moment. "Lucy is flirting with that groom again," Mama said.

I winked. She clapped her hands again.

"Her aunt has no idea. Let's see. Rachel is stealing anatomy books again," she guessed.

I winked. Where did she get her information? It was impossible to keep secrets from her, although I tried.

Mama clapped a third time. "I doubt her mother is half as sick as she acts. She only goes to Dr. Morrow so Rachel can borrow those books." Mama stared at me, unusually serious. "And your secret? I suppose it was Chelmsford?"

"Mama!" I squirmed in the carriage seat. "No. It was not."

She continued to study me, almost sadly. "I've never liked him. For you. He's nice enough, I suppose, for Lucy or Rachel. But not you, sweetheart. I'm sorry your father hasn't wanted to go to London for a Season. We can do better."

We. That was ominous. Mama was going to get involved in the matchmaking.

I gazed out the windows of the carriage at wandering sheep grazing on rolling green hillsides. *Have we arrived yet?* I wanted to ask. No. Still plenty of time for this tortuous conversation to continue. And Mama was not someone to be swayed or distracted.

But I could try to let her see that I could make the decisions on my own.

"Why? Why not me? Because I'm seventeen? Or because his rank is lower than Papa's?" I asked her.

She looked surprised. "None of that. He's just so—" Mama paused. "—bland." She stared out of the window.

I wasn't sure how to respond to her pronouncement.

"Like toast without butter. You need saffron-spiced sweet bread. Not dry toast," Mama said.

I had never compared Lord Chelmsford to breakfast buns, but I definitely preferred the flavored sweet breads. What was she saying? Of course there were other men out there, but how was I ever to meet them? Even if London was only a few hours ride away, it might be on the Continent if Papa forbade us from going.

"Lord Chelmsford is fine." I fiddled with the strings on my reticule again. The truth was, I did not know much about him. I just desperately needed him to protect my family, and I did not need a love match. As the only daughter in the family, I was the only one who could marry and ensure protection for Papa if anyone questioned his sanity. My brothers would be considered tainted by birth and at risk of losing their inheritance as well.

"Fine. Placid landscapes are fine. But I want more than *fine* for you, sweetheart. I want a Michelangelo." She patted my arm.

Mama and her analogies.

"First, he's a breakfast bun, now he's a painting? I can't keep up with you," I said.

She smiled at me.

"It doesn't matter, unless he decides he wants to court me." I picked at a loose thread on my dress.

Mama examined me closely. "And the new dresses you insisted we order last month? The extra music practice you've been doing? Does any of that have to do with the Chelmsford brothers reentering Society as eligible bachelors?"

I blushed.

"Keep your eyes open for other flavors," she said gently.

"Mama, you don't taste with your eyes," I said.

"You do when it comes to men," Mama said. "Promise me you'll wait until your father is ready for you to have a Season. You'll see what I mean."

"But he's stayed home for the last two years. We're missing another Season right now. What if he never wants to go back to London? Lord Chelmsford might be my only—"

She sat upright. "Listen to me, Eleanor. You will not marry stale bread simply because he is the only painting for sale in our neighborhood."

"I hate it when you mix metaphors," I muttered.

Mama patted my knee. "No daughter of mine will ever be so desperate that she has to settle for boredom, darling. You would not be content."

I pretended not to hear her, but I deliberated the whole way back to our estate. What flavor was Lord Chelmsford? Was he unbuttered toast? No feelings came to mind, no images or emotions. It had been months since I'd really seen him or spoken with him. Before that, our interactions were fleeting. Fun. Not flavorful.

Was he boring? Had I ever felt excitement? True, I did not relate to Rachel or Lucy when they sighed over the Chelmsfords. I didn't feel any special attraction, though we had always been comfortable and friendly. *But what if he's my only choice?*

CHAPTER 3

I pulled open the doors to the ballroom and made my way across to the piano. The late afternoon sun flooded through the ballroom's floor-length windows, making it difficult to see. Beams of light streamed over my shoulders as I settled onto the bench to play.

I only had an hour at most. *What if Sims finds me?* I worried. The butler was highly loyal to Mama, after all, not to me. I could meet John's friend later. As late as possible. Mr. Hauxton invited John to his father's estate for every holiday, and I never saw John anymore because of him. Now they were leaving together for a Grand Tour, which meant they'd travel together for at least two years. Maybe more.

It was a little hard to see the music with the glare on the paper, but I set out my favorite Beethoven sonata and took a deep breath. Just a few scales to warm up first. I squinted and tried to adjust the sheets.

I straightened and took a deep breath.

A shadow fell over the piano. "Ah, excellent. Have you finished?"

A pair of startling green eyes met mine. How had he crossed the ballroom so quietly? Had I been that focused? I stared at the stranger. Curly blond hair fell almost down to his collar points. A thick beard and mustache framed a handsome face.

It was John's friend. Who else could it be? John said he was an intellectual. I had expected a tall, thin man. With dark, tidy, straight hair. Very, very unattractive. With warts and bad breath. Nothing like this.

This man was stocky, almost my same height. Muscular. Unexpectedly handsome.

How dare John bring home a friend like this.

"Your footman sent me here. Said Lady Dunmore is resting and can't be disturbed," the stranger continued while I studied his face. "I won't have another chance to play for two years, so I couldn't pass this up."

Joseph! I thought. Why had he done this to me? At least he had not told Mama where I was. But now I would have no chance to prepare a Beethoven sonata or an Irish country air for the performance this evening. How would I impress Lord Chelmsford?

"Of course," I said. I was the daughter of the lady of the house. He was a guest. It was my duty to give way. But I was seething inside.

He came around the piano and said, "Allow me," then pulled the bench out from beneath me. Like a gentleman.

Which irritated me even more. I retreated as quickly as I could.

My foot caught on one leg of the piano bench and sent me stumbling backward. I heard a loud pop as I landed on the floor. My skirt crumpled beneath me. Pain seared through my ankle. "Is it broken? I think it's broken."

I leaned back on my wrists to steady myself and took a deep breath then let it out.

"I am sorry to meet under such circumstances," the man said. "I'm going to be insufferably rude and introduce myself. Mr. Percy Hauxton." The man bowed ridiculously low. "At your service. And you are Lady Eleanor?"

"Yes." I swallowed. It hurt almost too much to talk. My eyes watered because of the pain, and I tried to discretely wipe a tear.

Mr. Hauxton flopped on the floor and began to push my skirt up enough to see my ankle and part of my leg. He examined it closely.

"Really," I said. I'd never let a man see my ankles, let alone have one stare at them in such detail.

He blinked and glanced away as he slid my gown lower to conceal my ankle. He put his hands on it instead and began to feel the bones. "I am sorry you fell," he said. "Does this hurt?"

His touch burned through my stockings. "Everything hurts," I said.

"It doesn't feel broken," Mr. Hauxton said. "I've had my share of injuries and seen others. I feel certain it's merely a sprain, although it will hurt just as much."

"Merely?" I tried to sit up. I couldn't put any weight on my right ankle.

"Your slippers sustained the worst of the damage," he said with sparkling eyes. "I blame myself for their demise. My sister would be outraged or in tears over such an event. Most likely both."

It was hard to resist his humor, even when I was in pain. I could see a small rip on my slipper. "But I cannot stand. Surely, that is worse."

Mr. Hauxton knelt beside me. He hovered mere inches away. I could almost feel his breath on my face. I inhaled sharply.

He turned toward me, then froze, our faces nearly touching.

Mr. Hauxton backed away. "I do apologize. May I help you back to the bench?" He put an arm around my shoulders, offered me his other arm, and helped me rise to my feet.

I hopped to the bench slowly and collapsed onto it, exhausted.

"Stay there," he said, and he pushed the bench effortlessly toward the piano. "Are you settled?"

"What are you doing?" I asked.

"Well, I would still like to practice," he said. Mr. Hauxton settled himself beside me on the piano bench and smiled. "And so do you, I wager. If you'll move over a little."

My anger returned. I gave up my practice time for him. He

injured me, and now I would look ridiculous tonight. And he wouldn't even help me out of the ballroom? See me to a footman? He expected me to wait while he finished practicing?

But again, I was the daughter of the lady of the house. Even if my guest was rude, I could not be. I was too well trained. "Of course," I said, and I slid over as well as I could.

We barely fit together on the piano bench. Mr. Hauxton clearly trained in boxing and fencing. His sturdy leg muscles were a testament to that. Maybe he could beat Joseph in a fencing match.

"Can you reach the left pedals?" he asked.

"What?" My mind had wandered.

"If I play the right two pedals, can you play the other two?" Mr. Hauxton asked. "Let's experiment. Is this a French grand piano?"

"You realize I cannot use my right foot," I said. It throbbed with pain.

"Ah yes, I should have put you on my other side." Mr. Hauxton put his hands on my waist, slid me across the piano bench, and moved to the left side of the bench. "Better? Now I can reach the bass clef."

I didn't know what to think of the man. Audacious, certainly.

He began flipping through my sheet music. "Excellent taste. Can you play this?" He pulled out the sonata by Beethoven.

"You want me to play the right hand?"

"Yes, and I'll play the left. You know the piece already?"

"I have it memorized," I said.

"So do I," he said, and he tossed the sheet music back on top of the piano. "You start."

"You're serious," I said.

"Completely."

"But you wanted to practice alone," I said. "You won't have another chance for two years at least."

"I never said it had to be alone," Mr. Hauxton said. "You hadn't finished practicing, had you? We shall practice together. How fast do you like this piece?"

It was thoughtful for him to want to help me practice. But this was not the way I would have chosen to do so. I liked to practice alone. However, I could see that he was not going to be dissuaded. At least he didn't want me to sing with him. "You can work the pedal. It only needs one. I'll follow your lead."

"I await your cue," Mr. Hauxton said.

We began playing. We stopped and started, then stopped and started again. We sounded reasonably well, all things considered.

It was hard to stay angry while playing such peaceful music. It also required all my concentration to keep playing at the same pace as Mr. Hauxton and remember the notes.

I could feel the anger slipping away as I fell into the melody.

"Four hands?" he asked when we paused.

"Pardon?"

Mr. Hauxton wiggled his fingers. "You play two, and I play two. Four hands on the piano?"

I tried not to smile. "Absurd."

"Delightful," he said and raised an eyebrow.

I could not resist his absurd theatrics. I sighed dramatically. "Very well. Let's try."

We played the piece together. I transposed the left hand and simply played the entire piece higher on the keyboard. Mr. Hauxton played lower. Sometimes we had to cross our hands over each other. Our bodies pressed close together as we played, but it felt natural and easy. Mr. Hauxton was not at all self-aware or embarrassed, so neither was I. It all felt a little ridiculous or comical. But the music was enchanting.

When we finished, I couldn't help smiling.

"You see," he said, "delightful. Perhaps something simpler?"

Mr. Hauxton played a trill and then a triumphant march. He cleared his throat and began to sing, "Here's a health to the Queen and a lasting peace—"

I began laughing so hard that I forgot my ankle ached. "How did we go from Beethoven to *Down Among the Dead Men*?"

"So, you know your drinking songs?" he asked in between

verses. He boomed the song as loudly as he could. His rich, bass voice carried through the ballroom and straight into my heart.

"I have two older brothers," I said. "They sang them as lullabies."

Mr. Hauxton laughed so hard he couldn't finish the last verse. He simply trilled a few notes and pounded a magnificent ending.

"One last piece," Mr. Hauxton said, "before we change for dinner. I can't leave for the Continent without playing this one. May I play for one moment alone?"

He scooted closer to the middle of the piano. I had no choice. I could either sit with his thigh against my leg or fall off the bench. I had never met anyone who could act with such total unawareness of his impropriety.

"I need to play both hands," he said, by way of apology, I supposed.

We'd spent an hour together, and I was beginning to realize that Mr. Hauxton was unafraid of anyone's opinion. He would simply act as he chose, without concern for society's rules or expectations, and I reluctantly admired that. I could never live that way myself, but it was refreshing to meet someone so open and free and daring.

The music swirled around me, and I closed my eyes. It began quietly. A rich, calm melody, like water trickling over rocks. Angry at times, then peaceful again. It drew me in, building toward something, then never seeming to resolve any of the chords. This part of the song felt unfinished. I longed to add my own countermelody.

I opened my eyes to watch him play, blond curls shining in the late afternoon sunlight.

Mr. Hauxton attacked the piano. I had never seen anyone else play like that, with such energy and passion. With his whole soul. He leaned over the keyboard, ranging from the top of the treble clef to the lowest note at the bottom. I moved back to allow him room. He was completely lost to everything around him and almost unaware that I sat beside him.

The music rolled over me, soothing, relaxing again. It pulled at me in surprising ways, inviting me to feel things I did not want to feel. Not toward Mr. Hauxton.

I wanted to feel those things with Lord Chelmsford.

But my soul soared on the wings of his song. I closed my eyes again. Everything disappeared except sensation and sound building to a final triumphant ending which faded into a gentle echo.

I opened my eyes. The melody played over and over in my head. I felt refreshed and renewed. Even my foot felt a little better.

The last notes lingered in the ballroom air.

"Thank you," I said. It was hard to believe that this was the man who had taken my brother away from me for the last two years. And he had taken my practice time and twisted my ankle.

I had to remind myself of these things, because I was dangerously close to forgetting all about Lord Chelmsford and my plans.

"May I help you to a footman?" Mr. Hauxton asked.

I didn't trust myself to walk so close to him. All the way across the ballroom. If I were completely honest with myself, I had enjoyed sitting next to him a little too much.

"I think I'm recovered," I lied. I gripped the edge of the piano and put my weight on my left foot. I tested my right foot. "Ow!" I bit my lip in pain.

Mr. Hauxton glanced down at my lips and cleared his throat. He fiddled with his cuff links. "I hope your foot heals quickly. But my injuries usually require a week or two of rest before I can fully walk again."

I tried to take a small step and nearly fell again. There was nothing to hold. Just the vast, empty space of the ballroom in front of me.

"I can see you're as stubborn as your brother," he said. "But Barrington will tell you that I like to get my way." He put his arm around my waist.

I drew in a breath. His touch felt warm in the drafty ballroom.

Mr. Hauxton took my arm and put it around him. "Lean on my

shoulder. Otherwise, it will take the remainder of the afternoon to cross the ballroom." He smiled. "And I am hungry for dinner."

I had to admit to myself that my ankle hurt less now. Resting it for an hour had helped and even made it possible to walk, when I would not have been able to do so earlier. It still ached, but I could at least put a little weight on it. I was almost glad I had spent this time with Mr. Hauxton.

He held me firmly and I leaned into him each time I had to take a step. My head nearly lay on his shoulder. I wanted to blush. I had not worn gloves because I was practicing piano. Neither had he. I could feel the heat of his hand through the fabric of my day dress.

I gripped Mr. Hauxton's shoulder to steady myself and my hand slipped to his upper arm. I felt his muscle flex.

He didn't seem to mind. In fact, he grinned at me. Perhaps he had flexed his muscle intentionally. I would not be surprised.

This man was dangerous. He was strong. And gentle. And thoughtful. And kind. And—forward. I wanted to be angry with him, but it was difficult. I had never felt attracted to any of the Chelmsford brothers, in all the years I had known the four of them, like I had in the one hour I had spent with Mr. Hauxton.

Good thing he's leaving tomorrow, I told myself. *Just one day, then he's gone.*

CHAPTER 4

Mr. Hauxton's lilting melody played in my head the rest of the afternoon. I found myself humming it as Sibley brushed out my thick hair.

I had selected one of my new dresses, a light pink silk-satin dress printed with intricate designs. Brown scrollwork covered cream sleeves. Curling tendrils of light green ribbons ran throughout the dress. Ribbons of tiny rosettes decorated the shoulders and neckline. The pleated top formed a V-shape, drawing attention to my waist. The full skirt flared out over my hips. Thick rows of fabric decorated the bell-shaped sleeves. The stiff whalebone strips in the top of my dress forced me into perfect posture.

I debated. Which shawl? Lace or cashmere? The cashmere was softer and more comfortable to wear; the lace shawl was more elegant but scratched my neck.

Definitely the lace.

I made sure Sibley started my hairstyle earlier than usual to give us time to fight my unruly curls. My hair never wanted to part in the middle or lie flat. It took a lot of work to form a smooth row of uniform curls around my face.

Lord Chelmsford couldn't help but notice me. Especially with my limp. I brushed a hand over the curls as I studied myself in the mirror. What would Lucy and Rachel be wearing? I felt guilty even having the thought.

I approached the stairs with fluttery feelings of anticipation in my stomach. I was ready for Walter to fall in love with me. Lord Chelmsford. It was still hard to think of him with his father's title sometimes.

I sang the opening notes of Mr. Hauxton's tune softly. It seemed to fit my mood. But I meant to take each stair slowly. I tested my weight before I tried the first step.

I heard someone in the corridor behind me.

"You look like a meadow in springtime."

I turned around.

Mr. Hauxton had changed from his informal coat into a brown cut-away jacket with a tighter fit. It showed off his athletic build to advantage. The bow tie was off-center, and his cream satin vest already had creases. *His valet must have fits.*

He grinned at me. He waved his hand at my ensemble. "A field of wildflowers. The first blush of spring."

I went down the first step and tried to suppress a smile. I could see that he appreciated the last two hours of effort. But what was the point of being beautiful if it attracted the wrong man's attention?

"You are ridiculous," I said. Without thinking, I began humming again, this time varying the melody.

Mr. Hauxton said, "You had it right the first time." He followed behind me.

Insufferable arrogance, to think I didn't know the notes. "That you are ridiculous?"

He laughed loudly.

I lifted my chin. "I wanted to vary the tune," I said.

When I reached the bottom of the stairs, he was right beside me. "As I said before, this will go faster if you will allow me to assist you." Mr. Hauxton held out his arm.

I rested my hand lightly on it, and we began moving at a slow pace. My ankle still hurt when I tried to put any weight on it, although I tried not to limp.

"Crystalline dew on a rose petal."

"You are absurd," I said to him, narrowing my eyes.

Mr. Hauxton smiled widely at me. "Or perhaps the frost in winter," he said. "I feel a distinct chill just now."

My reserve crumbled and I laughed softly despite myself. Even if he only said these things because he liked to get a reaction from me.

"A tinkling laugh like droplets of rain," he said.

Still smiling, I turned to him. "Are you trying to provoke me? It will not work."

"A shimmering light. Can you lead me to the drawing room, O Evening Star?"

I huffed and pointed to the left. "We turn here."

"I simply find you so inspiring this evening." His mouth quirked in a half-smile.

"And I simply do not believe you to be sincere." I began humming again.

"Are you always this honest?" Mr. Hauxton asked me.

"No," I said. "But you are leaving tomorrow, and I will probably never see you again."

"You wound me," Mr. Hauxton put a hand over his heart and sighed dramatically.

He stared at the paintings around him, completely ignoring me, as we walked through the picture gallery. He continued to hum the tune exactly as he had played it. Like a governess trying to correct me. I stubbornly hummed a countermelody in perfect harmony to complement him. I could see him fighting a grin.

Joseph opened the drawing room doors for us. He nodded at Mr. Hauxton, then grinned and winked at me. Matchmaker. How dare he send Mr. Hauxton over to practice when I needed the ball-room? I would set Joseph to rights tomorrow morning. No more scones for a week.

Georgiana and Matthew talked together on a comfortable sofa

in the middle of the room, heads nearly touching, deep in conversation. Although they had been married for nearly two years, they still seemed to prefer each other's company to anyone else's. Mama and Papa chatted with Rachel and her mother, Mrs. Wickford, near the entrance to the drawing room.

I felt relief when I saw how simple Rachel's gown was. Instantly, shame washed over me. Still, I wanted to shine tonight, and it helped if Rachel's dress was a plain blue silk with no decoration and only a few tassels along the sleeves and shoulder.

But what was Papa wearing?

"Oh no. Not tonight," I whispered.

Mr. Hauxton followed my gaze across to Papa. His plain, loose-fitting jacket hung open over a light-colored vest and light pants. A single button at the top held the jacket together.

"He looks excellent, like any artist or intellectual in London," Mr. Hauxton said. "Perhaps a bit casual."

He looks completely eccentric, I wanted to say. No one should appear at a formal dinner looking like they came straight from the studio.

"Is it at least clean? No paint on it?" I whispered as we entered the drawing room, waiting to be called to dinner.

"Of course. But I will not be distracted from our discussion," he said.

"What discussion?" I wanted to sigh with relief. Mr. Hauxton, at least, had not suspected anything amiss with Papa. Would Lord Chelmsford be taken aback by Papa's appearance when he arrived?

"You think the piece needs improvement? More complexity?" He moved an arm behind his back and adopted a rigid stance, like Napoleon.

I couldn't tell if he felt amused or offended. "Yes, the second movement could use gentling. A counter melody. It feels unfinished. Why? Do you know the composer?" Without thinking, I stepped closer to him. The room was filled with the hum of conversation, and I did not want to shout or be overheard.

Mr. Hauxton stepped closer in response. "You could say that."

My heart beat wildly in my chest. But really, I had to stand this close to hear him. Before I could ask whether he had improvised the melody, John came into the room.

"Starving! About time for dinner, Hauxton. Stuck with Elle, old man?" John bellowed.

"John, welcome home," I said coolly. I had hardly seen him since he'd left for Cambridge, and this was my greeting? He had not even tried to find me when he arrived. True, I had been hiding in the ballroom, but still. He hadn't tried. Mr. Hauxton had found me, and John had not.

Mama and Papa turned back toward the room. Evidently, they had just finished their conversation with the guests at the same time that Georgiana and Matthew stopped talking.

John glanced back and forth between us. "What were you two talking about?" he barked.

The room fell silent as John asked his question. Rachel was watching me, too. I realized how close together we were standing.

Papa stared at Mr. Hauxton, who quickly backed away from me.

My cheeks grew warm. I did not want to explain that I'd spent an hour this afternoon, unchaperoned, alone with his best friend in the ballroom, when I had not even seen my brother yet. He might think the wrong thing. Mama definitely would. And I didn't know when Lord Chelmsford would arrive or what he would hear. Best to steer clear of this conversation.

"Music," Mr. Hauxton and I said at the same time.

"We were talking about music," I continued, trying to fill the silence. I looked around, hoping for a way out of this awkwardness.

Every eye in the room was on me. Mama glanced between me and Mr. Hauxton. She saw my blush. A calculating gleam shone in her eye. "Are you musical, Mr. Hauxton?" she asked.

I wondered how much time she'd spent in cross-examination with him before he'd escaped to the ballroom this afternoon.

"John tells us so little about his friends in his letters," Papa said pointedly. "Never know a thing about any of you."

Another awkward silence filled the room.

"Practicing duets together," Mr. Hauxton said. "In the ballroom. Lady Eleanor plays excellently."

My heart fell. This was exactly what I'd been trying to avoid. Don't let Mama know. They were only piano duets. She'll begin to scheme. Not tonight.

Mama grew interested. "Were you really?" She arched an eyebrow. "We must hear you perform together." She waved her hand vaguely at Mr. Hauxton and me. "A duet."

Oh no! I thought. *That sounds scandalous. I can't politely refuse, but I don't want to be paired off with him. I haven't rehearsed.*

But at least Lord Chelmsford wasn't here yet.

Just then Sims announced Lucy and her father, Mr. Maldon. My parents swept off to greet them.

John turned to Mr. Hauxton. "Sorry about them." He stared over at Papa. "Unbelievably honest."

"Your mother doesn't seem too bad." Mr. Hauxton sized me up. "A duet. Not too painful."

"No," I said. "Not unless you step on my foot again."

"I'll play the pedals," Mr. Hauxton said, "and you play the right hand. I didn't step on your foot. You fell." His look was one of challenge, but I could detect the teasing underneath.

"You practically pushed me," I said, but I smiled to let him know I didn't mean it. "And tore my best slippers. Cruel." We seemed to understand each other without speaking.

"Let me help you to a sofa or a chair. How is your foot?" Mr. Hauxton moved forward, genuine concern in his eyes. He took my elbow and began to maneuver me away.

"What am I missing?" John glanced between us. "What's wrong with your foot?"

"Nothing. Leave while you can, John," I said, as Mr. Hauxton helped me onto a cushioned chair. "First light tomorrow morning."

"Before Mother gets any more ideas, eh?" John gazed over at Lucy. "But there are a few things I'll miss while we're gone."

"You've missed those 'things' more than you've missed your own sister? She will still be here when you get back," I reassured him. "She's only sixteen. Perhaps you should go greet Lucy while I rest."

As John introduced Mr. Hauxton to Lucy, I rose from my chair and limped as gracefully as I could toward my parents on the opposite side of the room. There was only one carriage left to arrive. Lord Chelmsford's. I intended to be the first person he saw, and I did not want to be standing near Mr. Hauxton when he came.

CHAPTER 5

Papa set great store by punctuality. Lord Chelmsford was fifteen minutes late.

"Lord Chelmsford, the dowager Lady Chelmsford, Mr. Peter Chelmsford," Sims intoned.

I pushed back my shoulders, let out a breath, and curtseyed just deeply enough. These large hoop skirts made it hard to show that I had even dipped my knee. "Lord Chelmsford! We have missed you and your family. We've seen so little of you and talked to you even less. I think we've only seen you at church services."

I scanned his face for any signs of sadness. Or happiness. Or undying love. Anything. He bowed over my hand and smiled at me. I began to glow with happiness, but then Lord Chelmsford turned away. His eyes scanned the room to see who else was here. That was the height of bad manners. I was stunned.

Evidently his rise in social status had given him an elevated opinion of himself. But still. Everyone knew that a gentleman should give his full attention to the woman he was with. I glanced at Mama and she mouthed the words, "Burnt toast."

But he's my only chance, I thought desperately. *Without a Season or any house parties, I won't meet any other men. Maybe he's still mourning.*

My mother moved about the room, pairing people up to walk into dinner. Since Mr. Hauxton was new to the area, and our brother's dear friend from Cambridge, surely Mama would escort him in to dinner. Besides, as the younger son of an earl, he had nearly the same social standing as a viscount. A little less, it was true, but surely he was the guest of honor tonight. And how could she resist the chance to ask him impertinent questions?

I was wrong. A viscount, fresh out of mourning, took precedence.

Mama began pairing people up. "Lord Chelmsford, if you would accompany me into dinner? Lord Barrington will escort your mother, of course." She scanned the room. "Lord and Lady Dunmore will go together. I don't have the heart to separate them."

The guests graciously laughed.

"Mr. Hauxton, will you accompany Lady Eleanor? John, Miss Maldon? And Mr. Chelmsford, Rachel?" She glanced around. "Mr. Maldon, Mrs. Wickford can you go in together?"

I watched Lord Chelmsford offer his arm to Mama. His thick, dark hair was perfectly combed. Not a hair out of place.

Mr. Hauxton extended his elbow to me, his watch chain dangling loosely out of his vest pocket. I refrained from sighing in exasperation and rested my hand lightly on his arm. It wasn't his fault that Mama had paired us. I could at least try to be a pleasant dinner partner.

Lord Chelmsford turned his head back momentarily and I caught his eye. Perhaps Mr. Hauxton's attention would serve a purpose after all, if it drew the notice of Lord Chelmsford.

Except that Mr. Hauxton liked a challenge. He returned Lord Chelmsford's gaze and pulled me a little closer to him than strictly necessary. I tried not to notice how good it felt to have two men vying for my attention. *This must be what it's like to have a Season.*

I didn't see Lord Chelmsford at all during dinner. Between the enormous flower arrangement, the towering candelabra, and the platters of food heaped high, I could only hear Lucy's high-pitched giggle at regular intervals.

To my chagrin, I enjoyed Mr. Hauxton's conversation immensely. I was supposed to be sitting with Lord Chelmsford. Or his brother. Or near his mother. Anything to help further my acquaintance with his family. Instead, Mama had me sit between Mr. Hauxton and John. I asked them about their itinerary for the Grand Tour and heard all about Paris, Switzerland, Italy, Austria, and Germany.

I had missed talking to John so much, and Mr. Hauxton was so amusing, that I almost forgot what I was doing. Almost.

I held to my purpose. Waiting in the drawing room after dinner was excruciating. From my position near the door, I listened for any sign of movement from Papa's billiard room. I could hear loud laughing and an occasional groan. Sounds echoed in the entryway and picture gallery. Just like my piano playing did in the morning.

We had avoided any open arguments during dinner. This would be the real test. Could Papa keep his volatile opinions to himself? Would he even try?

Finally, Joseph opened the doors to the drawing room. Lord Chelmsford led the group with Papa; John and Mr. Hauxton followed. If I could catch his eye, perhaps Lord Chelmsford would join me on a sofa.

John saw me first, however, and bellowed, "Elle! Just the person. Hauxton needs to work on that duet you promised Mother."

Lord Chelmsford strode past me, his lips pursed. He seemed a little sulky, like a spoiled child used to being given the best toys. Mr. Hauxton came over and held out his arm. What could I do? I pasted a smile on my face, rested my hand on his arm, and hobbled over to the piano with him.

I felt a sad mixture of triumph and disappointment. I had drawn attention to myself, but Lord Chelmsford seemed put out. Mama would say he was a sauce that burned easily or milk that curdled or some nonsense. *What would it be like to live with such a man?*

Mr. Hauxton cleared his throat. Right. The duet. I glanced over at him.

"What kind of music do you usually play?" he inquired. "Something like 'The Battle of Prague'?"

I shook my head in disgust. "No. I play Beethoven. You saw my selections this afternoon."

"Ah, but we need a duet," he said.

We began to examine the sheet music. My attention wandered. I kept looking over at Lucy. She was seated between Lord Chelmsford and John and seemed to be dividing her attention equally between the two men. Lord Chelmsford seemed to be giving Lucy his undivided attention and pointedly ignoring me.

Mr. Hauxton kept trying to choose pieces for low voices, but I wanted to sing something higher. Finally, I lost my temper a little bit. "Why do you keep choosing these awful pieces? 'The Beggar's Opera'? Everyone sings that. Why do you insist on these pedantic pieces? Truly." I gazed directly into his eyes, daring him to tell me the truth.

I could see him resist and then give in.

"You're just like your brother," he said.

"No, I'm not," I protested.

"Yes, you are," he said calmly. "You're as blunt and honest as your father."

I stared at him, stunned. *Was it true?* I was so often horrified by Papa. Was I truly as abrupt and confrontational? I folded my hands across my chest.

"But in a good way," he reassured me. He laid a hand on my arms, pulling them down and putting a hand over them. Across the room, I noticed Lord Chelmsford look over at me. Perhaps his attention was not entirely on Lucy.

I moved my arm out from beneath his grasp. This man had no sense of propriety.

I pulled out a few other pieces of music. "So, why can't we sing the duets with the high notes?" I needed to sing a piece that I already knew, or my nerves would get the better of me.

Mr. Hauxton studied them. "Honestly? Most people can't sing those notes."

"I can sing those notes," I said with certainty.

"Hold on," he said. "Let me finish." He put his hand on my arm again and looked me in the eyes.

I took his hand off my arm.

"Most people can't sing those notes and make them sound good. Yes, they can hit the notes, but they strain. It's painful. I'd rather not hear it. And I definitely don't want to sing with it."

I folded my arms again. He was worried that I would embarrass him? I glanced through the sheets of music for the most difficult, most technical duet written for the highest vocal range.

Mr. Hauxton considered me. "Do you speak Italian?"

"French," I replied.

"Is Lord Chelmsford…academic? Or more of a sportsman?" he asked.

I stared at him, taken aback. Was he wondering whether Lord Chelmsford would understand a song written in Italian? "I believe he does not speak Italian, either," I said. "But he certainly knows Latin, and I can sing Italian, of course."

Mr. Hauxton grinned and handed me a piece of music. "'O Soave Fanciulla' from *La Bohème*."

"But that is a love song. I know what the word 'amor' means, even in Italian," I protested. But I did know the song by heart. I could sing it without missing a note.

He raised his eyebrows at me. "But Chelmsford doesn't."

"No. No love songs," I said.

"What else is there? Every duet is about lovers or someone dying," Mr. Hauxton replied.

We had to find a different piece. I already did not want to be seen singing together with him, and I knew the story of the opera. I understood the meaning behind the words. This was far too intimate, even if I had memorized the song.

Mama swooped down on us. "Ready? Oh! One of my favorites!" she said.

Before I could protest, she took the music from my hand.

Mr. Hauxton and I were about to sing one of the most romantic love duets ever written in front of the man I hoped to marry.

CHAPTER 6

Rachel performed first. She said she liked to finish before her nerves got the better of her, although I could never detect a hint of nervousness in her playing. Georgiana played "The Last Rose of Summer," but didn't sing.

Lucy spent an eternity complaining that she did not want to play too many songs. John and Lord Chelmsford took turns encouraging her. I did as well. She played too many songs. I did not mind. The longer she played, the longer I did not have to sing. Finally, I could delay no longer.

Mama handed the music back to me. Like she didn't trust me not to hide it or throw it in the fireplace unless she kept it close.

She knew me too well.

I had never sung this song with anyone else before, just on my own. Here we were, no practice, no rehearsal, singing in front of an entire room. A love song, no less. A very, very romantic love song. I prayed that Lord Chelmsford really didn't know Italian.

I gripped the sheet music. When we walked behind the piano, Mr. Hauxton took my hands and loosened my vise-like grip on the papers.

"You are crushing the music." He nudged my foot. "Breathe,"

he said quietly, "but don't screech." Mr. Hauxton smiled, then adjusted his glasses, which had fallen to one side.

I relaxed. It was just like his teasing in the ballroom this afternoon. He knew when I was nervous and how to dispel my worries. I took a deep breath, let the air out of my lungs and sat down. He adjusted the bench, pulling it farther away from the piano. I panicked. I didn't want to fall again.

"I can't reach," I said.

He slid it back into place, then seated himself beside me. His leg pressed against mine. Our bare hands touched where they rested on the keys. My heart raced.

His legs crowded under the piano, his knees hitting the underside of the keyboard. His feet tried to cover all four pedals.

And we were supposed to sing, too? This was going to be a disaster.

We began. Beginning was always hardest. Once my fingers touched the piano, I got lost in another world. I forgot anyone else was there.

Except that I was performing a duet. And someone else was playing with me. Every time he shifted to reach the far-right pedal, his leg pressed closer to mine. I could hardly concentrate at first.

Something unexpected happened. Singing felt effortless. I played the piece like I always did. We played with four hands on the piano and the effect was richer and fuller than ever before. Mr. Hauxton hardly knew the piece, but managed to keep up and cover any mistakes on the keyboard with the richness of his voice.

Our afternoon practice had actually helped. We knew each other's rhythm. Mr. Hauxton nodded, and I would turn a page. We were entirely in sync.

Usually, if I played or sang with Mama, she sped up or slowed down, and I had to change my pace. Not with Mr. Hauxton.

He had an innate instinct. Perfect timing that matched mine, and our voices blended as well. I'd tried to sing with John, but he had very little patience with me. And he'd been gone for years. I'd sung with Matthew, and we sounded passable. This was different.

I usually had to hold back to keep from overwhelming Mama, but Mr. Hauxton met me. His voice rumbled from deep within his chest, filling the room and pushing back against mine. I sang louder. He matched me, our voices blending into perfect harmony.

I hit every high note, filling my chest, pushing out the air, and holding the notes with ease. There was no strain. I was reaching for something just above me, stars in a twilight sky, and they came. The notes landed perfectly and lightly, like birds fluttering onto a branch.

My mind emptied of all thought except the story. I was aware of nothing except the sensation of singing and being transported to a peasant village in Italy on Christmas Eve. I was drenched in moonlight and could almost see the flickering candlelight. Faces blurred and the music carried me away.

Somehow the song sounded more beautiful than others because it was in Italian. I could feel the emotion behind it, the melodies blending in perfect harmony.

When we ended, the notes hovered in the air. Chills ran up and down my arms. I'd never sung like that in front of anyone. I'd never let them see how well I could truly sing, how powerful and strong my voice had become.

I wondered how Mr. Hauxton felt. Did he sing like that often? Did he play duets with others? Had he felt the same connection I had?

"Well done," he said quietly. Mr. Hauxton drew me up from the piano bench. He held my hand longer than necessary, and I could see something in his deep green eyes. His glasses were askew on his nose again.

I looked around the music room. Everything seemed sharper and more focused. Emotions coursed through me. Joy. Elation. And something I'd never felt before when I sang. Warmth. Peace. Understanding. Accord. I smiled at him, my eyes wide in wonder at what I had just experienced. He squeezed my hand.

Lord Chelmsford had noticed me, too. He was studying me. But

I could tell I had surprised him by singing with Mr. Hauxton. Mr. Hauxton had brought out the best of me as we sang together.

Lord Chelmsford frowned at me, as if I'd betrayed him with my talent and my rapport with Mr. Hauxton during the duet. I dropped Mr. Hauxton's hand.

How could I marry a man who wasn't proud of my singing? Perhaps he was jealous, and we would sing together instead some other time after Mr. Hauxton left.

But I had never seen Lord Chelmsford sing at any dinner parties or even at Christmastime. How much would I have to give up to have a marriage of convenience? To gain protection?

Papa and John had come over to congratulate Mr. Hauxton. Rachel and Lucy crowded around me, also voicing their congratulations, but viewing Mr. Hauxton with interest.

"I don't care if he's only a younger son," Rachel whispered to Lucy.

Mr. Hauxton glanced over at me, shock and hurt on his face. I did not think of him that way and wished that I could apologize to him for my friends. I knew how John felt about being a younger son, and I wished Mr. Hauxton had not overheard Rachel.

Mama had tears in her eyes. I went and joined her. She grasped my hands. "You have more talent than I knew, sweetheart. Such eloquence in your fingers. Such fluent harmony between your voices." She dabbed at her eyes with her handkerchief and patted my hands. "Even if you sneak away to practice. Bless you. I didn't know."

I sat, watching the scene around me. At least I had surprised Mama, which was hard to do. My stomach fluttered deliciously, and I wanted to keep this peaceful feeling forever. I wasn't sure what had just happened or what to make of it. I only had that experience because of Mr. Hauxton. Because it was a duet. I was used to singing alone. Being alone in a house that was usually empty.

But there was something important that happened when we blended our voices. A give and take. A push and pull. Something visceral between us that I couldn't deny.

Papa's agitated voice intruded on my thoughts. "And I was right! The National Gallery is crowded enough. Country doesn't need more of Turner's paintings. The Old Masters are enough for the Royal Academy. Why put Turner's watercolors on display merely because he died?" He was enlisting Mr. Maldon and Mrs. Wickford to support his old argument.

John's voice was equally loud. "But you haven't exhibited anything for years, either. Why shouldn't they exhibit his paintings?" He hadn't been in the same room with Papa for more than a few hours, and already they were arguing.

Matthew went over to try to help. I tried to think of a way to distract Papa's embarrassing outburst. I looked over at Lucy and Rachel for help.

Lucy spoke up. "I always liked your paintings, Lord Barrington. Wasn't your last one a tree?"

"Or was it a lake?" Mr. Maldon asked.

"I thought it was a sunset," Rachel said. "Very vivid colors. I liked it a lot."

I appreciated my friends' efforts, but they had made things worse. Papa shook his head, his dignity wounded. True, it had been almost three years, but his landscapes did all look alike. After the scathing reviews had come out, he had retreated from the art world and resigned from the Royal Academy. He had been even more difficult to live with ever since.

But it was the satirical cartoon that had done him in.

An idea occurred to me. "Papa! Mr. Hauxton has never had a tour of our picture gallery. You have so many paintings by the Old Masters. Perhaps you could show him your favorites."

"But he likes Turner!" Papa exclaimed. "He wouldn't appreciate Classic art."

I could see him softening, though.

Lord Chelmsford spoke up. "I don't care for Turner. Don't even know who he is, Lord Barrington." He scowled at me, as if to point out that he needed the tour far more than Mr. Hauxton. Which obviously was true.

Mama turned and faced the room. "Shall we walk back to the drawing room? Anyone who'd like a tour of the picture gallery along the way is welcome. I'd be happy to answer any enquiries," she said.

That did it. Papa couldn't stand to let anyone else exhibit his collection. "No, I'll give the tour."

Somehow Lord Chelmsford ended up walking with Lucy. He was captivated by the Rubens, a favorite of Joseph's. A floor-to-ceiling painting, taller than me, with an ornate gilded frame, and everyone in it was naked.

Rachel walked with Mr. Hauxton, examining some serene landscapes, and John and I were together. I was grateful for a rest from the conversation and already exhausted by the evening. Part of me had wanted to try to walk with Lord Chelmsford and another part of me wanted to avoid his scowls.

Papa had cornered Peter and was lecturing him on color palettes. John looked derisively at him.

"One more day," I begged John. "Try not to provoke Papa for one more day, and then you depart."

John nodded. He took my elbow. "Steady, Elle. You're really limping. Let me help you."

Papa's voice carried throughout the picture gallery. Now he and Mr. Maldon were comparing the cost of recent acquisitions. Mr. Maldon's newly purchased art cost more.

"He's going to be here all night," I whispered to John.

John yawned pointedly. He had as little decorum as his friend.

"Stop it," I whispered. "You'll only make Papa angry."

Eventually we moved back into the drawing room. The Wickfords had left for the evening, after Mr. Maldon and Papa began making extensive lists of every art purchase they had made over the last ten years. Most of the art on Rachel's walls was either a family portrait or had been painted by someone in her family.

Everyone else settled comfortably onto sofas or chairs. Papa stood in the middle of the room, still in full flow about his art collection. "Lady Barrington helped me select some of the best pieces on our Grand Tour. Can't buy the Old Masters here in England. We left right after we married." He winked at Matthew and Georgiana. "Best time of my life. They know how to respect artists in Italy."

"Had a grand time with Woodford when I went," Matthew said. "I believe we got the Rubens for you, Father."

Papa continued as though Matthew had not spoken. "National Gallery has it right. Educate the country with the finest examples. I once thought of donating a few paintings to it myself."

Mr. Maldon shifted in his seat. "I'd donate one if you would. One of my best, of course. Would it be worth a baronetcy?"

Papa seemed troubled. As if the thought of going back to London or facing Parliament was still too much for him.

Lord Chelmsford and his brother exchanged a glance. Lord Chelmsford smirked. "We have a few paintings at Chelmsford. Mostly family portraits. I could get rid of a few of those and not miss them."

Lucy giggled and Lord Chelmsford looked pleased with himself.

Papa turned on John. "What about you? The art you buy might end up here or over at Dunmore. I trust you'll purchase landscapes and portraits that reflect well on us."

"I haven't even left yet. I don't know which paintings will be for sale," John said.

Papa didn't seem satisfied. "I can't trust you," he pointed at Mr. Hauxton. "Rossetti and Hunt? Turner? No one respects Sir Reynolds or Raphael anymore."

I cringed. No matter how I tried to redirect Papa, he still managed to embarrass us.

"I wish we could go back," Mama said wistfully. "It was idyllic."

"And these two can't be trusted to buy the Old Masters. Who knows what they'll come back with." Papa sat down. He studied Matthew and Georgiana again. "You two need to go on a Grand Tour. Did Lady Barrington a world of good."

Any quiet conversations around the room stopped.

Dread filled me. *Not now,* I pleaded silently. *Not in front of everyone.*

"You can't be serious. I review all the accounts daily. I can't leave for Europe now," Matthew said softly.

"Something John could have been doing." Papa shot a glare at John. "If he'd come home on holidays."

This was one of my fears. A family quarrel at a formal dinner. With Papa's temperament and John's, I should have known this would happen.

"But I'm not the heir!" John exploded.

Papa advanced toward John. "And I was only a vicar! But now I'm the earl, and you may be, too, someday."

Matthew seemed at a loss for words. I thought Georgiana was used to our family by now, but even she seemed shocked. She whispered something in Matthew's ear.

"We didn't know when to tell you," Matthew said finally. He looked around the room at Lucy and her father, at Lord Chelmsford, his mother, and his brother, and at Mr. Hauxton. "Travel would be difficult right now in Georgiana's condition." Matthew took her hands. She smiled at the room.

"Do you mean—" Mama exclaimed. She swept over to Georgiana and embraced her. Matthew seemed embarrassed and proud. Lord Chelmsford and his brother eyed the door as if they wanted to leave.

I wanted this night to end, too. Why would Lord Chelmsford ever want to align himself with our family? *Would he suspect Papa's true condition?* I would never marry if anyone knew.

Lucy and I exchanged glances. *Help me,* I pleaded silently.

"Perhaps a game of cards?" Lucy suggested.

Yes! I thought. *Maybe losing to Lord Chelmsford would make up for singing so well.*

Lucy moved toward the card table.

"Thank you," I mouthed to her when no one else could see. *Dear Lucy. Loyal Lucy.*

Lord Chelmsford and Mr. Hauxton joined us. I arranged myself across from Mr. Hauxton. I intended to partner with him and lose spectacularly.

Mama watched the four of us settling in at the card table, a speculative gleam in her eye as she considered the couples. Papa opened his mouth, and I quickly interrupted him.

"Can we stop all this reminiscing about Europe, Papa? Lucy and I feel left out. You know daughters seldom get a Grand Tour," I said.

Papa turned to Mama. "Why not?" he said loudly. "Eleanor is absolutely right. Times have changed."

My hand froze over my stack of cards. Surely, he didn't mean what I thought he meant. *Was he serious?*

"Why don't I buy the art myself? You and Lady Eleanor can accompany me on another Grand Tour of Europe."

CHAPTER 7

Silence greeted Papa's pronouncement.

Matthew spoke first. "You can't leave me alone to manage the estates."

Papa turned around to face Matthew. "First you can't leave because you're in charge of the estates, and now I can't leave because you're not in charge of them. Make up your mind!" he yelled.

"You can't just walk away—" John began.

"What would you do if I died tomorrow? You'd figure it out. So figure it out today. I'm leaving. You'll manage." Papa grinned. Once he latched onto an idea, he never let go.

I could almost see the lists and plans forming in his head. I picked up my cards. It wouldn't be hard for me to lose this game. I wouldn't even have to try. All of the threads of my carefully woven plan were unraveling in front of my eyes. What did Mama think of this?

"Capital idea!" Mr. Maldon clapped Papa on the back. "Can I commission you to purchase a few paintings for me as well?"

Papa slid out from under Mr. Maldon's hand. "You could not possibly afford the Old Masters from Italy."

Mr. Maldon rubbed his hands together. "Eh? No, no. Mining is going well. Get me at least three or four good ones, Barrington."

We began to play. I looked at Mama. She looked pointedly at Mr. Hauxton and smiled at me. "We'll begin packing in the morning." That was all. If Mama agreed with Papa, there was no hope of changing their minds. I tried to think of any argument for staying, but I knew the determined look on her face.

She was probably tired of Essex, too. If Papa wouldn't go to London, Mama would rather go to Europe.

Mr. Hauxton kept tugging at his vest, wrinkling it even further, and his tie was almost entirely undone. His glasses lay on the table, and he didn't seem to realize they were there. He kept looking over at John with a furrowed brow, then to my father.

I studied Lord Chelmsford over my hand of cards. My only chance. Gone. Even if he was sulky and had an inflated opinion of himself. No marriage was perfect. At least it would have been a marriage. A way to escape this house.

Instead, I would return from our Grand Tour, perhaps as old as twenty, without having had a Season or being presented at Court. Even if, by some miracle, I ever did have a Season, I would certainly be older than all the other debutantes.

But in reality, I would return with no prospect of marriage and no chance of a Season. How would I ever marry? I laid down the wrong card and hastily picked it up again.

Lucy kept up a constant chatter to keep Lord Chelmsford content, and he responded as though she were the only person at the table. It was as though I had disappeared already. As soon as he knew I was leaving, Lord Chelmsford had seemed to dismiss me from his mind and focus on the future in front of him: Lucy.

Mr. Hauxton was unusually quiet during the game, too. He played a card. It was the wrong suit.

I watched Mr. Hauxton fiddling with his watch chain and wondered what he must be thinking of my family, who had invited themselves along on his Grand Tour. He bounced his leg up and down and stared at his cards without seeming to see them.

He was the sort of man who charmed everyone he met and didn't mean any of it. He had paid attention to me because he hurt my ankle. And because he wanted to best Lord Chelmsford. And because we both knew he was leaving, and it was harmless to have a short flirtation.

But my heart raced every time I saw him, and my mind went momentarily blank when he entered a room. My hands shook, and I could hardly focus to see my cards.

Lucy won another trick.

Now Mr. Hauxton and I would spend months or years traveling together. With my parents and John as chaperones the entire time. Constantly moving from city to city. But no one went on Grand Tour to get engaged.

The lace on my shawl itched and distracted me. No, Mr. Hauxton was not a candidate for marriage. He was a younger son. My brother's friend. Impulsive and unaware of social boundaries. Insincere.

I would be a spinster forever.

Mr. Hauxton and I did, indeed, lose spectacularly. But dear Lucy played brilliantly, and at least Lord Chelmsford left happy.

I, on the other hand, was miserable. I was leaving for months, probably years, and would not see Lord Chelmsford again. What would happen in that time? Lucy and Rachel were getting old enough to marry soon. Would the Maldons and Wickfords have intimate dinner parties with the Chelmsfords? Would Lord Chelmsford go to London for a Season? Their father used to go to London each year and often took his sons.

John had planned to travel with Mr. Hauxton for at least two years. Would I be gone as long as him? How long would Papa stay in Europe? Two years was too long to hope Lord Chelmsford would wait. And why would he, after tonight? Who would want to align themselves with me when they truly came to know my family?

Mama thought Papa's idea was brilliant. John raged. Matthew acquiesced. Mr. Hauxton hid away in the ballroom or practiced fencing with Joseph. Joseph said Mr. Hauxton only won because he let him.

Papa held firm.

The servants packed quickly. John delayed his departure. Everyone was inconvenienced. I had no say in anything that happened.

I couldn't decide whether the feeling in my stomach meant I felt dread or excitement or both. I didn't have time to think or feel in the whirlwind of activity.

When I told Mama my worries that I would never marry, that I would end up a spinster or on the shelf, she reassured me that there were men in Europe, too. "There's more than one way to fry a fish," she said, "so keep your eyes open for new flavors. We've already discussed this. Now, just pack the essentials. We'll buy our gowns in Paris."

I rarely understood Mama's analogies and didn't feel any better. I stayed up late preparing for the journey, packing more than the essentials, and assured myself that I would sleep during the endless days of carriage and train travel once we crossed the Channel.

I wasn't sure how Mr. Hauxton felt about us coming along on his Grand Tour with John. Suddenly he had an older couple who would move slower than him and a young girl who had to be chaperoned. We complicated things.

I knew how John felt about Mama and Papa accompanying him, and I tried to stay out of his way.

I had a plan. A goal. Marry a peer. Gain protection. Leave my unpredictable parents behind. Specifically, I was going to marry Lord Chelmsford. I'd been working toward this for months, the entire time Lord Chelmsford was in mourning. Practicing piano. Ordering new gowns. Waiting for his mother's mourning period to end.

And now my whole life spilled upside down, like a salt shaker. Mama would appreciate that analogy. Like one of Papa's bottles of brilliant paint, tipping over and staining the floor of his gallery. Like a lid crashing down on a piano mid-melody.

My parents upended my life and I felt at odds with myself. Loose. Drifting. Unraveled. There was no anchor anymore. What did I want? This was John's trip. Mr. Hauxton's trip. Mama's idea. Papa's obsession. Did my wants matter, even if I knew what they were?

I was the youngest. The extra. The shadow. The echo after the song finished.

But I also felt a curious sense of freedom. After Papa's embarrassment and retreat from London, we had lived in exile for so long. I'd rather explore Europe than stay confined to Essex for two more years. After all, there was no guarantee that Lord Chelmsford wouldn't prefer Lucy or Rachel. Or someone else entirely.

If it was a choice between traveling with my parents or hiding in the ballroom every morning to avoid Georgiana, I'd rather travel.

CHAPTER 8

June 1854

I studied the turbulent sea as our ship churned its way toward France. It reminded me of Papa, unpredictable as the waves and weather.

Perhaps it was best we leave England. No one could discover his true condition if we were constantly moving between cities.

I glanced at the other passengers. *What kind of people lived in Europe? Criminals fleeing prosecution? Families fleeing debtor's prison? Couples who could not marry honorably? People avoiding scandal? Beau Brummell, penniless, after he fell from grace. Was this the company we had sunk to?*

Papa's raised voice interrupted my thoughts. "We'll begin in Belgium and move down toward Paris. Then Italy. By boat."

"That was years ago. People go to Switzerland before Italy now," John insisted.

"You have to factor in the weather. We're leaving at a different time of year than you did. We don't want to cross the Alps when it snows," Mr. Hauxton said, looking at John, "nor do you want to sail when the seas are rough." He motioned toward Mama.

Mama didn't respond to anyone. The rocking of the ship affected her more than the rest of us, and the weather was calm today. I went to her and put a hand on her back.

"But I know the countries. I've done this before," Papa began again.

"You went everywhere by carriage," John said. "Not railway. It was twenty years ago. Things have changed. Switzerland first."

I rubbed my mother's back and handed her a peppermint lozenge. "Mama, did you take the boat to Italy last time?" I asked.

She nodded.

"Were you sick last time, too?"

She nodded again.

I stared meaningfully at Papa. "The whole way?"

Mr. Hauxton looked over at me and our eyes met. Again, without having to tell him, he knew my worries and concerns.

He studied Mama. "Crossing the Alps is reputed to be quite the adventure," he said. "Judge Wills summitted the Wetterhorn this year."

John opened his mouth and Mr. Hauxton subtly motioned to him to stay silent. Mr. Hauxton already knew Papa well enough to realize he would love a challenge.

Papa considered Mama, weak, leaning on me. His brows knit together.

Mr. Hauxton stared out over the sea and spoke casually. "Several paintings were inspired by the St. Bernard Pass. *Napoleon Crossing the Alps.* I believe you like the works of Jacques-Louis David. Or do you prefer Delaroche's more recent version?"

Papa hit his fist on the boat's railing. "Absolutely not! A farce! No elegance at all. David's is the only masterpiece." He chuckled. "Turner tried to paint the pass twice. Failed both times. Absolute abominations. The hospice is unrecognizable," he said.

John's face flushed. He was so volatile at times, just as quick to argue as Papa. But if he argued, Papa would do the opposite.

Mr. Hauxton motioned for him to stay silent again. "I've always wondered what the hospice actually looks like on the summit."

"So have I," Papa agreed.

John finally caught on. "You could paint it, too. Or sketch it."

I flashed Mr. Hauxton a grateful smile. He knew how to pacify my father's anger, how to guide his thinking, how to direct his decisions. Instead of attacking him head-on, like John, he understood that Papa wanted to engage in discussions. He knew how to handle Papa and John both and prevent arguments. Mr. Hauxton knew how to get his own way and make my father think he had still made the decision.

I felt uneasy, however. He seemed to intuitively understand my parents. And I didn't want anyone to know too much about them, especially Papa.

The pier in Calais drew within sight. After three hours on deck, I felt decidedly wind-blown and chilled. The briny smell of fish and seaweed tickled my nose.

Our boat knocked against the shore, and sailors scrambled to shove a thin wooden plank across the foamy waves. *That was it?* I delicately placed one foot in front of the other, praying I would not slip. Water slapped against the rocks beneath me, spraying salt water everywhere and making the soles of my shoes slippery.

Finally, I reached a set of stone steps set into the quay. I wobbled on unsteady legs as I climbed. My ankle had nearly healed, but I was worried I might injure it again.

Mr. Hauxton, behind me, put a hand on my back. I jumped as though scalded and tried to continue climbing but found myself still unused to walking on land.

He offered me his arm. "May I, Lady Eleanor?"

I battled with my pride. I did not want to be an inconvenience. I did not want John to resent our presence on his Grand Tour.

"We are holding up the line." Mr. Hauxton jerked his head backward.

I glanced down the stairs and felt a wave of dizziness. Papa, Mama, John, and a train of servants carrying trunks all waited for me. Some balanced precariously on the slick plank. I took Mr. Hauxton's arm.

He led me up the stone steps toward the quay. "First time on the sea?"

I hardly trusted my voice, but I wanted to prove I belonged on this journey. "Yes," I managed, as I watched the steps carefully. Up another. Almost halfway there.

"You're doing much better than your mother. No wonder she has never taken you sailing." Mr. Hauxton led me gently up another stair. "Truth be told," he turned his head and then glanced back at me, "you're doing better than your brother."

I glanced over my shoulder. Papa had Mama on one arm and John on the other. They looked equally sick. I teetered as I turned my head back toward the stairs.

Mr. Hauxton caught me tightly around the waist. His touch sent shocks through me. My heart raced with the fear of slipping and the unexpected contact.

He helped me stand, quickly removed his arm from my waist, and offered me his elbow. "The stone stairs become moist from the sea spray." Mr. Hauxton indicated the slick rocks beneath our feet. "You did well to wear your half-boots."

"I did consider my dancing slippers but decided against it."

He paused, his walking cane in mid-air.

"Because a certain gentleman crushed them while I was practicing in the ballroom."

"Ah, naturally. One could not wear those slippers to cross the Channel." Mr. Hauxton helped me up another step.

Our conversation distracted me from the queasy feeling in my stomach. "I felt fine until we waited to disembark, and the boat began swaying in the harbor. It wasn't until after the journey was over that I began to feel unwell." I took another step. I was beginning to trust my legs.

"It happens to me, too. I believe most people feel that way." Mr.

Hauxton led me to the top of the quay and onto Calais Pier. "There. You have reached the summit. You are a seasoned traveler already."

He let go of my arm and dug a collapsed spyglass out of his pocket. "Care to have a look?" He extended the bronze contraption and passed it to me.

"Thank you." I shaded my eyes with one hand and squinted through the eyepiece. I felt better now that I could survey the ocean in its entirety. Gulls cried overhead as they dove toward the fishermen's boats. Waves splashed against rocks, washing over them and leaving a white foam behind in small pools. I longed to walk along the beach and feel the gritty crunch of sand beneath my feet. Mama and Papa had never taken me to the sea before.

I could see old nets and seaweed scattered along the shoreline. Patches of sunlight slid through the clouds, changing the colors of the water. Broken timbers littered the sandy beach below us. Steamships slid up and down the waves, their hulls fighting to make land as screaming puffs of steam joined the clouds above. Sailors and passengers bustled up and down the quay.

I returned the spyglass to Mr. Hauxton. "It's almost exactly like Turner's painting of Calais Pier," I said. "Except the quay is not quite so dilapidated."

Mr. Hauxton studied the sea for a moment, then lowered the small telescope and smiled down at me. The brightness of his eyes still startled me. There was so little difference in height between us that his face somehow seemed closer than it should be. "We are lucky the clouds are not grey today," he said. "Your mother would not have survived the crossing."

I nodded. Salt air blew across my face, lifting the locks of hair near my cheeks. My loose bun had been blown by the breeze as we crossed the Channel. I closed my eyes and raised my cheeks to the sun.

"Is there any better feeling in the world?" I asked and opened my eyes.

Mr. Hauxton watched my face intently. I returned his gaze. The ocean air lifted his blond curls, playing with the tendrils in the wind.

"The wind has made a mess of your hair." I lifted my hand to touch it and stopped myself just in time.

Mr. Hauxton scrutinized my own errant tresses. He reached over and tucked a wisp of hair behind my ear, brushing my ear and neck as he did so. Behind us, I could hear footsteps approaching.

"Train station is over here, old man. Can Elle walk?" John's voice boomed across the pier.

"Certainly!" Mr. Hauxton yelled back across the crowds. He tucked the spyglass back into his pocket. "This, indeed, is the best feeling in the world," he said as we wound our way through knots of people toward a tower of luggage.

My ankle felt a little sore, but I tried to keep up. At least I wasn't limping anymore.

"Soon to be replaced by the worst of experiences." Mr. Hauxton smiled down at me. "Crowded train carriages filled with smoke."

"Or will it be the inns?" I challenged him.

"Definitely the beds," he said.

"The innkeepers." I tried again.

"Sharing a room with Barrington." He mimicked snoring.

"Not understanding the accents."

"The weather." Mr. Hauxton guided me around a group of women waving to their husbands returning from a fishing expedition. The smell of brine and rotting fish wafted up to me. My stomach clenched. He coughed.

"I daresay it will be the smells." I liked sparring with Mr. Hauxton. He didn't seem to mind.

He let go of my arm as we crossed the square to the train station. "That will be both the best and worst of traveling."

An enormous structure towered over the harbor, the entrance to a newly built train station. Arched windows covered the front of the building. Porters and attendants scurried around, hauling trunks over rough stone.

Inside, shouts rang out over the sound of hissing steam and

squealing brakes. An enormous clock covered one wall. Signs for "Calais-Lille-Paris" hung near a gleaming emerald green train while birds swooped overhead. Ornate gilded railings framed the front and back of each ruby red passenger car.

"That is the most adorable train!" I said. "Not at all imposing."

Mr. Hauxton threw back his head and laughed. People around us stared.

"Adorable? A Crampton locomotive?" he asked, still in a loud voice.

"Sssh," I said and glanced around. I lowered my voice to a whisper. "And yes, it's nothing like the black beast we took to the Great Exhibition."

"Why should I be quiet?" Mr. Hauxton asked, raising his voice even louder. "You'll never see these people again."

I hurried away from him toward Papa, who helped me into a car. I found a cushioned wooden seat across from Mama and drew the curtains shut.

Behind me, John and Mr. Hauxton climbed into the train carriage. "You'll want to see the countryside," Mr. Hauxton said, leaning over me, and drew the curtains open again.

Mr. Hauxton paced around the carriage, looking for a place to store his walking stick. John pulled his hat off his seat just in time, so Mr. Hauxton did not crush it when he sat.

I watched him settle next to John. Mr. Hauxton was a mystery to me. He paid attention to me like no one else ever had, so solicitous and kind. But it was also stifling at times. As a proper Victorian woman, I could not complain. I was expected to thank him for taking care of me. But I did not want him to pay too close attention.

I had seen humor and warmth in Mr. Hauxton, but he also had a distinct lack of propriety, no sense of privacy, and a touch of resentment when Rachel called him a second son. Perhaps that was why he and John got along so well. They both felt discontented with their prospects.

Mama glanced at me. "Why so quiet? Thinking about Chelmsford?" Her voice startled me as the train gave a lurch and a whistle and began moving forward. Only Mama could speak loudly enough to be heard over a train whistle.

Mr. Hauxton glanced toward me. I met his eyes briefly and looked back at Mama. "No. No. Not Lord Chelmsford," I said.

Mama nestled discreetly, yet comfortably against Papa on the rich velvet upholstered bench across the aisle from John and Mr. Hauxton. I wanted that someday. I wanted the ease and comfort and complete acceptance they felt with each other. Whether they agreed or not, and often they disagreed, they cherished each other. I contemplated Mr. Hauxton.

Mama followed my gaze over to him. "Already lost your taste for toast?" she murmured quietly as she closed her eyes to wait.

Had I? What flavor was Mr. Hauxton?

Images of stormy clouds over a turbulent sea came to mind. Mr. Hauxton was the tang of sea-spray, the calm of sunlight after a storm, the aquamarine of ocean waves, and the warmth of crackling fire when our hands met. He was a mist of scents and shimmering shadows, ripples on water, a feeling of calm, and a reassuring warmth.

I could not afford to develop a taste for anyone other than a peer. Best not to sample other flavors. Best to distance myself from Mr. Hauxton. He was not, after all, the oldest son in his family. And I feared my family needed the kind of protection he could not give.

CHAPTER 9

Bringing us along on their Grand Tour not only increased the number of passengers, it tripled the number of attendants. With three valets and two lady's maids, as well as guides and translators, we created quite a scene anytime we arrived at an inn or tried to board a train.

We arrived at the British embassy, a towering stone hotel near the Elysée Palace. I stepped back to take in the view. The enormous stone façade rose above the street. I had to tilt my head back to see the top of the building. Row upon row of tall windows covered the building.

"I forgot how large it is," Mama whispered to me as we entered the marble foyer. Columns supported a spiral staircase and a crystal chandelier dangled overhead.

The British ambassador to France and his wife rushed forward to greet us. "Come in, come in!" Mr. Charles Stuart called. "May I introduce you to my wife, Lady Elizabeth Stuart? Now, with which of you did I correspond?"

Mr. Hauxton gave a slight bow.

Mr. Stuart missed the gesture at first, since Mr. Hauxton was sandwiched between Papa and John. "Mr. Percy Hauxton? Ah, there you are. The Duke of Woodford sent a message ahead. Lady Elizabeth has rooms set up for you, as long as you need. Six weeks? Two months?"

"Thank you." Mr. Hauxton introduced all of us, but he had to raise his voice. The servants were just starting to unload the luggage and the clang of metal wheels echoed in the entryway.

"Up we go!" Mr. Stuart said, and pointed to the first floor above him.

I couldn't help turning my head every direction as we made our way up the marble stairs. I stopped near the top to survey the gleaming entryway from above. I had never seen such grandeur. I felt remarkable, simply by association, and a little awed.

"Steady now," Mr. Stuart said and laughed. "You'll grow used to the sight."

Lady Elizabeth threaded her arm through mine as she steered Mama and me toward our rooms. "It's so rare that I get to spend time with women my age," she nodded at Mama, "or shop with their daughters." She smiled at me. "Most people only stay a few weeks, but His Grace requested that Mr. Hauxton be given as much time at the embassy as he would like."

I entered my bedroom. A thick red and yellow rug covered the floor. An exotic medallion pattern was woven into the rug's design. It felt soft and plush beneath my feet. Ornate mirrors hung around the room and a tall furnace heater filled one corner. The bed looked thick and freshly aired with crisp sheets. I could hardly wait to lie down and sleep after the exhausting days of travel we'd already had.

"Dinner is at seven o'clock," Lady Elizabeth said, squeezing my arm. "Ring for hot water if you need it."

Nothing prepared me for the dining room. Perhaps the entryway should have given me the first clue. Or the splendor of my bedroom. Or the wallpaper in the hallways. Or the sheer size of the palace-like embassy.

I felt like I was living in a fairytale when I entered the room. The dining hall ran the length of the building, with towering ceilings, inset mirrors on the walls, tiered chandeliers, and a table that could easily sit a hundred people. Columns ran up the walls to a crown molding embellished with plaster medallions. Heavy drapes hung across a towering glass window that overlooked the luxurious gardens.

I had come to Europe hoping that my father could hide his eccentricities here. But there were easily seventy-five people at dinner tonight. And this was not a special occasion.

Dinner was a formal affair, as lengthy as our meals in England. I ate quietly, observing the people around me. It was all overwhelming. So many people.

Lady Elizabeth had the advantage of hiring French cooks and the food was exquisite. Mr. Hauxton engaged her in conversation, as well as all the people around him. I couldn't hear them across the table, but he seemed as eager as a schoolboy in his favorite class. His face wore the same intensity I had seen at home when he talked about music. I had never seen him so animated or so charming.

I could hear Mama, who sat near Mr. Stuart, ask about the spices in each dish. Evidently, she was compiling a list of new recipes to try when she returned home. I wanted to remind her that she no longer cooked our meals herself, but this was neither the time nor place to do so.

On my other side, I could hear Papa. He had found some fellow art enthusiasts, who were telling him which museums to visit and where to find art supplies for painting. I could hear them advising him on how to purchase artwork.

"And what do you paint?" one of the men asked Papa.

"Landscapes. England needs more landscapes in her gallery," Papa said.

One of his new associates shook his head. "Portraits. I'm telling you. Lord Stanhope won't give up until he gets a portrait gallery.

The man who can donate portraits by the Old Masters will be the hero of the day."

Papa nodded thoughtfully.

"Which artists are you trying to acquire?" a third man asked.

"I'm here to buy a Michelangelo for England," Papa said loudly, and the table went silent.

I cringed. Michelangelo sculptures and paintings rarely left Italy, cost a tremendous amount, and were notoriously difficult to ship over long distances. How could he even hope to do that? If that was his intent, we would be in Europe a long time.

And how would I fill my time? I could not imagine eating dinner, night after night, with so many people.

I caught Mr. Hauxton's eye as he paused in a conversation. Had he been watching me? He gave a start and turned back toward Lady Elizabeth. She glanced at me, then resumed their discussion.

But as soon as there was a lull, I could feel her studying me. I felt uncomfortable being singled out by the ambassador's wife and hoped she would simply let me disappear into the crowd after dinner.

But she had other plans.

CHAPTER 10

After dinner, we settled into the drawing room, which was equally large and equally adorned with columns and gold-leaf on the walls and doors. The ornate upholstered seats seemed too exquisite for sitting, but Lady Elizabeth settled herself next to me and insisted. "It is like living in a palace, I assure you. But you do live here and must make yourself at ease."

I tried to imagine how long it would take to walk around the room. No wonder so many rumors surrounded the spy network in Paris. One could easily have a private conversation anywhere in the room.

But people tended to stay together in small groups of five or six and leave half of the hall empty. Lady Elizabeth leaned forward and patted Mama's arm. "Now let us discuss gowns."

I lost attention quickly as they debated the merits of each modiste. I could feel Lady Elizabeth's eyes on me, and I had the feeling that she had not come over to discuss tassels and lace.

I leaned back and tried to overhear a nearby conversation between Mr. Stuart, John, and Mr. Hauxton. I was eager to avoid Lady Elizabeth's attention.

"Vienna has a legation, you see. Then they sent me off to St. Petersburg. Spain, Portugal, and Brazil after that," Mr. Stuart said.

Lady Elizabeth saw that I was distracted. "Oh, don't let him get started on this," she laughed. "Next he'll be telling you his war stories. Are you considering diplomatic service?" Lady Elizabeth neatly turned the conversation away from her husband. I could tell she knew his stories about Napoleon by heart.

John looked disappointed. I knew that history was a favorite subject of his.

And now we were all part of the same conversation. I was not able to evade her or outsmart her.

"Yes. My father is the Earl of Shelford and my brother is Viscount Arbury," Mr. Hauxton answered her.

"Of course! I should have recognized the resemblance. I think His Grace did mention that. So, you're hoping to follow the family tradition? Or work with the duke?"

Mr. Hauxton hesitated. "I'm not sure. I'd like to, but I've heard the Foreign Service prefers men with titles. Some people don't give any respect to younger sons. I don't know if that has been your experience, Mr. Stuart." He glanced over his shoulder. Evidently, he knew I was listening.

And he still thought I shared my friends' prejudices. I needed to apologize for them next time I had the chance to speak with him.

"My husband is the exception among ambassadors, to be sure," Lady Elizabeth answered quickly. "But my father is an earl and politically active as well. Your father's past service should help you, Mr. Hauxton. And you, Mr. Barrington? Did you come on a Grand Tour to practice your French, as well?"

John shifted in his chair. We'd never talked about his ambitions as a family. "Actually, I favor the Home Office. I'd like to get a position in the House of Commons or work my way up to a secretarial position. Hauxton and I make an intimidating team. With me at home and him abroad, we could be a powerful force in government."

Mr. Stuart nodded. "Indeed."

Papa stared at John, confused. "I've never heard this before. House of Commons? Thought you'd be a good vicar."

"Yes. There are plenty of seats up for election. I'd like to do some good," John said.

Papa harrumphed. "Vicars do a lot of good."

I shifted in my seat, so I could see the group better. Mr. Hauxton's jaw was set. I couldn't tell whether he wanted to defend John or himself, or both of them.

Lady Elizabeth also turned in her chair to join the conversation more fully. "You need not worry about a lack of title, Mr. Hauxton. With Woodford's backing, and our recommendation, you would go far. Especially if you marry well." She cast a look toward me and smiled. "Will you walk with me, Lady Eleanor?"

She did not wait for my agreement but drew my arm through hers and pulled me forward. We began moving at a regal pace, surveying the enormous room as we made a slow circuit along its outer edge. Lady Elizabeth guided me toward an unoccupied part of the drawing room. "Do you know why I have a title and my husband does not?" she asked.

"You are the daughter of an earl," I said.

"I married Mr. Stuart, whose father was the fourth son of an earl," Lady Elizabeth said. "We have had to work hard for our position here. While it is true that his lack of title is a significant barrier, I do not think it matters as much as Mr. Hauxton worries. Talent and charm will take a man far in this work."

I wondered why she was telling me this. "I'm sure that will reassure him," I said, not sure how else to respond.

Lady Elizabeth turned toward me. "Oh, but my dear, I wanted to set your mind at ease. Your mother has been telling me they wish to find a cottage closer to Versailles," she said. "She dreamed up a story about how loudly you sing in the mornings and how your father's paint fumes would disturb the others at the embassy. Perhaps I have lived in France too long, but I fear I have become a romantic. I chided them for separating true love. You may stay here with me as chaperone if you wish to remain close to Mr. Hauxton."

"Mr. Hauxton?" I stammered.

"Young love," she sighed. "How long have you and he known each other? Before the Grand Tour? Is that why you're traveling together?"

"Oh no, you mistake the matter. There is no arrangement between us," I hastened to reassure her.

"Not yet? Mmmm." Lady Elizabeth studied me. "Really, you must stay here while your parents hide themselves away. I would love to have another woman here with me for more than a few days." She glanced across the room at Mr. Hauxton, talking animatedly with her husband and a knot of other men.

I considered it briefly. Leave Mama and Papa? Spend my days with a stranger? Make conversation with people I didn't know every night? My stomach tightened. I had never been away from my parents.

The men were standing up now and moving across the room. Several men were gesturing wildly. Evidently, the conversation was hotly contested, and Mr. Hauxton was the center of attention.

"Indeed, there is no understanding between us. And I do sing quite loudly in the mornings. I will be content to stay with my parents." It was not quite the truth. I wished to be in Paris some of the time, with its action and excitement, rather than out in the quiet countryside. And I loved the splendor of my bedroom. I didn't want the simple kind of cottage bedchamber that Papa and Mama would think was quaint and adorable. But I could never live in the embassy on my own. Night after night.

"Come, Lady Eleanor. I am trained to detect lies. I am not a diplomat's wife for nothing. Your parents' story rang of fabrication instantly." Lady Elizabeth stopped walking and studied me.

Panic rose in my chest. I felt tight bands constrict as my lungs struggled for breath. What did she suspect? She was used to espionage, to detecting secrets. I must distract her from speaking about my parents. Perhaps, we should stay away from Paris as much as possible in the future.

What could I say that was the truth? I must tread lightly if she truly could detect falsehood. Nothing about my parents and certainly nothing about Papa. "I admit I feel a sort of...fascination with Mr. Hauxton. I've never seen a man like him. He's completely different, one moment to the next. He was nothing like this at home, at Barrington. When he's among his peers, he comes alive, so vibrant and argumentative. When we are alone, with family, he's quiet and thoughtful. Gentle at times, and loud at others. I don't know which is the real man."

Lady Elizabeth nodded her head and sighed. She tugged me forward again, her voice lowered to a whisper, even though we were still far away from any other groups. "I felt the same way when I fell in love with my husband. He was so much more complex than the other men who wanted to court me." She patted my arm. "It is quite all right to be honest with me. I am also adept at keeping secrets."

I also spoke in a low whisper as we continued around the room. I threaded my fingers together. "Truly. I have no matrimonial interest at all." I squirmed under her intense scrutiny and looked across the room instead. My gaze fell on Mr. Hauxton. "I am merely curious. I cannot make him out."

"And yet you have not taken your eyes off him all evening," Lady Elizabeth said softly. "Nor can he keep his eyes from you. You will make an excellent diplomat's wife, and he was born for the service. Your mother has taught you how to run a large household. You'll handle the embassy well. You already speak French beautifully and you have months to perfect it. Most women don't have the luxury of a Grand Tour."

We were drawing near to the crowds of people. I wished she would continue to whisper, but she spoke at normal volume now. "I'm sure they'll give you a small embassy to start after you marry. This may feel overwhelming at first, but Paris was not our first assignment. Mr. Stuart does not plan to leave this post for four or five more years. Perhaps by then you will be ready."

"No, no, Mr. Hauxton does not feel any regard for me, I assure you," I said. I tightened my grip on my fingers, trying not to look mortified, and glanced to see if anyone were listening.

As though he could hear his name across the large room, Mr. Hauxton's eyes briefly left the circle of men and the heated debate and found mine. We locked eyes for a long moment. He watched us walking, and I realized I had neglected my own conversation. I turned back toward Lady Elizabeth.

She smiled triumphantly. "I assure you, Lady Eleanor, he has been watching you as intently as you are watching him. He is merely more subtle."

I shook my head. "I'm sure you are mistaken."

She peered at me intently, then said, "I already told you—I do not make mistakes. Even when people lie to themselves, I can detect a lie. If you grow restless, visit me anytime while your parents are in Versailles." Lady Elizabeth patted my arm one last time and left me with the group of arguing men.

She had steered me quite close to Mr. Hauxton, then left me awkwardly on my own. Matchmaker.

I watched him arguing. He raised his hands to make a point and leaned in, then threw his head back to laugh the next moment. Mr. Hauxton casually turned his head to the side to glance at me. He knew I was watching him. He was like one of my father's falcons, able to observe his prey from the side of his eyes.

My cheeks grew warm, and I saw a smile slowly grow across his face as he continued talking to the men around him. I couldn't let him think I was blushing because of his attention.

I saw a flash of movement in the corner of my eye. Thinking it was another young woman, I quickly turned, and said, a little too loudly, "What a warm evening!" and fanned my face. I found myself facing the enormous ceramic tile heater. White bricks filled the corner, floor to ceiling. What I had mistaken for movement was simply the flicker of flames in the grate.

I heard someone choking. I risked a glance at the small group, my face truly red now. Mr. Hauxton was coughing to cover his laugh, but it turned into choking, because he was laughing so hard.

Mr. Stuart pounded Mr. Hauxton on the back. When Mr. Hauxton recovered, his grin covered his entire face. He gazed at me, flicked his eyes to the heater, raised his eyebrows, and then looked back to me.

Even from here I could see the twinkle in his eye. He looked divinely handsome when he smiled. I took a deep breath and let it out. Mr. Hauxton continued to smile and stare.

"Mr. Hauxton? I say. You make a good point." Someone nudged him, and he looked around at the group as though lost.

"What?" Mr. Hauxton had completely lost the thread of the conversation.

"Could you restate your argument for Monsieur Stuart?" the man asked.

Mr. Hauxton rejoined the conversation, although he kept his body turned slightly toward mine. He had one eye on the men and one eye on me, as though one audience were not enough. He had to be sure that both the men and I were watching him.

Across the circle of men, Lady Elizabeth raised an eyebrow ever so slightly at me, tipped her head toward Mr. Hauxton, and a ghost of a smile crossed her lips. She barely nodded, and I gave her the smallest of nods in return.

I turned back to warm my hands in front of the heater. This time I was not trying to hide any awkwardness. I was trying to hide my smile. Lady Elizabeth was right. Mr. Hauxton was watching me. To the point of distraction.

And I had successfully distracted Lady Elizabeth from inquiring about my parents' real motives as well.

CHAPTER 11

The summer flew by. We settled into a quaint, comfortable cottage in Versailles with tiny bedrooms. Tiny compared to the British embassy, at least. I tried not to feel too bad about it. I found paths to walk and explored the countryside. Protecting the family and preserving our privacy were more important.

Papa mostly spent his time in museums, sketching the Mona Lisa, studying other portraits, or trying to recreate landscapes at home. "I wonder if Stanhope needs this one," Papa would say after meeting with each art dealer. It was always *"What does England need?"* now instead of trying to find paintings for Barrington Hall's picture gallery.

If Papa was thinking about Lord Stanhope and the Royal Academy, perhaps he would consider returning to London. He might be willing to attend a session of Parliament, since the summer exhibits took place in the latter half of the Season. It was a lot to hope, but Papa was acquiring a lot of artwork.

Mama went to museums and galleries with Papa but spent most of her time in the kitchen. Here, in our smaller rented cottage, she could cook to her heart's content. With her own French chef to teach her.

That left me with a lot of time to play piano, and it didn't disturb anyone. I had to admit that my mother was brilliant. We were all probably happier here than we would have been at the embassy. Even if it did feel like I had traded my exile in Essex for an exile in Versailles.

We saw John and Mr. Hauxton occasionally. They spent as much time in Paris as possible. The Stuarts hosted several formal dinners with French officials and diplomats from other countries. Mama and Papa—and therefore, I—missed most of them.

I wandered among the streets of Paris with Mama and Lady Elizabeth. If we put her off entirely, she would grow suspicious. We got fitted for new gowns, ordered gloves and slippers, ate at small cafés, and tried perfumes together.

Mama invited John and Mr. Hauxton to Versailles a few times and cooked new dishes on the nights they came. Mr. Hauxton helped me practice French. I could hear his accent improving, and he swore that mine was getting better as well. Flatterer.

But summer was ending. Many residents of the embassy were leaving to spend the fall and winter in Italy. Mama received a letter from an old friend inviting us to visit her in Vienna. Papa insisted on leaving Paris before the winter set in and the Alps became impassable. John and Mr. Hauxton argued strenuously against spending the winter in Vienna instead of Rome, but my father was intractable. He didn't want to go where the crowds would be.

We visited the embassy one morning before our departure to do the last bit of shopping before we boarded another train.

"Could you recommend a bookseller? Need new tomes for the library at Barrington Hall," Papa told Mr. Stuart.

"Yes, of course. The Galignani brothers. Won't find better. Great garden and reading room. Give them my name and you'll get excellent service."

"Oh yes, but they write for his newspaper anyway. The Galignani Messenger you've been reading is published by them," Lady Elizabeth chimed in. "And no one writes a better guidebook. I'm sorry I can't come with you this morning."

She pulled me aside while Papa went to find John and Mr. Hauxton. She studied me, a serious look on her face. "Have you been happy here, Lady Eleanor?"

Her question startled me. "Yes. I've finally had a chance to play and sing with no interruptions. The country walks are lovely. We have a stream—"

"I blame myself," Lady Elizabeth interrupted. "You should be engaged by now. You put on a brave face." She patted my cheek and left her hand there. "Darling girl."

The room suddenly felt warm. I glanced at Mama to see whether it was time to leave yet.

Lady Elizabeth sniffed sadly and withdrew her hand. She pulled herself up. "But never let it be said that I am not a strategist." She tapped her head with her finger, then took my hands in hers. "I have spoken much of the advantages of marrying to Mr. Hauxton. The best posts are given to married men. Only the unmarried men get sent to St. Petersburg. And I enumerated the qualities he should seek. Intelligent. Discreet. Like you."

I was none of those things. But why did that make me feel disappointed instead of relieved? Mr. Hauxton was the farthest thing from discreet. How could he ever hope to be a diplomat? He could talk an elephant into an alliance with a mouse, but he couldn't keep a secret to save his life.

"Don't look so morose. If I don't hear of your engagement soon, it'll be the first time I've been proven wrong. Do write to me, dear," she said, and walked away.

John and Mr. Hauxton decided to accompany us. Mr. Stuart insisted it would not be safe otherwise. We had learned that, like London, there was wisdom in carefully planning our path through town and avoiding certain streets.

As we approached the bookshop, lanterns hung at intervals beneath stone archways. Tall trees lined the portico-covered walkway. Artwork filled every pane of the windows from the street to the top of the building. I'd never seen anything like it, not even in London.

Bookshelves, floor to ceiling, as high as our entryway at home, filled the store. Light streamed in through glass panes in the ceiling above us. Assistants waited near ladders, ready to retrieve books from the higher shelves. Stacks of books filled tables. An entire section of the store held nothing but musical arrangements.

Mama and I gasped and turned toward each other.

"Eleanor." Mama seized my arm. "This shop was not here last time I came to Paris. Select a few songs for Dunmore and Barrington Hall, will you?" She drifted off in a haze of happiness.

I turned to examine the shelves. Although the store was filled with people, it was quiet like a church. Each wing of the store soared high like the nave of a towering cathedral. I felt like I needed to whisper.

I wandered over toward Papa. "I'm looking for the music. Is there anything in particular you wanted?" I asked.

He grunted and continued to flip through lithographs of famous paintings.

John waited with me. "What should I pick out?" he asked.

"This is exquisite." Papa motioned to a store attendant. "Will you place these Botticelli prints aside? We will add others to our purchase."

"Father—" John prompted. He shifted his weight from one leg to another. Since he had just graduated from Cambridge, he had no townhouse in London yet or residence of his own. Just a bedchamber at Barrington Hall, which Papa owned, and Matthew oversaw the Dunmore estate.

"Pick anything," Papa replied. "Philosophy. Science. History. I'll buy the art books."

"I wish I had a library," John muttered and moved off.

Mama wandered over with a stack of books in her arms, which she gave to the attendant.

"This poetry will go to Dunmore," Mama said. "The library at

Barrington Hall is well stocked in Byron. What do you have from Mrs. Browning?"

I picked up a book of poetry by Alfred Tennyson and showed it to Mama. She quietly slipped it to the attendant while Papa wasn't looking.

I wandered over to the display of musical arrangements. So many composers lived in Europe. So many more songs, arias, operas, concertos, and symphonies were available here than in England. I closed my eyes and inhaled. The scent of books and ink was intoxicating.

I collided with someone and a warm hand steadied me at the waist. My eyes opened.

Mr. Hauxton quickly put his hand behind his back and began perusing the sheafs of paper, a half-smile on his face. "Is this going to happen often?" he asked.

"What? You ruining my best slippers? I hope not. I will run out of slippers." I picked up the top selection of music on his stack without looking. I still felt a little breathless from the feeling of his hand at my waist.

"No, not ruining your slippers. You closing your eyes and running into me. I seem to recall that was what occurred." Mr. Hauxton indicated the music in my hand. "That is only for men's voices."

I glanced down. "So it is." I hadn't even looked at it. I was simply trying to hide my embarrassment behind the paper, but he had caught me.

Mr. Hauxton took the sheets from my hand and his fingers brushed mine. Even though I wore gloves, the sensation flustered me. "What else have you found?"

He had only a few sheets of music selected so far. I searched along the table for something more suitable.

"More than I will buy." Mr. Hauxton rifled through the songs.

"Why? Whose library are you buying for?" I asked.

"My father's library at Shelford, but mostly my mother will use the songs." He moved along the table. "I need some pieces with low notes for women."

So many stacks of music. I selected one song. The Bridal Chorus from *Lohengrin*. No. "Tornami A Dir" from *Don Pasquale*. I scanned it quickly. No. Another. "O Soave Fanciulla." Definitely not. I put it down quickly and tried to find something for one voice.

Mr. Hauxton picked it up. "For whom are you buying music?"

"My oldest brother." I knew it wasn't entirely true. I would select pieces I liked, regardless of where the music was kept or who owned it.

"The heir. Everything handed to them." He sifted through sheet music. He held up a piece and turned it over, scanning the lines.

"I would choose this piece for myself. But I live the life of a younger son," Mr. Hauxton said. He examined the music.

I ran my hand across the stacks of music as well. "My friends were inexcusably rude at Barrington. Lady Elizabeth thinks you have great potential, even if others do not."

Mr. Hauxton tilted his head and considered me. "And you?"

I watched him. He had none of the usual energy or fight about him. I wondered what had happened to make him that way. I missed his exuberance. "You are far too melancholy today. I like it better when you're argumentative."

Mr. Hauxton grinned at me and straightened. "I have missed you this summer." His glasses were halfway down his nose from squinting at the small writing. I wanted to push them back up and straighten his always-untidy pocket handkerchief.

Instead, I busied myself with rearranging the stacks of paper. Mr. Hauxton's hand found mine. I stilled and gazed up at him. His brilliant green eyes had darkened to a deep emerald green in the dim light of the store. He met my eyes and let his hand linger just a moment too long, gently caressing the top of my hand, before moving on to the next stack of music.

I returned his smile and tried to break the tension. "You've grown dull, Mr. Hauxton, spending so much time with John. You complain nearly as much as he does."

He moved around the table to stand beside me. "The embassy dinners were tedious without you and your parents."

Please don't ask me why we stayed away. I've got to change the topic.

I moved further down the row of music, so Mr. Hauxton was not standing quite so close. I pointed to the stack of songs he had collected. "More complaints? You and I have both seen real poverty on the streets of Paris. When have you ever known neglect? Your eldest brother and mine are the closest friends of His Grace. They move in the highest circles of the Upper Crust. You and John will, too. I daresay your father will set you up with your own town house in London. Come now. I cannot lament your circumstances. Even if you had a boring dinner partner."

Mr. Hauxton laughed so loudly that several customers looked at us. One of Galignani's attendants came over. I handed him my stack of selected musical arrangements and started to leave.

"As you command," Mr. Hauxton said. He picked "O Soave Fanciulla" back up from the stack. "I will purchase the entire store. But only if you sing this duet with me, my nightingale. Tell me, does your father know that his wife and daughter read the same poetry as the artists he despises? That he harbors enthusiasts secretly sympathetic to the movement he despises?"

I scoffed. "I take care not to flaunt my purchases. May I ask you to do the same?"

Mr. Hauxton bowed ridiculously low and his glasses slipped down his nose. I headed over to find Galignani's guidebook for Switzerland, but I could hear his laughter continue all the way across the store.

At least he was no longer morose. I had discovered the way to deal with Mr. Hauxton. Direct contradiction. He seemed to love an argument as much as Papa. And I had inadvertently given him a secret to keep from Papa as well.

All the same, I could not focus as I stood in front of the guide-books. I stared at the rows and rows of books, my mind a blank. All I could remember was the feel of Mr. Hauxton's hand on mine, warm, even through my gloves.

And I also couldn't help thinking about his older brother. Perhaps Mr. Hauxton had enough social connections to help me after all. Even if he didn't on his own, surely his family did. Maybe an alliance with him wasn't entirely out of the question. After all, we had received preferential treatment at the embassy. Mr. Hauxton's connections held more sway than my father's.

Not that I wanted to throw myself at Mr. Hauxton. But perhaps he wasn't off the menu after all.

CHAPTER 12

Late August 1854

I sat on a blanket-covered rock by the side of the road. We were stranded. Granted, it was the most beautiful place in the world to be stuck. And stuck we were. Wheels in dirt ruts. Carriage at a dangerous angle. A sharp mountain peak jutting up behind us, cracks and fissures running through the rock face. Other travelers passed us on foot, staring curiously at our predicament.

I decided to focus on the mountain peak while Papa and John argued about what to do. Mr. Hauxton came over to check on my mother and make sure we had enough shade while we waited.

I still couldn't believe we were leaving Switzerland already. We had spent a week in Bern, a week in a small village called Rüeggisberg, and two weeks in Geneva. A few months ago I had been planning my wedding to Lord Chelmsford. Theoretically. Since he hadn't even started courting me and was still in mourning. Now, here I was, hauling a few dresses around in a trunk and traveling all over Europe.

The crossing from Dover was easy compared to ascending the Great St. Bernard Pass.

"The guide is explaining that they have to dismantle the carriage, carry it over the pass, and reassemble it in Italy," Mr. Hauxton explained. Evidently, he spoke German as well as French.

"And how do we get to Italy?" Mama asked, a touch of hysteria in her voice.

"Walk. Unless you want to hire someone to carry you. They have mules for the steeper part of the climb." Mr. Hauxton's voice was even. Blunt. Like my father.

I had discovered that traveling with someone stripped away the veneer of drawing room superficiality and civility and left room for honesty. Then again, Mr. Hauxton had been forthright and shared his opinions openly from the moment we'd met.

Mama stood. "Of course I can walk. It's lovely scenery and I am a great walker. If Napoleon could cross this pass, so can I." She glanced over at me and lowered her voice, as though she did not want Mr. Hauxton to hear her. "Mules?" she asked. "Do we really have to ride mules?"

"Shall I read to you from the guidebook?" I flipped through Galignani's red-covered bible. I had it nearly memorized by now. "There are chairs for 'females or timid persons or invalids.' We have to hire eight porters to carry you over the mountain if you don't want to ride a mule or walk."

Mama glared at me and raised her voice to her normal speaking level. "I am neither timid nor an invalid. I will ride the mule when it is necessary and not a minute earlier."

Mr. Hauxton stifled a laugh.

I flipped through the book. "It says 'the path is bordered by precipices on each side,' but if you sit with your back to it, you can 'escape much of its horrors.'"

Mama's face grew pale. "We did not cross the Alps last time. We rode on that blasted boat. Perhaps I would prefer that."

A true laugh escaped Mr. Hauxton.

"Why haven't we started?" Mama glanced anxiously at the sky.

"What if it rains? Read that section on thunder from the guidebook."

"Your husband hasn't realized this is our only option yet," Mr. Hauxton said. "Even though he made the arrangements himself several weeks ago."

"In that case, we may be here a while." Mama smiled and sat back down.

"'An Englishman has said that he who never witnessed a storm among the Alps, cannot conceive any idea of the continuity of the rolling and burst of the thunder which roars round the horizon of these immense mountains.' Is that the part you wanted?" I shut the book. Part of me wanted to see the magnificence of a storm like that, to experience something so dramatic.

Mama's face went paler than it had been before. She closed her eyes. "Perhaps I should help your father make up his mind." She pulled her shawl tighter.

"I will read you to sleep, Mama," I said. "Perhaps you would like a nap instead."

She stared at me.

Mr. Hauxton came over and held out his hand. "I don't think you're helping her."

I hid the book behind my back. "You don't really want the book. You merely wish for me to stop reading."

He smiled slowly at me, staring straight into my eyes. He took a step closer. I did not move. If he wanted to intimidate me, it would not work.

Mama marched over to Papa. She would be well enough. The sky was clear. It was my book. He had no right to take it. But I was curious to watch him try.

Mr. Hauxton advanced. "Lady Eleanor." He took another step.

I gripped the book tighter against my back.

"May. I. Read. Your. Book." He moved forward along the trail with each word. Soon we stood nearly nose to nose.

"No," I said simply, although I found it hard to concentrate.

Mr. Hauxton gazed down at me through his spectacle-rimmed

eyes. I could smell something, a new cologne he had purchased in Paris. I couldn't place the scent.

He continued to stare at me, his arms moving slowly toward my book. "What if I say please?"

I felt my resolve slipping.

Mr. Hauxton's hands covered mine in a flash as he tugged at the book, brushing my fingers and the small of my back. His touch seared me through the rough traveling clothes.

Part of me wanted to lean into his touch. I pulled back to cover my reaction. "You cheated! And you do not want the book. You merely do not like to lose."

Mr. Hauxton held the book up and examined it. "Are you admitting defeat?"

I brushed the front of my dress. "Hardly. The contest was unfair," I protested, thinking of ways to get my revenge and get my book. I wondered how forward I could be, with Mama and Papa nearby. I enjoyed a challenge as much as Mr. Hauxton did, and it certainly didn't hurt that his touch sent tingles through me. *Are they talking to the interpreters or watching me?*

He held the book barely out of my reach, but his eyes dared me to grab for it.

"Hauxton!" John yelled.

Both Mr. Hauxton and I startled. We turned toward Papa, John, and the waiting group of valets, lady's maids, and servants hired to carry our carriage and luggage.

"Can you interpret, old man? Mother insists." John waved him over.

Mama waited with her arms crossed, tapping her feet, and looking toward the sky.

I felt a surge of disappointment as Mr. Hauxton sauntered over toward John, swinging the book behind his back.

John gestured toward the translators. "Can't make out a word. What language is Swiss anyway? German, French, or Italian?"

"Yes," Mr. Hauxton hollered as he walked away, "all three."

• • •

"Napoleon rode a white horse, not a donkey," Papa muttered as I walked past him.

We began to hike. The dirt path was soft, moss-covered in places, and my boots were sturdy. The August air was warm. The weather in Switzerland was so different from Essex. I gloried in the feel of a mountain breeze on my skin. Yellow, purple, and blue wildflowers waved along the road. Sharp peaks and spiky trees interrupted the sky.

I breathed in the sunshine and continued to walk up the steep trail. I'd lost track of anything except the blue sky overhead and the worn rocks beneath my feet. My mind wandered while I watched the clouds drifting in overhead.

Mr. Hauxton had become the unofficial arbiter between Papa and John. We had fallen into a pattern already. A problem would arise. Papa would stake out a position, and John would argue the counter point, whether or not he really believed it. Mr. Hauxton would listen calmly and wait. One of them would ask for his opinion, and Mr. Hauxton invariably had the logical solution. He could make them both feel like they had gotten their way. I appreciated his diplomatic approach.

Papa and John were simply too much alike. Both artists, but with completely different tastes. Both argumentative, with quick minds and strong opinions. Mr. Hauxton didn't mind giving his view, but he was able to see the merit in any argument instead of staking a position and holding to it at all costs.

I wondered if Mr. Hauxton felt some contempt for Papa and his constant schemes or John and his constant opposition to my father. I knew that I did. Somehow it was alright for me to feel that way, but I didn't want an outsider to see and understand the family dynamic so well. *I'm ashamed that he knows us so well and sees our squabbles. And scared that he'll see more than it's wise for him to know.*

I continued to walk and think as I gazed at the darkening sky. I pulled my shawl around me. The crisp mountain air had a distinct chill to it now, though I found it invigorating.

Already I loved Europe. I loved travel. I loved seeing new

terrain and hearing new accents. I reveled in the flavors of new foods. I couldn't fill my sketch books fast enough to record the landscapes and people I was seeing.

The sun had disappeared behind a bank of clouds, and the sky grew dark. I hiked along the narrow trail, which became increasingly steeper. Bits of slate and shale began to appear along the sides of the road.

The easy rhythm of the walking allowed my mind to wander. Walking was far better than sitting in the carriage or a train for hours, my legs numb from going over the bumps in the road or the feel of the train track beneath us. I wished more of our days were like this, hiking through the Alps while a trail of servants carried wheels and axles and trunks behind us, as ridiculous as it was.

Except that the sky had indeed grown grey now. Perhaps Mama's premonition was correct. *How long had I been woolgathering?*

I reached a small inn that marked the beginning of the steeper climb. An elderly man rushed out and began speaking in a language I did not recognize. He grabbed my hand and led me toward the stables. I glanced behind me. Mr. Hauxton was not far behind. He nodded, and I followed the man.

My guide seated me on a mule and began escorting me up the rugged road. I had ridden horses often enough to feel comfortable on a mule, but I struggled a little to adapt to the swaying motion of the gentle animal.

The mule steadily worked its way up the winding path toward the top of the pass. My guide, who seemed older than Papa, kept up a constant stream of conversation without checking to see whether I understood him or not. I didn't.

I turned my head to try to catch a glimpse of anyone else. Mr. Hauxton followed closely behind. His eyes were intent, studying me. He quickly glanced away and began to inspect the cliffs.

I couldn't see John, Papa, or Mama anywhere.

"Where are my parents?" I asked the guide and gestured down the steep trail. A few loose pebbles scattered beneath the mule's feet. I clutched the lead tighter and leaned forward. The guide shrugged.

"Mr. Hauxton?" I yelled.

He looked away from his careful study of the mountainside ravine.

I clutched the lead of my mule tighter. "Do you see John or the others?"

He turned around, then back at me. He shook his head and resumed his study of the Alpen ledges.

I gazed at the wild scenery, the treacherous drop along the side of the trail, and the darkening sky. The mule plodded along past craggy cliffs. Shards of slate slipped beneath the mule's feet. I felt an urgency to reach the summit, but I knew the mule and the guide could go no faster.

Clouds rolled across the sky. I could see a small building atop the crest of the hill. I checked behind me again. No other animals or guides. Still just Mr. Hauxton. I pulled my shawl tighter around myself. We were alone.

CHAPTER 13

Mr. Hauxton and I reached the top of the St. Bernard Pass at nearly the same time. My guide helped me dismount and left with the mule. I could see a stable and the famed hospice across the clearing. Dogs roamed freely.

I turned around to drink in the sight at the top of the mountain pass. The viewpoint overlooked the Italian side of the valley. A mountain lake filled the valley below, patches of sunlight breaking through the clouds to reflect on the azure water. Wind rippled the surface, sending out small waves. The breeze bent the grasses against the steep slopes and sheered-off rock faces. Spruce and pine trees from the hillsides reflected on the glassy lake.

Mr. Hauxton wandered over. "Glorious, isn't it?"

The sharp line of blue-grey mountains ringed the valley. The delicate pink flowers of Alpine rock-jasmine fought to grow through the slate. Pockets of white edelweiss and brilliant green moss grew around us in unexpected places: along the trail, poking out of tree trunks, protruding through the shale. Purple columbine rose in spiky rows of blooms, while scarlet martagon lilies rested beneath them. Above us, an expanse of dark blue sky covered one valley while grey clouds rolled across the other.

"The mountains and storm clouds remind me of Turner's painting," I agreed. "But do you think it's safe? My parents? John? Will they make it?"

"Our group was the last to start hiking, and we arrived at the inn at different times. Perhaps the guides held John and the others back." Mr. Hauxton gazed out over the valley. He turned toward me. "They barely let you and me start the climb on our mules. I'm sure they're safe."

We stood together, drinking in the view from the top of the pass. The clouds streamed down like a veil, thin but, I hoped, harmless. What had seemed ominous as I climbed now looked like a gauzy curtain of clouds shot through with rays of sunlight.

I tried to convince myself that my parents were, indeed, safe. I needed a distraction. "Do you see that?" I pointed to another winding trail, heading down the slope toward Italy.

"It's an old Roman road," Mr. Hauxton explained. "My guide told me all about it."

"You could understand him?" I asked.

He glanced down at me with a hint of a grin on his face. "I have a headache from trying."

We contemplated the valley together. This was a place of transition. Of division and unity. Switzerland on one side, Italy on the other, but one road connected them. It was a place of turmoil and peace. Napoleon had snuck his army through here but had also given a farmhouse and land to the lovesick guide who aided him across the pass. What did it hold for me?

I couldn't concentrate on the scenery any longer. "But if they began riding after us, and the storm develops...What if there is lightning in those clouds?" The shadows shifted as the sun moved behind the cloud, and I grew suddenly cold.

Mr. Hauxton glanced around the clearing. "If they were unsafe, the dogs could search them out. This is a rescue hospice. The guide is not worried, nor am I." Mr. Hauxton paused and took me aside. His face grew unusually tense. "May I ask you something, Lady Eleanor?"

His earnest tone drew my attention. "Of course."

"Will you call me Percy?" Mr. Hauxton's green eyes sparkled as the sun came out from behind a cloud.

My heart fluttered. "Of course," I said again. "And you may call me Eleanor."

"While I'm not overly concerned about your family's safety, we're in a bit of a bind, here, Elle." Percy began pacing. "Walk with me?"

Elle? Percy spoke to me as casually and comfortably as John. How long had he thought of me as Elle instead of Lady Eleanor?

I followed him as we explored the paths around the hospice and stables. "Even the wind smells different up here," I said. "The wood smoke from the monk's hospice. The pine trees. The wind is cold, but the smells are delicious." I shuddered as we entered a patch of shade.

Percy glanced at my shawl. "That thing is useless up here," Percy said. "Please, take my coat." He drew it off and draped it across my shoulders.

The weight of the garment comforted me at once. The warmth of the wool enveloped me. Percy's warmth. Wearing it felt intimate, like an embrace. I felt suddenly shy.

"Go ahead," Percy said, watching me. "I won't take it back."

I tugged the jacket around me. "Thank you. You must be freezing."

"I'm impervious to cold," Percy said. "A little-known fact."

I knew he was lying, but I appreciated the gesture too much to argue.

"We should get you inside, but here's the thing. I've been watching the others go up the path while your father and John—"

"While they argued and wasted valuable hiking time?" I asked.

He found a log and brushed it off with his handkerchief. He sat down and motioned for me to join him. "Well, yes. If we'd left earlier, they might have made it up before the storm blew in or the afternoon grew too late. But we're stuck here together."

Comprehension dawned. Percy didn't give me permission to

call him by his Christian name because he felt close to me. He had another reason.

"You're worried how this looks," I said. "While I'm worried whether my parents fell off a cliff or died."

Percy nodded. "They're fine. But listen—I don't think anyone knows me or has any connections to the diplomatic world. You never know. A scandal like this would sink my career before it began."

I stood and walked over to a fir tree. I let my hand glide over its needles. I'd never felt anything so soft and yet so sharp at the same time. Kind of like Mr. Hauxton. Except I had to remember to call him Percy now. My heart sank. I had wished for a little more intimacy, it was true, but not in this way. Not when he resented it. Not when I worried about my parents' safety.

"What do you propose?" I asked, leaning over to pick up a pinecone. I rolled it in my hands, examining its jagged edges.

Percy came up behind me and put a hand on my shoulder, turning me around. "I'm trying to protect you as much as I need to protect myself." He took the pinecone out of my hand and held my hand. "Neither of us wants to be forced to marry because we were unchaperoned tonight."

His hand enveloped mine, warming it in the late afternoon. Why did he look at me like that when he had no romantic intentions? His eyes said one thing, but he told me another.

I could hear the barking of the famous St. Bernard dogs in the clearing. The guides must have told the monks that we had arrived. I pulled my hand from Percy's. "Then perhaps we should not let the monks discover us alone in a secluded wood."

I found my way back to the clearing. A pair of St. Bernard dogs came bounding over and licked my hands.

Percy was right behind me. He said quietly, "Follow my lead. I'll think of something as we go."

That sounded like Percy. Spontaneous. The opposite of me. "I believe it is you who is following me right now." I threw a grin over my shoulder and proceeded toward the hall. I had no idea what we were going to do, but I wasn't about to let Percy get the upper hand.

The monks led us into a large stone hall filled with rough wooden tables and benches. Travelers sat in groups. Percy pulled a monk aside and quietly explained our lack of luggage and asked for separate rooms. The monks were discrete. Almost silent. They were not our concern. The other travelers were.

While one monk bustled off to find us rooms and some of the night clothes they saved for emergencies, another gestured toward the tables. A third promised to set off for the stables after talking to us.

Percy translated for me. "He says they can send the dogs back down to the inn. If there's anything amiss, the dogs will find them. If nothing's wrong, the dogs will stay at the inn overnight. And he says not to worry, little one."

My throat felt thick and I couldn't speak. The monk patted my hand. He whistled to his dogs and headed out the door. We moved over toward a table near a large window.

Percy whispered in my ear, "I've got an idea. Trade places." He slid onto a bench that faced the cavernous dining hall. In a louder voice he said, "You can watch the sunset from there, darling."

I tried not to show any surprise. After we sat down, I mouthed the word, "Darling?" I raised my eyebrows at him. I shrugged off Percy's oversized coat, so I could eat.

Percy settled onto the bench casually. He put an elbow on the table and leaned forward. In a whisper he said, "They seem to be couples here. Mostly. Maybe newlywed. I don't see any families. No brothers or sisters. If we act like we're married, we stand a better chance of blending in."

A monk served us each a bowl of warm vegetable soup, a thick slice of dense brown bread, and a hunk of the Swiss cheese I had grown to love. After the day's exertion, and my worries about my family, it smelled divine. I took a bite and began eating.

Percy reached across the table with his right hand and took my left. He grinned and began rubbing his thumb over my knuckles.

I had taken my gloves off to eat and could hardly concentrate on my food.

"Aren't you going to cause the very scandal you're trying to avoid?" I asked between bites of soup. "If people see you behaving like this?"

Percy let go momentarily to rip off a chunk of bread. He dipped it into his soup. "Ah, only if we are noticed. But if we blend in so completely, no one will remark on a thing." He cupped my cheek gently, looked into my eyes and sighed.

"What are you doing?" I whispered.

"There are at least four other couples doing the same thing," Percy said.

I darted my eyes to the side. I couldn't see very well with my back to the crowded room.

"You're not convincing anyone," Percy whispered. "Darling."

I leaned my head into his hand and closed my eyes. *Why does this have to feel so good?* Knowing it was all an act ruined it for me. Mostly.

"I doubt anyone acts like this in public," I said, gazing into Percy's piercing green eyes. "That would be scandalous."

Percy looked both smug and exasperated. "It's true. It's a hospice, not a grand hotel. The people who hike up here are a different sort."

Almost instinctively, I turned my face to the side and kissed his palm. Percy's smile split his face from side to side. I smiled slowly in return as I rested my cheek in his hand. His eyes sparkled with warmth and humor.

I was surprised at how easy and natural it had felt. It scared me a little. But no, I had wanted to wipe the smug look off his face and surprise him. That's what I told myself. Even if I welcomed the warmth from his hand and hated the thought of dinner ending.

Down the bench we heard a woman sigh and the man speaking in German.

"They think we are adorable," Percy said. "It's working." He took my left hand again and resumed eating. "Maybe you should do it again. But somewhere higher." He tapped his lips.

Was he serious? The thought was far too intriguing, and I dismissed it quickly.

"You are ridiculous," I said and pulled away. "Not a chance."

Percy rubbed my knuckles again. "But I am right," he said. "I am watching the other couples carefully. We fit right in." His glasses had slid halfway down his nose, as usual.

I reached across the table and pushed Percy's glasses up his nose. He grabbed my wrist and began to play with my fingers.

I tried to discreetly tug my arm away. "I am hungry," I said. "I would like to finish my soup before it's stone cold."

"I'm hungry, too," Percy said. He gazed into my eyes and gently pressed a kiss to the fingers he held. He returned my hand to the table, never breaking eye contact.

I felt my heart rate quicken. The cheese on my plate suddenly became very interesting. Perhaps I could count the holes in it. I took a slice, put it on my bread, and took a bite. A large bite. One that I could chew for a long time to avoid conversation.

What was happening between us? Something was changing, and it would not ever be the same between us. *But what is an act and what is real?*

Percy's eyes scanned the room casually. I could hear laughter and conversations in several languages. A few of the St. Bernard dogs flopped near the fireplace.

"You can hardly restrain yourself," I said. "Is it painful? Not being able to talk to anyone?"

Percy shook his head ruefully. "How did you know?"

"It's what you do. Everywhere we go," I said. "Meet strangers. Trying to avoid them must be difficult."

"On the contrary. It's good practice," Percy said. "Lady Stuart insists that I must learn more discretion if I hope to become an ambassador. More observation and less participation."

I smiled at Percy. "But it's not who you are."

Percy smiled back, "No, it's who you are. Always on the edges. Adept at keeping secrets."

What does he suspect?

I tore off another piece of bread. "I will keep this quiet, Percy. As long as John does, too, your career should be safe."

Percy studied my face. He said quietly, "We both should be safe. What other secrets are you keeping, Elle?"

I finished my bread and cheese and concentrated on finishing my soup. "Just the scandalous poetry purchases."

Percy laughed loudly. The German couple looked over at us and smiled again.

"You can't do it," I said. "You cannot avoid drawing attention to yourself. It's in your nature to laugh, to make friends, to be the center of every conversation."

"Then we are doomed to marry," Percy said. "But you are wrong. I can play a part when I need to." He finished his last bite of soup and scraped the bench backward. He held his arm out toward me and raised his voice. "Darling? Are you cold? The stove looks inviting."

I shivered as I joined him near the fire. "The temperature drops at night, doesn't it?"

Percy drew my shawl around me, then tucked his coat around my shoulders once again. "We are on top of a mountain." He shrugged, then grinned. "I would not know. I am impervious." He guided me toward the center of the stove where the flames were warmest.

I rubbed my hands and arms as the heat of the fire and the warmth of his jacket gradually permeated the chill. I thought of Percy's reaction to the prospect of a forced marriage. If word reached others that we had spent a night without chaperones, did he really consider that doom? Woe? The worst of ills? After pretending to be married to him, I felt quite differently than he did. I had enjoyed it a little too much.

Another dog joined us, begging for attention. I scratched its head and behind its ears. It reminded me of Papa's hunting dogs.

"Are you sure they are safe?" I worried about my parents. "With the steep cliff and the thunder."

Percy put an arm around me. "I am sure they waited at the inn before proceeding. We will see them tomorrow. The dogs are famous for their rescues." He pulled me toward him.

I looked around. To my astonishment, Percy was right. The level of decorum was lacking. Each couple was more casual than I had expected. We were not in my drawing room or a formal parlor. Seven other women rested their heads on their husbands' shoulders. I counted.

I was tired. I was scared. I was pretending to be married, so we would not draw anyone's notice. And Percy's jacket smelled really, really good. If only I were as impervious to Percy's charms as he was to the cold temperature.

But I was not. I rested my head on his shoulder. I closed my eyes and let the warmth of the fire wash over me. I felt my fears dissolving in the circle of Percy's arms as we stood in comfortable silence. I wished this were real.

I heard someone approaching and decided not to open my eyes or break the spell. Someone spoke rapidly in a language I only half understood. Percy answered briefly. I heard laughter and the footsteps went away. I opened my eyes.

Percy gazed down at me. "I told you I could play a part when I needed to. I've been silent for ten entire minutes, Elle. And it worked. They think we've been married for years. We look so comfortable with each other, they said." He put a hand on my cheek. For one moment his eyes darted to my lips.

Surely, even he would not be so bold. Not in public.

Percy swallowed and cleared his throat. "Let's find our rooms. I fear your parents will not make their way to us tonight."

The temperature dipped even lower as we moved away from the fire. The night sky twinkled with stars through the windows. The light had grown dim in the hall. Evening had fallen.

CHAPTER 14

Percy and I waited in the brisk morning breeze. On one side, visitors streamed down the mountainside toward Italy. On the other, I watched for any sign of my family.

"And the dogs would have come back?" I asked again. "If my family was—" I took a deep breath. "—injured?"

Percy put an arm around me. The last travelers had left an hour ago. Only the monks and dogs remained at the pass, and they were busy preparing for the next day's guests.

"Yes. The dogs are well trained," Percy said.

He and I watched the trail together. His closeness blocked the mountain wind sweeping the summit.

I had asked the same question at least five times. Percy answered me every time. Calmly. Kindly. Reassuringly. Even though there was no need to pretend for anyone, he still comforted me and held me close.

This was going to make it hard to stop pretending.

At last I spotted mules on the trail. Percy moved away instantly. The cold morning air rushed around me. A mixture of relief and sadness swept over me.

Mama dismounted from her mule like a queen and rushed to

embrace me, then Percy, then me again. "Eleanor! Darling girl! You made it! I worried all night. Your father saw those cliffs and panicked." Mama clung to me.

John laughed. "By the time he got over his fear of heights, the storm rolled in and the monks wouldn't let the mules attempt the hike. They weren't worried about us, just the animals."

John tore Mama off my neck and took her into the hospice to rest.

Papa fell off his mule and tried to walk on shaky legs.

"May I assist you into the hospice?" Percy asked. I could see him fighting a grin.

Papa shook his head. He viewed the mountains in wonder, although his face looked sick. "It's so high up here."

"It is the third-highest pass in Switzerland, Papa," I said. "You summited one of the tallest peaks in the Alps." I managed to keep a straight face.

Papa's headshaking turned into nodding. He pointed at Percy. "Perhaps you can help. Need to talk." Papa gulped.

"Are you well?" I asked. I put one arm around Papa's waist, and Percy put an arm around my father on the other side. The three of us began walking slowly.

"Eleanor. Compromised? Have to. Marry?" Papa could hardly get the words out.

"No. We were surrounded by monks the entire time," Percy said.

"Separate rooms, Papa. They had planned accommodations for several and so few arrived. No need for concern." I shared a look with Percy.

"Alone. All night. No chaperone." Papa drew a deep breath. He seemed to regain some of his strength. "See here, Hauxton, I wouldn't wish a forced marriage on anyone, but if you and my daughter were alone all night..."

"Lord Barrington. I give you my word. We were in full view of the other guests and monks the entire evening. Surely, they were chaperones enough."

Papa turned toward me. "Ellie, child? You are unharmed? The precipice is so steep. The whole way up I imagined you falling off your mule."

I couldn't recall the last time he had used my childhood name. "Yes, Papa. Mr. Hauxton rode directly behind me, and my guide stayed close the entire way. It didn't rain until well after we reached the summit and had dined."

Papa laid a hand on my shoulder, then looked down the valley to Italy. He stepped back from the edge of the viewpoint. A few loose pebbles scattered, and he scrambled backward even further. He put an arm across me. "Back up, dear. I still think the boat would have been better."

He nodded briskly to Percy. "Very well, Hauxton. Thanks for watching over my little...over Lady Eleanor." Papa strode toward the hospice without looking back once at the magnificent view or trying to paint Napoleon crossing the Alps.

We were alone. Percy stretched and chuckled, probably in relief. "Catastrophe averted. Well done." He rolled his neck back and forth. "I think I'll explore the paths with John. Care to join us?"

A catastrophe. That's how he viewed a possible marriage to me. It stung a little. "No, I'll need to check on Mama."

We gazed at each other. "If you're certain," he said.

"Go on," I said. "John will want to abuse Papa behind his back, because he is afraid of mules and mountains."

"Then I'd best let him get started." Percy looked at me a long moment. He smiled, then left.

It was over. I watched him cross the clearing and heard him whistling. Relieved. But I would miss this closeness. We wouldn't have chances to be alone anymore. Now that I had felt a connection with Percy, the normal distance felt farther away than ever before.

After lunch and a rest, we rode down the winding trail into Italy. Papa led the way down the mountain. He seemed eager to reach the bottom. Once we reached the verdant valley, we left the mules behind and feasted on our first Italian meal while we waited for the servants to reassemble the carriages. Eventually, we began riding toward the nearest train station.

John and Percy rode in one. Papa, Mama, and I rode in another. I wished the carriages were larger so we could all ride together. I missed Percy's conversation already.

At least the trains had more space than the carriages. Six people could fit in a compartment instead of four people in a carriage. I liked riding on the trains.

I began a new piece of embroidery. The Calais Pier with a stormy sky, like the one we'd seen over the St. Bernard Pass. I worked on it during train rides to keep myself occupied.

Percy came and sat with me to help select embroidery thread colors.

"And how are you an expert on embroidery thread?" I asked.

"I am an artist," he replied, and insisted that I use a darker shade of grey for the sky. I would have thought it was merely an excuse to let our hands brush each other's as we pointed to the linen and dug through my embroidery basket. If it had been anyone else.

But I did enjoy it all the same.

I had a lot to think about as the train chugged toward Turin. I loved the tall Italian cypress trees that looked nothing like the English countryside. It was nearly September. We'd been gone almost four months.

What had Lucy and Rachel been doing? How many social engagements had they had? That was long enough for sixteen or twenty more dinner parties. Plus social calls once a week. And maybe four summer picnics. And four excursions. Not that I was counting. But it was well over thirty or forty events. That was enough to fall in love.

I would have been betrothed by now.

Had Lord Chelmsford begun to court anyone? Did I still care? I tried to remember what Lord Chelmsford looked like. I couldn't think of anything.

Instead I imagined green eyes encased in lopsided wire-rimmed spectacles. I remembered the comfort and warmth and ease of standing in front of a fire, Percy's arm pulling me toward him.

Did he feel anything like I did? Was he really pretending, merely to avoid a scandal? Or had those looks been genuine? Surely, there was something real there.

But Percy had made it quite clear that he would go to great lengths to avoid marrying me. Or being forced to marry me. Was it the same thing? Did I fit into his ambitious future life? Did I want to be a diplomat's wife? Images of the mirrored dining hall filled with nearly one hundred people flashed in my mind. It was a daunting thought.

⚜

We flew through Turin, Verona, and Venice in our haste to reach Vienna before the snowstorms began. Percy and John spent time together, as they always had, and I was left with my parents.

But now I missed Percy. I'd had a taste of saffron spice. And I liked it. But how would I get a chance to sample more with John always around?

Winter arrived in Vienna at the same time we did.

CHAPTER 15

October 1854

Percy and John took apartments in a fashionable quarter of Vienna. Papa wanted to settle in Baden bei Wien, a spa resort town nearly two hours away by carriage. I quickly pointed out that, in winter time, the warm waters would attract many people. And the art museums were all in Vienna. Somehow, Mama and I managed to convince him to take up apartments in the center of town.

Our apartments occupied one floor of a building overlooking a round plaza, Michaelerplatz, in the First District. A white church with statues over its entrances protruded on one side. Windows lined the cream and yellow stucco buildings, five stories high.

Streets led off in several other directions, the buildings shaped like wedges. People, horses, and carriages traveled every direction, rattling over the cobblestones. A café occupied one corner, and a bank inhabited the other.

An arched gateway adorned an entrance with the most ornate statues I had ever seen. Tall columns topped the statues leading into the Hofburg Palace. A green copper dome sat atop the massive structure.

A shop named Loden-Plankl occupied the entire bottom story of the building across from the gate. Warm woolen jackets and clothes filled its windows. I promised myself I would go back as soon as I could.

Roman ruins ran directly along the road. I thought of Percy and wanted to show him the crumbling blocks of stone embedded in the cobblestone road or examine the outlines of ancient buildings which lay in our path.

I couldn't believe my luck. Vienna. The heart of the city. For six months, or until winter ended. And we finally lived in the same city as Percy and John. Surely, we would see them often.

Mama arranged a visit to the Schönbrunn Palace gardens before the plants actually froze. She thought it would be nice for us to meet the friend who had written to her. I thought it sounded uncomfortable.

But off we went. I wore half-boots and a new wool cape to combat the chilly breezes.

We arrived and found a knot of people near the entrance. Two short women, about my age, waited by the garden gate. Percy and John glanced at each other and quickened their step.

A tiny, blonde woman chattered away. She looked about fifteen years old. Her head didn't even reach the bottom of my chin. The other wore her rich, dark hair back in a bun. It accentuated her heart-shaped face and dramatic eyes.

An older man and woman waited with them.

Mama rushed to grab her friend's hands. "Catherine!" she cried. "It's been too long!"

"Anne!" The woman greeted Mama, then gestured toward the brunette girl. "My daughter, Miss Charlotte Harwich." She indicated the dainty blonde girl. "Miss Cecelia Duxford." Then she waved at the man standing beside her. "And Mr. Duxford. He works for the Foreign Office here in Vienna."

John stepped forward and held his arm out to the women. "May

I accompany you on a tour of the gardens?" He flashed his most handsome smile.

Miss Duxford quickly took his arm.

Percy stepped forward and held out his arm to Miss Harwich.

I tightened the cape around me and held onto the clasp. I'd never seen him pay attention to another woman. His focus had always been on me. It sounded childish to even admit the thought, but I had grown used to having Percy all to myself.

"Sir?" He inclined his head to Mr. Duxford. "I should like to speak with you. Will you walk with us as well?"

"No, no, wouldn't dream of interrupting the young people. You go on. Plenty of time to talk later, young man. This is a garden, not an embassy." Mr. Duxford chuckled at his own joke.

"Shall we sit while my husband sketches the statues?" Mama asked. "The rest of you go on, like Mr. Duxford said. I want to hear all about Catherine's music school."

I trailed behind the others. John walked with Miss Duxford on his arm, thoroughly engaged. Percy walked with the quiet Miss Harwich on his arm, apparently having a one-sided conversation.

Mama intended for me to become friends with Miss Harwich. Instead, Percy strolled alongside her. I watched them from behind. It seemed like a young couple courting. He fawned on her, asking her questions, drawing her out, entertaining her. Miss Harwich's raven hair shone in the sunlight. She laughed at all of Percy's jokes and dipped her head shyly the rest of the time.

He treated her the same way he treated me. Just as friendly and attentive. Just as kind and solicitous. I didn't mean anything more to him than anyone else. I felt lost and forgotten.

I pulled my cape around my shoulders and clung to it. Gravel crunched under our feet. Breezes blew around us as clouds drifted across the sky. Fading greenery lined the hills, and the naiad fountains no longer ran with water. Hedges lined the walk from the mustard-yellow palace up toward the Gloriette colonnade on the hill ahead of us. The only sound came from cooing doves swooping in and out of the cage-like aviary.

I wished I had brought a sketchbook, like Papa, to capture the waves of the clothing on the classical statues lining one walkway. I wanted to focus on something other than the couples in front of me.

I gazed at the faceless stone statues, some without arms, some without heads. Incomplete, yet whole. Artistically broken to mimic the ancient relics. Abandoned.

Others had detailed, lifelike visages. I would recognize them if they rounded the corner of the foliage which divided the statues from the other parts of the gardens.

"Come on, Elle." John yelled over his shoulder. "More to see. Never finish at this rate."

I reluctantly left the row of statues. We made our way to Schönbrunn Hill. I gasped when I glimpsed the view and stopped in amazement. My cape fell off my shoulders and I retied the ribbons to snug it back into place.

A gigantic Roman ruin covered the hillside. Weather-worn columns supported a crumbling façade. Underneath a towering arch, cracked blocks and stones led to a carved fountain with two frolicking statues. Pitted stairs on either side wound beneath more shadowed archways. Fallen stones lay artistically arranged among the rubble.

Percy waited for me to catch up to him and Miss Harwich. I quickened my pace.

"It's called the Ruin of Carthage," he explained.

"Did you study before you came? Ask the local monks? Or your mule guide?" I teased.

Percy laughed. "Guilty. I read the guidebook." He turned to Miss Duxford. "Have you seen it before?"

"It's only a folly, not a real ruin." Miss Duxford slid closer to Percy. "Let's try the maze."

"I'd like a moment to study it," he said. He looked away from Miss Duxford and back at the ruin.

"I love a maze! Is it easy to get lost?" John asked and offered his arm to Miss Duxford. She switched her attention back to him.

"I've seen this several times, too," Miss Harwich said.

John offered his other arm to her. They headed toward the large row of hedges, taller than their heads.

Miss Duxford seemed put out. I got the sense that she preferred not to share the secluded hedge walk with Miss Harwich.

I could hear Miss Duxford begin to interrogate John as they walked. "Now tell me all about your family. Do you have brothers? Mmm. And how many estates are there? Mmm."

Percy and I stood side by side, contemplating the folly. He didn't even watch Miss Harwich leave. I enjoyed the comfortable silence between us. It felt good to be alone with Percy again, like the day had grown warmer and I could finally breathe.

"I can't wait to see Rome," I said. "To see the real ruins, in spring."

He nodded. He seemed to be memorizing the sculptures.

I considered the intricate patterns carved into the stones above the columns. "How do they carve faces out of stone? And the columns—I've never seen lines like that, so exactly and evenly spaced."

"Did you see the Great Parterre figures?" Percy asked.

"Their dresses," I said.

"The lines and movement."

"The way they flowed."

We studied the folly again. It was like singing a duet in silence. Completely in sync. Reading each other's thoughts. In total harmony.

"I could stay all day just to examine the figures on the fountains." I shivered. "If it weren't almost winter."

I started to walk toward the maze. "I have to come back."

Percy joined me reluctantly. "When it's warmer. I want to sketch the friezes."

I pulled my cape tight around myself. "And the tops of the columns."

"The capitals. Yes. Corinthian. And the pattern in the great archway," he said.

We entered the maze. I could hear the others in the distance. The hedges muted the sound and dappled sunlight filtered through the leaves. I loved being alone with Percy, knowing we shared a love of ancient ruins.

"Rome would have been warm." He kicked at the gravel on the path as we wandered idly along the path.

I didn't want to rejoin John too soon, and I matched my steps to his. "My father can never say no to my mother's wishes."

"My father is much the same way." Percy slowed a little as we walked.

I enjoyed the feel underfoot of crunching dry leaves on the dirt path. There was no reason to hurry. "Is your mother as whimsical as mine?"

"More so. And my father indulges her." He grimaced playfully. "Theirs was a love match."

"And you do not approve of love matches?" I asked. Something heavy settled on my heart. Was he in earnest or not? "You would not be equally as indulgent, were you to fall in love?"

"A spare must plan carefully. There is no room for indulgence or whim," Percy said, avoiding my gaze.

I could not make out his tone, so I tried to make my tone teasing. "Will you not marry for love? Will you strategize and calculate and plan? Even that?"

Percy examined the hedges nearest him. "Especially that. And you? Do you approve of your parents' match?"

I hesitated. *How could I answer that without saying too much?* "Theirs is a love match, too. My father and mother understand each other."

Percy laughed loudly. A few birds scattered from the bushes around us. "Always so evasive. I believe you scheme just as much as I do. Tell me this: will you seek a love match, or will you seek the richest duke you can find when we return to England?" Percy jabbed me in the ribs with his elbow. "Truly."

We walked in silence for a moment. I was beginning to believe that Percy was serious. It was hard to imagine him seeking a marriage of convenience.

I jabbed him back. "Tell me. Will you seek a love match, or will you scour the *ton* for the perfect diplomat's wife? One who can help you get appointed to an embassy?"

Only the sound of leaves crunching underfoot broke the silence.

"How are you enjoying Vienna?" Percy asked in a light tone.

"Are you trying to change the subject?"

"I am not trying. I did." He grinned at me.

I swatted his arm. "Very well. Let us discuss the weather. Or our travels, instead. Which did you like best? The innkeepers or lumpy beds or horrid smells?" I brushed my hand along the hedges. The thick branches bristled against my glove as dry leaves crumbled beneath my touch.

Percy would not answer my question. He would marry strategically, avoiding families tainted by scandal, like mine.

As I stopped walking to readjust my cape again, Percy bumped into me. I put my palm on his chest to steady myself at the same time his hand found the small of my back. I froze.

A few dry branches hung overhead, casting us into shadow. Our faces were inches apart. A breeze ruffled his tousled hair. Percy's brilliant green eyes searched mine.

He held me close, the warmth of his hand welcome in the chill fall air. "Will you seek a love match?"

I wondered what he saw in my eyes. I tilted my face up toward him. His chest felt firm and solid beneath my hand. I swallowed. My mouth suddenly felt dry. What would it be like to run my fingers through that wavy blond hair?

I could see longing in his gaze, but something held him back. I did not dare to move, and I hesitated.

He thought I was a catastrophe.

Just then, Miss Duxford's voice came through the hedge. "Over here! Is that you, Lady Eleanor? Almost there."

I had forgotten that the winter hedges were neither overgrown nor covered with leaves.

He dropped his arm, and I moved backward. He began walking around me.

"Percy." I stood still, not sure what to say.

He turned around, waiting for my reply.

"I—" I could not formulate a response. I intended to marry solely to protect myself and my family. I had never thought a love match could be a possibility for me.

He strode away, shaking his head. I couldn't keep up.

We zig-zagged our way to the center of the maze and rejoined the others. I could not help feeling I had missed an opportunity, that I had let Percy down.

But he hadn't answered my question, either.

I swatted the bushes with my gloves and watched the crushed leaves fall to the ground.

Percy accompanied Miss Harwich through the gardens the remainder of the afternoon.

CHAPTER 16

November 1854

When we returned to our apartments, Mama informed me that I was now registered in classes at Mrs. Harwich's music school. "They need singers for their Christmas concert, and enrollment at her school has been declining ever since her husband died. I'll enlist John and Mr. Hauxton as well. Miss Duxford is already enrolled."

She wasted no time. The next day Mama arranged another outing. This time we were going to meet the Christmas concert director in order to promote Mrs. Harwich's school. Evidently there was a great deal of competition, and spots in the concert were limited.

We crossed the plaza in front of our apartments in Michaelerplatz and found the entrance to the Spanish Riding School near the large gates. Papa had secured tickets to see the all-white trained stallions. John and Percy waited near the doors. Mrs. Harwich came bustling up with her daughter, Miss Duxford, and a man I'd never seen before.

When Mama suggested we meet the concert director, I imagined an elderly man with white hair flying in every direction. Mr. James Felsted was nothing like I imagined.

Winter sun danced on his artistically tousled curls. His chestnut brown waves reminded me of the young Austrian emperor who had just married his young wife Elisabeth a few months ago. 'Sisi' was only sixteen years old when they married. And I was now eighteen with no prospects.

But this man worked all over Europe. He knew Johann Strauss. He was probably older than John or Percy. Maybe younger? Definitely unmarried.

And he could smile. A blinding row of perfectly straight, unnaturally white teeth.

My heart beat a little faster.

"Greetings, fair ladies." Mr. Felsted bowed toward us. "I have awaited your arrival impatiently. Now, may I meet these goddesses?"

John spoke up. "My father and mother, Lord and Lady Barrington. My sister, Lady Eleanor."

"This cannot be your mother. Surely. I thought she was your sister." Mr. Felsted took Mama's hand and raised it to his lips.

Mr. Felsted sighed dramatically. "But there are four beautiful women and I only have two arms. Whatever shall I do?"

"You'll manage." Papa snorted. "Stop keeping them out in the cold." He escorted Mama indoors.

Mr. Felsted held up both of his elbows. "Whom may I accompany? Lady Eleanor?"

Giddy butterflies tingled in my stomach. He was a bit ridiculous, but he must be immensely talented. Perhaps he was just nervous.

Percy pushed past John to get a better view of Mr. Felsted. He raised an eyebrow at me. "I believe I made arrangements to escort Lady Eleanor. My apologies, Mr. Felsted." He held out his arm to me.

The butterflies intensified. Percy wanted to escort me. Out of all the women, he chose me. Not Miss Harwich. Hopefully, I could sit between them and still get to know Mr. Felsted.

John held out his arm to Miss Duxford, who took it reluctantly. She was also eyeing Mr. Felsted. I turned my head back to make sure Miss Harwich had an arm. I hadn't liked the feeling of walking alone in Schönbrunn gardens. Mr. Felsted smiled perfunctorily and offered his arm to her.

After we entered, Mr. Felsted craned his neck to see who else had arrived. "Let's get a seat at the front. I see four seats up there."

"I'd rather let my parents and brother sit up front," I said. "John wants to convince my father to buy more horses."

We moved one row back, on a red-upholstered bench in the center of the viewing area, so Percy and I sat beside Mr. Felsted and Miss Harwich.

I peered through the columns that surrounded the boxed seating area. The arena had several tiers of balconies, divided by towering marble columns. Chandeliers floated on the medallion-covered, plastered ceiling of the pristine white room, yet a thick layer of dirt covered the floor.

"What a strange combination," I said quietly. "Chandelier ceilings and dirt floors." The grandeur of the room awed me.

Percy rested his hand on my arm. "Opulence and simplicity."

"The Ballet of the White Stallions," I said. "I think we read the same guidebook."

"A palace for animals?"

"That's the one," I said.

Mr. Felsted didn't hear me. He was trying to position himself so he had a clear view of the two balconies. On his other side, Miss Harwich was positioned behind a column and her view was almost completely obstructed.

I leaned across Mr. Felsted and tried to speak to Miss Harwich. "Shall I move along the bench, so you have more room? Can you see?"

Miss Harwich shook her head. "I mean, yes, please, if you would, and, no, I cannot see."

I nudged Mr. Felsted, who had just settled himself. He was taking up half of the bench. "Miss Harwich can't see. Could you move down, please? If I move over?"

"But of course." Mr. Felsted's smile was too large. He moved right next to me, his leg brushing mine.

I shifted in my seat, trying to angle myself away from him. Mr. Felsted slid along the bench, his thigh brushing up against mine. I moved over again, as far as I could. Mr. Felsted grinned at me.

I was sorry I had positioned myself next to him as well as Percy. However skilled as a singer, he was encroaching on my side uncomfortably.

Over my head, Percy shot an icy glare at Mr. Felsted. "Miss Harwich, can you see now?" he said loudly.

Miss Harwich nodded.

Percy stared at Mr. Felsted, who didn't move. Percy tilted his body toward mine and laid his arm on the bench behind me to allow me more space to scoot over. I squirmed on the bench, so my leg didn't touch Mr. Felsted's.

Mr. Felsted returned Percy's stare, then slid closer to Miss Harwich. I felt sorry for her.

Percy's leg nearly brushed up against mine, but it wasn't uncomfortable like it was with Mr. Felsted. It was safe and reassuring beside him. I knew he was protecting me, not leering at me. I wanted to lean into him and let him hold me, like he had in Switzerland.

I turned at an angle so my back fit along his chest, with barely an inch separating us, to get farther away from Mr. Felsted. I could feel the heat of Percy's body. It was going to be hard to pay attention to the show.

Across the large, indoor arena, a door opened. Eight white horses entered in procession. Tall riders in military-style jackets lifted their hands in salute as they passed through the entrance. Somewhere behind us, a live orchestra began playing. Music filled the arena.

The Lipizzaner stallions promenaded around the walls. The riders filed the snowy-white horses past the ground-level box where we sat. The animals reared up on two legs. I took a deep breath. One stallion kicked in the air, its rider still on its back, and landed. I'd never seen anything more beautiful.

Percy fidgeted with his cuff links. Finally, he bent down so our faces were nearly touching. "They're born dark and take ten years to turn white," he whispered in my ear.

I inclined my head back toward him. "One in every hundred horses stays dark."

He looked down at me. "They're considered lucky." His glasses were askew, and his breath smelled like peppermint.

I squirmed around and straightened his handkerchief. "I really did read the guidebook, too."

I couldn't wait to hear what random fact Percy could come up with next, and how his breath would feel on my skin. I loved sitting with him. It was easy and comfortable. And delicious. I still felt like I had butterflies in my stomach, and I wondered if he felt the same way.

The stallions jumped in circles; all eight horses coordinated perfectly with each other. Unfortunately, the animals finished their routine as the music drew to a close.

Mr. Felsted stood as soon as the applause ended. He put his shoulders back and struck a pose as he gazed around the arena. He looked like a show horse waiting for a trainer to put him through his paces. He also had Miss Harwich trapped.

I tried to exit the row as quickly as possible to give Miss Harwich room to avoid Mr. Felsted. What would Mama think? We were supposed to be impressing him and persuading him, but had Percy or I offended him? Would he allow Mrs. Harwich's school to perform in the city-wide concert?

I needed to remedy this somehow. Convince him to let us sing in his concert. In a way that didn't involve sitting anywhere near him.

CHAPTER 17

Mr. Felsted became a regular part of our social circle. It evened out the numbers. Three women, three men. It was exhausting to watch Miss Duxford flirting with all three men, trying to divide her attention among them, while Miss Harwich remained aloof. I tried to avoid entertaining Mr. Felsted as much as I could, without seeming to avoid him. That was exhausting also. Sometimes I missed living in the quiet cottage in Versailles.

Mr. Felsted hinted loudly and often that private lessons might improve our chances at winning a solo in the concert. Finally, Papa paid for lessons to quiet him, on the condition that I practice at John's apartments.

I had never visited John at Cambridge or Eton. The outer rooms were surprisingly well-kept, since Percy frequently lost his walking stick or mislaid his watch, even though it was attached to his vest by a chain.

John had a small office. Every piece of paper was lined up, edges precisely matching. Carefully stacked rows of books filled his shelves.

"You'd make a good estate manager," I told John, as I examined his ledgers. Neat, clear handwriting filled the books. Perhaps John maintained the order in their apartments.

"The only thing I manage is my quarterly allowance," John said.

Sketches of horses covered one sheet. "What are these other pages?" I asked.

John closed the ledger. "A proposal I'm working on."

John's valet, Parker, who served as his butler as well, announced Mr. Felsted. The rented apartments had a piano in the drawing room. I moved into the room and was surprised to find Percy sitting in one corner.

He sat with folded arms and legs crossed over one another. He held a book in front of him with one hand. Percy merely nodded when we greeted him and continued reading.

John said, "Hauxton's going to chaperone for me. I've got to finish these numbers. You don't mind, do you, Elle?" He went back to the ledgers in his office.

I felt relieved. Percy, on the other hand, muttered something under his breath and crossed his legs again. He wanted to be here as little as I did, but I hoped for more sympathy. I hoped he knew this was not my idea, but my father's.

Mr. Felsted seated himself at the piano. "Let's warm up first, shall we?" Mr. Felsted ran through some scales and warm-up exercises.

My voice was a little out of practice from disuse the last few weeks, but I warmed up quickly.

Mr. Felsted flashed his toothy smile. "Impressive! You've got quite a range. Very natural sounding on the high notes."

I glanced at Percy. He hadn't turned any pages yet but stared at the floor.

"Let's work on the breath control." Mr. Felsted left the piano. He came around so that his back faced Percy. "Take a deep breath and let it out slowly. Let's see how long it takes you." He considered my stomach and chest, then let his eyes rest on my chest.

I smoothed the front of my skirt as I inhaled. I wanted this to end immediately. How could I do that without creating a problem for Mrs. Harwich? I pushed the air out slowly.

"Very good," Mr. Felsted said as I let out the last of my breath. "Now try again, and I'll show you where I want you to breathe."

Mr. Felsted came around behind me. He put one hand on my stomach. "Take a deep breath. Push my hand out."

I pulled my stomach in to avoid him, rather than pushing it out to fill it with air. My lungs barely expanded. Where was Percy? Could he see this?

Mr. Felsted whispered in my ear. "Gently." His warm breath tickled my ear.

I raised my shoulders and tried to shrink away. I pushed the breath out as fast as I could, not even thinking about breath control.

I wanted this lesson to end, but I didn't know how to tell him. Mr. Felsted had maneuvered us behind the piano, so Percy could not see.

If I offended him, would he take revenge on Mrs. Harwich? Refuse to allow students from her school to perform? My father was paying a lot of money for these lessons and for the school to participate in the concert. My mother desperately wanted to help her old friend.

But I did not like the feel of his hands on my stomach.

He tightened his hold. "Now let's work on the exhale. That was too quick." Mr. Felsted angled his body to block my view of Percy entirely.

Mr. Felsted put a hand on the upper part of my chest.

Every muscle in my body tensed. I took a shallow, shaky breath and held it, hating the feel of Mr. Felsted's hands on me.

"Now breathe again. Deeper breaths," Mr. Felsted said.

What could I say to let Percy know I needed help?

But just then he tore Mr. Felsted's hands off me. "This lesson is over."

I could hear the menace in his voice.

Mr. Felsted glowered at Percy, but Percy held his ground. He moved in front of me, blocking Mr. Felsted.

Heavy footsteps crossed the drawing room.

"He's gone," Percy said and turned toward me.

I waited until I heard the door of the apartments close, then I let out my breath.

Percy searched my face. "Are you well?"

I shook my head, then my whole body began shaking. I couldn't form words. I felt so violated by Mr. Felsted.

I stared across the room, pulling my arms around myself. I couldn't control my breathing, taking deep gulps but never getting enough air. My chin trembled and I covered my mouth to stifle a sob.

"May I?" Percy opened his arms wide. "Could I be of any comfort?"

I nodded. Percy peeled my arms off my shoulders and wrapped them around himself. I stood stiff, still breathing hard. My heart still raced, and I could not believe that I was safe yet.

He took a hand and gently pulled my head to his shoulder. Finally, I collapsed, letting Percy hold me, grateful for the refuge of his embrace.

I began to cry silently, though sobs wracked my body. I felt like my stomach would be sick.

Percy held me close. He put his head gently on top of mine and stroked my hair. "He's gone, Eleanor," he whispered. "You are safe. Shall I get your brother?"

"NO! No." I heaved great breaths, trying to gasp for air. I did not want anyone to witness me in this condition or know what had happened. Slowly, the crying stopped. I pulled back and gazed up at Percy, tear tracks staining my cheeks. "Thank you," I whispered.

He ran a finger along the ridge of my cheek, wiping away an errant tear. He led me to a sofa in front of the fireplace. He searched for a soft blanket and tucked it around me, then sat next to me and took my hands. "Let me get your brother. We need to tell your father." Percy's voice was gentle, but insistent.

I didn't want to talk about it. I felt ashamed of the encounter.

What if Percy or John thought I liked those attentions or encouraged Mr. Felsted?

I stared at the dancing flames in the hearth. Finally, I said quietly, "No. I don't want to talk about it or answer questions. I just want to forget it ever happened. But how will I explain this to Papa? That I'm not taking lessons anymore? Or tell Mama that I won't be singing in the concert?"

A hint of anger flared in Percy's eyes. "You cannot let a scoundrel like him get away with that behavior."

"Please, Percy." I could feel myself shaking still. I pulled the blanket higher over my chest. The fire crackled and popped.

"No one has the right to touch you like that, except—" He stopped abruptly. "Are you shaking?"

I sat silently, waiting for him to finish. Except who? Was Percy imagining someone else holding me like that? Himself?

Percy's thumbs absently stroked the top of my hand. "You're shaking."

He crossed the room to find another blanket. "No one has that right, except your husband, when you marry. But I'm sorry you lost your tutor."

"What about you?" I asked.

"Me?" he asked. "I don't have that right, either, Elle." But his gaze held a look that made me wonder if he had briefly considered it.

I felt my cheeks grow warm. "I meant, could you tutor me? You have musical training. You write your own compositions. I can tell my parents I prefer you as a tutor."

But now I wondered. What would it feel like to be held in Percy's arms instead of Mr. Felsted's? When I wasn't crying or distressed? When I was secure and not at risk? Just like we had been moments before. Just like in Switzerland.

Percy tucked another blanket around me. He took a deep breath and paced around the room. I followed him with my eyes. My breath had nearly returned to normal, but I still felt weak. I decided to stay on the sofa. I didn't trust my legs yet.

He went back to his chair by the window, then paced over to the piano. He picked up some sheet music and stared at it. He put it down and walked back to his chair.

"Will you help me, Percy? Please. Will you keep this quiet? Even from John? I have no wish to relive it."

I heard another long sigh.

"Yes," came his reply from the corner. He turned around and grinned at me. "But you'll probably screech."

Percy came and put his hand on my shoulder. He spoke in a serious tone. "Perhaps we should not start today. You look done in. Come back tomorrow."

CHAPTER 18

Percy wasn't home when my maid and I arrived for the first tutoring session. Sibley discretely disappeared somewhere. John kept me company while I waited. I couldn't remember the last time we really talked. Before he left for Cambridge. Maybe even before Eton.

"What are these graphs?" I looked over John's shoulder at a list of numbers and figures.

John motioned to me to sit down. "Horse breeding schedules. Trying to figure out how long it would take to get established. I'd have to ask Father for a loan to start, but I need a plan."

"Are you serious about this?"

The papers covered his desk.

"More than anything." John pushed a ledger toward me and slumped down on his desk. "What else am I supposed to do when we return?"

I started to read his proposal. "I thought you were going to work for the Foreign Office."

"No, that's for stuffed shirts like Hauxton." John grinned and glanced over his shoulder.

"Did I hear someone call my name?" Percy entered the small room that John used as a study.

"If you heard me say 'stuffed shirt,' then yes, I was talking about you." John paused in his calculations. "How was Miss Harwich?"

"And this comes from the man who spends all day making calculations, even though we've left university." Percy nodded to me. "Miss Harwich and her mother are well. Are you ready to leave this stuffed shirt and do something worthwhile?"

We crossed the hall to the drawing room with its modest piano.

"I'll chaperone from here!" John called from his study.

"Really? More calculations?" Percy called back and turned to me. His eyes twinkled. I always liked seeing this lighter side of him. I wondered if he was in a good mood because of his visit with the Harwiches or if he and John were always like this.

"I spoke with Mrs. Harwich this morning. The choir committee—"

"Mr. Felsted," I said.

"Yes. Mr. Felsted, who is the head of the choir committee, does not need a school choir in the concert."

I sat on the piano bench. "So what's the point of tutoring me? I can just quit."

"No. Your father made a generous donation to the committee—"

"He bribed Mr. Felsted," I said. "When he paid in advance for my lessons."

Percy joined me at the piano. "And the committee will consider allowing one or two solo or ensemble numbers. A quartet perhaps. If Mr. Felsted approves. If the quality is high enough for his standards."

I snorted. His standards.

Percy blinked. "What was that sound?"

I shook my head. "I didn't screech."

Percy tried to compose his face. I could see him fighting a grin. "No, but we don't want *that* in your singing, either."

He rifled through sheets of paper, looking for songs. "Miss Harwich and I decided to audition three numbers. Miss Duxford will sing a solo. Miss Harwich will sing a duet with you. Barrington and I will join you to sing a quartet."

I snorted again. Mr. Felsted would never approve our musical selections.

"No. I'll tell Papa I changed my mind about lessons." I drew myself up. Majestic. Queenly. Why spend time practicing and watching Percy fawn over Miss Harwich, if Mr. Felsted was already set against us?

Percy exhaled and scrubbed a hand over his face, knocking his glasses askew. "Really, Elle. I see why your brother calls you the Duchess sometimes."

I moved toward the door. Glided. Serenely. "Good day, and I thank you for your time."

He stopped me. "You've got to help Miss Harwich. Her mother's school is facing closure and they have no other income. They need someone from the school to perform in this concert."

Percy's face was so earnest. I pulled my shawl closer around myself and considered him. Was he interested in Miss Harwich? Or did his concern stem from another reason? The thought of rehearsing with Miss Harwich, of watching him shower attention on her, was too much for me.

And the thought of performing in front of hundreds or thousands of people. My parents had taught me the value of privacy.

"I sing alone as a respite to leave everything behind. The thought of performing in a concert is overwhelming," I said.

Percy gaped at me. "But a voice like yours should not be hidden. It's meant to be shared. What good does it do if no one else hears you?"

I shifted uncomfortably. It sounded so selfish when he said it that way. "I don't want attention or praise."

Percy smirked. "You cannot help being magnificent, Eleanor. You will have to learn to live with it. But don't decide now. Practice today, and you can decide later," Percy said. He drew back the piano bench and settled himself. "Let's warm up."

⊙⊱⊰⊙

Miss Harwich was already at John's apartments when I arrived the next day. I couldn't back out. I would rehearse. I might even audition. But Mr. Felsted would never agree to let me perform, so I would not have to worry about that.

Miss Harwich and Percy stood with their heads together, bent over a piece of music. I'd grown accustomed to his attentive nature. I'd assumed that our closeness and understanding was unique to us. I'd expected to practice alone with Percy and now I felt like the odd one out.

I stepped back while he bantered with Miss Harwich over musical selections and discussed the dynamics of each piece.

"'Still, Still, Still,'" Miss Harwich insisted in her soft, gentle tone. "We must sing in German for a Viennese audience. Miss Duxford will sing 'Ave Maria,' but we should rehearse it in case she falls ill. Lady Eleanor and I can practice with her at my mother's school."

Percy sighed dramatically. "Very well, you have convinced me. Come, Barrington, shall we at least have our way on the selection of the quartet piece?"

John joined them near the piano. I noticed he managed to get between Percy and Miss Harwich and silently cheered for him. I'd seen Lucy and Rachel overlook my brother, and I wanted him to at least try to gain Miss Harwich's attention, if he wanted it.

She pulled a piece of music from the pile and showed it to John. "'Stille Nacht.' It's a great favorite here." She gazed up at him with her heart-shaped face and deep, dark eyes.

"Then it is decided," John said.

John rarely had the patience to sing with me at home. But Miss Harwich had asked him to join the quartet, and now he was going to sing. Perhaps she would not overlook him as my friends had.

Percy joined me on the sofa. "This is going to take a lot of work," he said in a low voice. He nodded his head toward John and Miss Harwich. "I had no idea your brother was so incompetent."

"I thought you sang together," I said.

"He can sing. He can't woo," Percy said. "Look at them. Neither of them can discuss a topic without my help. I need you. I don't want to do this alone."

I stared at him, too relieved to react.

"Come on, Elle, don't be obtuse. John's smitten."

I glanced at John. Suddenly he laughed much too loudly at something Miss Harwich said. He was smitten with Miss Harwich? Percy was only helping John?

"Of course." I fiddled with the tassels on my skirt. Why did they put those things on clothing? They never laid flat.

Percy put a finger under my chin and tilted my head up, forcing me to look at him. "What did you think?" He seemed genuinely puzzled.

"He's not the only one who can be obtuse," I muttered, then clapped a hand to my mouth. "I'm sorry, Percy. That was uncivil of me."

He laughed, then spoke even more quietly. "Did you think I was smitten, too? Don't mistake compassion for courtship, Elle. I'm worried about them. That is all. Her father died. Her mother's school is on the edge of closing. They need to participate in this concert."

"Of course," I said again, letting go of the tassels and smoothing the front of my skirt. I smiled at Percy.

"They're not like us," Percy said. He covered my hand with his and held it still. "You and I are capable of conversing intelligently without aid. Let's go rescue them and pretend to rehearse."

We headed back to the piano.

And now, instead of dreading rehearsals, I thought I might enjoy them. *Us.* Percy said "us." Comparing John's courtship of Miss Harwich to his relationship with me. I could sing all day if he asked me to.

CHAPTER 19

Rehearsals continued throughout November and December. I would arrive at John's home, talk with him until Miss Harwich arrived, then we would all practice.

I looked forward to my afternoons. I realized I had missed my brother and enjoyed our renewed closeness. I wanted to grow closer to Percy, too, or form a friendship with Miss Harwich, but our practices only allowed for a superficial kind of bond.

At least we laughed a lot. Percy and I tried to keep things light and give John plenty of opportunities to stand near Miss Harwich.

She was a remarkable musician. Between her mother's lessons at the school, rehearsals with Miss Duxford, and practices with Percy and John, I'd never felt more content. Music provided a challenge and filled my days. I was spending more time than ever doing the thing that made me happy.

Papa visited the many museums in Vienna, as he had in Paris, sketching and trying to recreate paintings. Mama visited cathedrals, spent time singing with Mrs. Harwich, and tried to find every Viennese bakery she could. She discovered several new torte and kuchen recipes, to everyone's delight.

The day of Mr. Felsted's examination arrived, just two weeks before Christmas. Winter snow covered the streets and blanketed the tops of the buildings.

I rehearsed with Percy beforehand at John's apartments. Miss Harwich would meet us at her mother's school.

"I can't face him," I said quietly to Percy as we finished practicing. "How will I sing in front of him?"

He rested his hands on the piano keyboard. "Can you forget what happened?"

I shook my head. "I'm sure he hasn't. He will not give me a fair chance. He will select someone else." I took a deep breath and pushed it out. "Miss Duxford. I hear she is taking private lessons from him."

"You are right. He may do that." Percy played a few scales. "I am sorry for Miss Duxford. But I cannot regret spending these weeks practicing with you."

I sat down next to Percy on the piano bench. We warmed up our voices. Just the two of us.

"You promised me a duet," Percy said. He dug around in a pile of loose sheets on top of the piano. "Ha!" He waved a piece of music in front of me.

"I cannot see it if you continue to move it about." I grabbed his wrist to make it stop moving. I always took my gloves off to play the piano. The unexpected feel of his skin on mine shocked me.

Percy grinned. That familiar look of challenge flashed in his eyes. He held the sheets above my head.

"No, Percy. Just give me the music, if you want me to sing it."

Percy dangled it. "Do you promise?"

"Why? What song is it?" Now I was on my guard.

He corrected his mistake. "Promise before I tell you which song it is."

"You are impossible," I said. "Are we warming up our voices or learning to wrestle?"

"Don't tempt me," Percy muttered, and quirked an eyebrow.

I couldn't continue to meet his gaze. "Very well. I promise. Will I regret it?"

Percy arranged the sheets on the piano. "Not at all. It's your favorite. 'O Soave Fanciulla.' I bought it in Paris."

I pursed my lips. "I put that one back on the stack. With all the other duets."

"And I picked them all up and purchased them," Percy said. "Now you may thank me."

I choked on a laugh. "Once. We can try it once."

"Four times."

"Twice."

"Agreed," Percy said. "I've already learned the accompaniment."

He had spent weeks learning it? We had stumbled through it at Barrington Hall, but I could tell he had really learned it. I felt a little nervous, as though the moment had added weight. It wasn't a casual decision, like it initially seemed. This meant something to him.

Percy began playing. He sang first. I began to drown in his rich voice until suddenly I had to hit the first, piercing note. But it was as effortless as the first time. Clear, high. The interruptions, the back and forth, the seamless transitions. We hit our notes together, the music pulling us in. Pure and sweet, full of the longing of a couple falling in love. This time when we sang, "amor," there was real emotion behind it.

The tug of his voice was as real as a physical sensation, our voices tangling and intertwining. I responded by pouring my heart into the song. I felt myself sway closer to Percy on the bench as the longing in the song matched a yearning of my own.

And yet my character pulled away in the song, and his character had to pursue her until they came together. Percy's pleas resonated in me, and I couldn't tell whether it was Mimi or myself responding. The song built to a climax until it resolved gently, with both of us singing together, "amor, amor, amor," as the notes lingered in the air.

When we finished, Percy put a hand on my shoulder, his face intense.

"Elle," he said in a husky voice and drew me into an embrace. I wrapped my arms around him, my heart beating wildly.

He traced a finger down my cheek and his gaze dropped to my lips.

I could hear John swearing in the other room.

Percy began to pull away, but I kept my arms around his neck. He looked toward the open doors. We both knew John was working in the other room.

Percy pulled my head onto his chest and wrapped his arm around me. He rested his head on mine for a long moment. I closed my eyes. This was what it felt like. This was what I wanted.

Then he let go.

I wanted to call him my amor. I wanted to hear him call me that. But John was waiting to leave and could walk in at any moment.

"Let's find John. I believe it's time to leave," I said, my voice squeaking a little.

Percy ran his fingers along the inside of my palm. I took a deep breath and smiled at him.

He grinned at me. "I have a surprise." He began playing a melody similar to the one he'd played at Barrington.

"You changed it," I said. "Varied the melody. It's much gentler."

"You said it needed a counter melody," Percy said as he played. "I've been revising it."

"It's beautiful. So relaxing. You've taken out the intense parts," I said, laying my head on his shoulder as he played and hoping I would hear John before he entered the room. "It's much softer. You must have been working on it for weeks."

He tilted his head down toward me. "I think of you every time I play."

That was the first moment I thought I might be in love.

He finished the piece. Memorized. He knew it by heart.

I could hear my heart beating in response. Percy took one of my hands in his. He moved an arm behind me on the piano bench and slid closer. He searched my face, an intense gleam in his brilliant green eyes.

"Are you ready to face Mr. Felsted?" he asked.

He had done all this to distract me. To prepare me. To reassure me. Weeks of practicing the duet's accompaniment until it was flawless, of reworking his own composition to suit me.

I gazed up at him, my head still on his shoulder. "Certainly. If you will be there with me," I said. "Thank you, Percy."

"It is my pleasure," he said and grinned.

I rubbed my gloves together and pulled my cloak tighter around me. We made our way along the icy sidewalks. The frosty winter air whipped my cheeks. We each walked as though we were alone in our thoughts.

Regardless of what I told Percy, I still felt uneasy about confronting Mr. Felsted, and yet my thoughts were filled with amazement at the lengths to which Percy went to anticipate my concerns and alleviate them.

We arrived at Mrs. Harwich's school. Someone had placed rickety wooden chairs along the length of a hallway. I settled myself between Miss Duxford and Miss Harwich.

A row of men sat across from us, all the way down the hall. John perched himself in a chair directly across from me and Miss Harwich. He and Percy hardly fit in the small chairs meant for younger students.

I could see Percy reading a book next to John, but every now and then he would glance up at me while John was watching Miss Harwich. I squirmed in my chair and tried to shift to get a better view of Percy.

John noticed me. I studied the grooves on the wooden floor until John started watching Miss Harwich again. When I looked back at Percy, he winked at me. I couldn't help smiling.

The wait seemed interminable. Finally, Miss Harwich, Miss Duxford, Percy, John, and I entered a classroom together. Mr. Felsted conferred with other committee members at a table in the back. Mrs. Harwich rested her fingers on the keys of a well-worn piano. She glanced nervously at us.

Finally Mr. Felsted deigned to notice us. "We'll practice together, then I would like to hear your pieces." He smiled at Miss Duxford. "I know Miss Duxford has worked hard on hers."

After some scales and simple songs, Miss Duxford sang "Ave Maria" flawlessly. Her voice soared over the high notes and rested softly. Whatever else he was, Mr. Felsted was a good teacher.

Next, Miss Harwich and I faced Mr. Felsted together, side by side. Beside me Miss Harwich shook slightly. Perhaps I was not alone in my concerns. I whispered to her. "Did you ever have one of his lessons?"

She nodded. "Just one."

"Me, too," I said and tried to smile. "Let's bear the bell. Do the trick. Tip top."

Miss Harwich took my hand and pressed it. "Thank you." She let go.

I ran my hands down the front of my emerald green velvet gown to smooth the rows of fringe. I closed my eyes and remembered the feel of Percy's arms around me.

The piano began. I took a deep breath. As the familiar notes played, my fear subsided. We began singing "Still, Still, Still." Miss Harwich's deep, rich alto voice supported my high soprano. I felt a surge of gratitude for our blossoming friendship and tried to blend my voice with hers, so it did not overpower her.

Percy and John were standing at the back of the room. I focused over Mr. Felsted's head and focused on Percy instead. I sang with every bit of emotion I felt toward Percy. I knew I was beginning to feel something deep. What, I wasn't sure. Perhaps *amor*. But it was something warm and comfortable and safe. The opposite of Mr. Felsted.

I could see Miss Harwich looking over Mr. Felsted's head toward John.

We both finished with our heads high and our shoulders back. We had sung nearly as well as Miss Duxford. Mr. Felsted glared at us.

Percy and John came up to join us for "Stille Nacht." Mr. Felsted scowled at them. We had no chance, but we sang our best anyway. I felt Percy's voice strengthening me, Miss Harwich's quiet friendship, and John's unwavering loyalty. It was a moment that touched me, regardless of the audience or the outcome.

Afterward, Miss Duxford said in her gentle voice, "Too bad there are so few spots left in the concert." She probably meant it, but she didn't seem very concerned as she left the room on Mr. Felsted's arm.

Miss Harwich waited outside the school while her mother secured the locks.

John hit his gloves against his legs. "Well done, Miss Harwich."

"Thank you. You sang well, too, Mr. Barrington," she said, seemingly too shy to meet his eyes.

The winter wind whistled around us. I tightened my cloak around myself and drew up my hood. I pulled my gloves on carefully, pushing them onto my hands one finger at a time, then rubbing my hands together.

John nodded brusquely, then said, "Well."

"So," Miss Harwich said, staring at John's collar.

"Suppose we're finished with rehearsals," John said. He tugged at his collar.

"I suppose so," Miss Harwich said.

Percy and I exchanged a glance. Perhaps John was hopeless and needed help after all.

"Miss Harwich, I have heard so much about the Christmas market," I said. "Would you and your mother be kind enough to accompany my family? Perhaps your mother could arrange it? I am most curious and would love a local guide."

Her face lit up. "Oh yes. Perhaps on Christmas Eve. It is magical. Mr. Barrington, Mr. Hauxton, will you join us, too?"

John didn't say anything. Percy nudged him.

"Absolutely," John said. "Until then, Miss Harwich. Mrs. Harwich." He bowed stiffly. "Unless Mr. Felsted selects our musical number?" He looked hopefully at Mrs. Harwich.

"I will inform you if your arrangement is chosen," Mrs. Harwich said. "Thank you for rehearsing so long. You all sounded beautiful. Until Christmas Eve."

CHAPTER 20

Mr. Felsted selected Miss Duxford's solo of "Ave Maria." That was all. At least Mrs. Harwich's school would be represented in the city-wide Christmas concert. Most of the other prestigious schools had three or four musical numbers.

I felt bad for Miss Duxford. Her father had a small income working for the Foreign Office, and she relied on revenue from other concerts to supplement their meager means. Mr. Duxford had never advanced far in the ranks nor did he have many connections among the aristocracy.

I also worried about what would happen if Mrs. Harwich's school failed. We would leave in a few months, but I knew I would carry my friends' concerns with me.

We didn't see Miss Harwich again until Christmas Eve. We planned to meet the Harwiches near St. Stephen's Cathedral since we lived in different parts of town.

Papa inspected the crowded streets. "Hope they aren't late. It's cold."

"We'll get some mulled wine to warm up," Mama suggested.

We made our way to a wooden stall at the entrance to the

Christmas market. Cut trees rested in pails, decorated with intricately folded paper ornaments and candles.

"Oh! Christmas trees!" I took Mama's hands. "Can we buy one?"

"No need, dear. I've asked the servants to surprise us with one when we get home," she said.

I laughed. "But now I will not be surprised."

"Then do not tell the others," she said.

Intoxicating smells overwhelmed me. Ginger and spices, mulled wine, the savory smell of rosemary and roasting sausage. My stomach growled.

"I'm glad we didn't eat before we came." I moved toward the sausage stand.

"Start with these, Elle," John's voice said behind me.

Percy held out a paper cone filled with roasted chestnuts.

I reached out. "Ouch!"

He picked one up and peeled back the brown skin, revealing a creamy center.

"How can you hold those?" I shook my hand. "They feel like they came right out of the fire."

"They did. Right there," Percy said. He and John grinned at each other.

John pointed to a man with a cart a few feet away.

Papa took one. "They'll warm your hands at least." He wandered off. He bought a cone of chestnuts and began to examine the roasting mechanism. I could hear him asking the vendor questions.

Percy offered me the meat of a chestnut. It nearly melted in my mouth.

"One of my favorites," I said. "But I've never eaten them when they were so fresh."

He peeled another for me.

"Don't get me started. I still have my eye on the sausages." My stomach growled, and I popped another chestnut in my mouth. It was still warm, and I had to chew quickly.

John laughed. "That was not very proper, Elle. You'll never be a duchess if you eat like that." John took the cone of chestnuts from Percy and peeled another.

"Sounds like a terrible life," Percy said. "I'd rather have roasted chestnuts than be a duke."

"At last we found an advantage to being a younger son," John said. "Roasted chestnuts!"

I ignored them both and walked over to the stall where I heard the sausages sizzling. I ordered a wurst with mustard and a cup of mulled wine.

I'd never eaten food while walking on the street before. The combination of hunger, a chill wind, and the intoxicating smells made the food taste better than it could anywhere else.

I took another bite of the warm sausage encased in a crunchy bun. The crisp tang of mustard burst through the other flavors. There was nothing like this in England.

Miss Harwich joined us, already holding a cup of warm mulled wine. "Isn't it amazing? The candles and the Christmas trees. The singing." She looked around. "It's my favorite part about living in Vienna."

"I love all of this," I said to her. I turned back to John and Percy. "I like Christmas better in Austria."

"Agreed," Percy said. He offered me his handkerchief and pointed to a spot of mustard on my face. "Especially the food."

I couldn't decide whether I was more mortified that I had mustard on my face or that Percy had told me in front of John and Miss Harwich.

I dabbed at my cheek. Percy pointed to the edge of his mouth and grinned. So the mustard was by my lips. That's why he'd noticed. I felt a little better about it.

I wiped my lips, folded the handkerchief, and tucked it into my reticule. I searched for something to say to cover my embarrassment. "I am so envious that men get to go on a Grand Tour so often and women so seldom. If it hadn't been for my impulsive parents, I would have missed all of this."

"And yet, the novelty can wear off." Miss Harwich finished her wine and set down her cup. "I enjoy Christmas, yes, but the rest of the year can be—" She paused.

"Is it lonely?" I thought of Miss Duxford, who had stayed home with a slight cold. "With so few other women your age?"

The group began walking through the stalls. Miss Harwich and I walked together, with Percy and John behind us. The steam from my mulled wine warmed my face.

"It's not the loneliness," Miss Harwich said sadly.

John offered Miss Harwich a chestnut. She accepted it and peeled it with the expertise of experience. "It's the finality. Knowing that things will never change. People come and go on their way through, but I stay here."

"Will you never return to England?" I asked.

Miss Harwich hesitated. "My father did not manage his money well. He did not leave any debts behind, but he did not leave very much for us to live on. We could not live in the same style in England as we do here. We could not work and be part of the *ton*. I'm sorry to be so personal, Lady Eleanor."

Miss Harwich's warmth and depth surprised me. She sometimes seemed so cold and unreachable. I enjoyed getting to know her and was glad she finally trusted me enough to tell me the truth.

I threaded my arm through hers. "I am glad. Thank you for telling me."

We stopped at a booth filled with wooden toys, intricately carved and painted. The merchant held up some small, hand-stitched balls and began juggling them for us. He held them out to me.

I nodded my head. "John, am I going to have a niece or a nephew? When will we hear from Matthew?" I asked.

"Not for a while, I daresay." John picked up a wooden top and spun it. "I say, Miss Harwich, have you seen these?"

I selected a carved man on a string that moved up and down when the string was pulled. And a doll. Just in case. I took the brightly wrapped packages and paid the craftsman. They slipped in my arms.

"May I?" Percy reached around. His arm wrapped around my waist for a moment to steady the falling bundles.

I startled and turned, the parcels beginning to spill out of my arms.

Percy scrambled to catch them. "May I hold your packages?"

His fingers brushed mine as he fumbled to take them. It was all so ridiculous, and yet I got lost for a moment in his piercing green eyes. Our hands met beneath the stacks of neatly wrapped purchases. Even through my gloves, I could feel his warmth.

"Thank you," I managed to reply.

John and Miss Harwich had finished playing with the wooden toys and were waiting. Watching us.

I tried to think back to our previous conversation. "What was your father like?" I asked Miss Harwich.

She began walking. "He loved to travel." She spoke over her shoulder. "Like yours, Mr. Barrington. We moved to Paris, Berlin, Geneva, and Rome. We went all over, really, before he started the music school."

Something settled inside me. A feeling of pity. Or was it relief that I had escaped her fate? "Why not come to England and visit me? In a year. I should love to have you visit. John and Percy, persuade her."

I glanced behind me. Miss Harwich followed my gaze.

John's eyes grew wide. He stared at Miss Harwich. Percy tried to compose himself when he saw John's reaction, but he laughed.

Percy got himself under control and said formally, "Yes, Miss Harwich. Could your mother spare you for a Season?" He gave a half-bow in her direction.

"I'm not sure I'll be in London. I may simply return to Barrington Hall," I said. "But I should love your company there."

Percy shot me a curious look. He probably knew why my father had avoided London for the last two and a half years. Nearly everyone did. But for Papa to continue to refuse to go would become an issue as time went on.

I inspected some colorful candles in a wooden pyramid to avoid him. I gave the blades at the top a spin to watch the delicately carved figures move.

Miss Harwich shook her head. "No, I am afraid my mother could not run the school alone."

"But you—you must see Essex," John stammered.

"The school requires our constant attention." Miss Harwich sounded resigned. "I have no dowry left or funds for gowns." She pinked a little at the admission.

"If you should change your mind," I said, "you will have a place to stay."

"Yes," John said. "Certainly."

I felt closer to Miss Harwich than ever before. I smiled at her. "Most likely, I will not have a Season either. Come, show us what else you love about the Christmas market."

We walked through the crowded stalls until our fingers and toes were nearly numb. Scales hung next to piles of dried fruits and candies. Bright cloths covered the tables. Signs listed prices in German. A band played Christmas carols in the distance. The hum of conversation filled the air as small children ran between us and around the stalls.

When it was time to leave, Miss Harwich said, "You cannot leave without trying gingerbread." She dragged me to a stall.

An aroma of ginger and other spices mixed in the air. A small, elderly woman stood in a stall with trays of brown cookies decorated with icing.

"This is what I've been smelling!" I sighed. "Oh, Miss Harwich. You are the truest and best of friends." I was surprised to see a sheen of moisture in her eyes. She must have been lonelier than I realized.

John bought cookies for all of us. One bite, and I was in heaven.

"John, can we buy a few to take home?" The warmth of the ginger filled me. "I'm going to need more of these cookies."

John laughed and gave the woman more coins.

Percy took the stack of paper-wrapped cookies. "Shall I add this to your purchases?"

I couldn't answer. My mouth was full. I simply smiled and nodded.

Wine, roasted chestnuts, sausage, and gingerbread. It wasn't anything like the meal we would have tomorrow on Christmas, but I suspected that I liked this *al fresco* meal better.

As we wound our way home together through the quiet streets of Vienna, I glanced aside at Miss Harwich. How similar were our circumstances? What if my father decided he never wanted to return to England? Would I ever be like her, exiled in Europe for years? No. Surely, Papa wanted to see his new grandchild. He was the earl. He could not leave his responsibilities behind forever.

But for now he seemed content to let Matthew run the estates. He seemed happier than he had been in years. What if Papa decided to stay on the Continent, where no one knew our past, for the rest of his life?

CHAPTER 21

We entered our apartments and gave our cloaks to the servants. To the surprise of everyone but Mama and me, a small tree filled the center of the drawing room. It rested in a pot on a round table. Intricately folded paper stars rested between the branches. Servants scurried around, lighting colored candles on the tree. Their soft glow cast shadows throughout the room.

A large repast awaited us in the drawing room. Mama poured tea for anyone who wanted it. There was mulled wine and coffee for the others. Dense Austrian tortes and traditional English tarts sat side by side on trays.

Mr. Felsted, Mr. Duxford, and Miss Duxford had joined us after the outdoor Christmas market. Miss Duxford did, indeed, seem ill. She acted more subdued than usual, only smiling and carrying on with one man at a time.

"What games shall we play?" Mama glanced at John. "The young people, I mean. Lord Barrington and I are happy to talk with Mrs. Harwich and Mr. Duxford."

None of the parlor games that involve penalties or possible kisses, I begged John silently with a look.

John cast a calculating look at Mr. Felsted and Percy. "Tableaux vivants," John announced. "Shall we stage paintings for my father to guess? No Rubens."

Only Percy and I laughed. Evidently the others had not seen the floor-to-ceiling images of naked women in the museums like we had.

Mr. Felsted eyed me and Miss Harwich. Perhaps he had seen the Rubens paintings. I stared pointedly at John.

"In pairs, then. Miss Duxford and Mr. Felsted together?" John asked. "Miss Harwich, if you would partner with me? And Percy, old man, could you take on Eleanor?"

We rearranged ourselves to sit in couples. Mama spoke up. "Try the hallway on the other side. You can plan your tableaux vivants over there. The servants can bring you anything you need."

Mr. Felsted and Miss Duxford went first. It took them a long time to plan their "living picture." The servants brought fabric and random vases for us to use as props while they were gone. Finally, Mr. Felsted and Miss Duxford returned. They arranged themselves at the pianoforte. Mr. Felsted adopted a wild look on his face. Miss Duxford struck a pose as though holding a flute.

"'*The Magic Flute*' by Mozart!" Papa shouted. "Although that is not a painting."

After them, Miss Harwich and John went out into the side hallway. When they came back, John seemed pleased with himself. Miss Harwich looked as stoic as ever, although her cheeks seemed slightly flushed.

John hunched down on the floor, his nose twitching like a rabbit. He began hopping. Miss Harwich held her hands together in prayer, draped in a blue cloth, her eyes lifted to heaven.

"Albrecht Dürer! *The Young Hare* and *The Praying Hands*. But you're not allowed to move. Honestly, do none of you know the rules? Eleanor, give us a proper scene," Papa mumbled.

It was our turn to plan which painting we would stage. Percy and I walked out of the drawing room and began making our way down the side hallway.

"What do you think?" Percy asked. "Something different from what they've been doing?"

"How about something horrible? Enough of these gentle images. No praying. Let's go for Shakespeare." I mimicked stabbing him in the heart.

Percy grabbed my arm. "Not so fast, Lady Macbeth." He tucked my arm into his side and looped it over his own. "No murders tonight."

We reached an alcove with a small bench, perfect for two people to sit down. We stopped there, then glanced up. Now I understood why Mr. Felsted and Miss Duxford had taken so long to plan their tableaux vivant. Mama had instructed someone to hang a mistletoe ball overhead. Several berries were conspicuously missing.

Percy cleared his throat. I looked down from the mistletoe to Percy's face.

"Romeo and Juliet?" he suggested. "Star-crossed lovers?"

I nodded without breaking eye contact, my face still tilted up to him. We stood inches apart.

"That would be horrible enough," I said. "I could die slowly."

Percy untangled my arm from his side. "Or perhaps a happy scene after all." He slid his fingers between mine, then moved one arm around my waist. He waited for a reaction. "This isn't like what Felsted did?" Percy jerked his head toward the drawing room.

I shook my head, still gazing into Percy's eyes. "Not at all."

Percy drew me closer to him. "So, *Romeo and Juliet*?" he asked, his eyes filled with longing.

I nodded again and put my other hand on his chest. Time slowed to a standstill.

Percy put one hand on the side of my face, letting his thumb slide over my bottom lip, then cupping my face. "Why didn't it work for them?"

I had a hard time thinking.

"Tragic," I whispered. "Not enough mistletoe."

Percy looked up. The arm around my waist pulled me closer to him. I swallowed. Percy's eyes went to my lips.

My pulse quickened. I had wanted this for so long.

Percy lowered his head toward mine. I moved my arms up around his head to close any distance between us. I loved the feel of being held in Percy's embrace. Warmth exploded through me as Percy's hand moved from my waist to the small of my back.

I could feel his lips hovering above mine. Nearly there.

I waited for Percy. I didn't say anything but gazed up at him. I had imagined a future with him. Here it was, a moment away. Slowly, he brushed my cheek with the back of his hand.

I felt his breath above mine.

"Are you sure?" Percy spoke so low I could hardly hear him. I nodded, letting my fingers drift up to play with his hair. It was as soft as I had suspected.

The arm at my waist tightened. Percy's other hand moved up my back, drawing me closer to him. His lips caressed my own, soft as a feather, hesitant. He kissed me again, softly, then again.

All of my doubts and worries vanished. Nothing existed but this moment. Only Percy. I felt loved, wanted, needed more than anyone or anything in the world. If Percy had any uncertainty about my feelings, I wanted to answer his question right now. I pulled Percy's head toward mine.

Percy deepened the kiss and pressed me closer to him. I felt like I would never be the same again. Like I couldn't breathe, but I never wanted this to end. Every nerve tingled with awareness.

I moved one hand onto his chest, over his heart. It raced as wildly as my own. Then Percy did the only thing that could have made this kiss perfect. He whispered, "*Amore mio.*"

We had no trouble acting like a pair of devoted lovers. Percy insisted on the romantic balcony scene, since it was Christmas Eve. Mama guessed *Romeo and Juliet* right away, before my father.

"Yes, but which artist?" Papa complained. "That scene is

overdone."

A feeling of contentment settled on me. I even felt at peace with Mr. Felsted. Everyone laughed their way through a game of charades, where the riddles got more and more ridiculous, and then we sang a few favorite Christmas carols.

Miss Duxford rested while we sang. Her voice had grown quieter and quieter during the night. I was worried. She needed to be able to sing tomorrow to establish her own reputation, and Mrs. Harwich needed her to represent the school.

Finally, after another slice of chocolate torte for everyone, the party broke up for the evening. I watched Percy and John leave with a mixture of reluctance that the festivities were over and anticipation for the next day.

For the first time, my emotions were clear to me. I was an eighteen-year-old woman feeling the first stirrings of love. I knew my own heart well enough to understand these feelings had moved well past infatuation.

Lord Chelmsford was a distant memory. A safety measure. Percy, however, was real. He was present. He was gentle and tender. And I was falling in love with him.

I settled into bed but could not get comfortable. I picked at an invisible seam on my blanket and fiddled with the tassels on my pillow. I couldn't forget the feel of Percy's arms around me. The way we always thought of the same ideas. How he looked out for me and carried my packages at the Christmas market. The way our voices sounded as we sang together. His attentiveness. When I spoke with him, I felt like I was the only person in the entire world who existed for him.

The more time I spent with Percy, the more good qualities I saw in him.

I always knew when Percy entered a room. His eyes followed me wherever I went. We conversed easily. We argued even more easily. We were falling in love. Perhaps we were already in love, yet something held Percy back from declaring himself in words.

I would leave him no doubt about my feelings tomorrow.

CHAPTER 22

My stomach fluttered with giddy anticipation as I waited for Christmas dinner. The smells wafted throughout our apartments.

"What is that?" I asked Mama. "Onion pie again? I love onion pie."

"Shall we find out?" she replied.

I settled into my chair. "Perhaps you could." I didn't want to leave the drawing room. Percy would arrive momentarily.

"Come with me. No use sitting about. Someday you'll need to instruct your cook on how to make Christmas gravy."

Mama tugged at my arm. She marched me through the maze of rooms toward the kitchen.

"Did Hauxton make good use of the mistletoe?" she asked. "I hung it for you, dear."

"For me?" I tried to avoid answering her.

"I did not hang it for Miss Duxford. I assure you; she does not need it." Mama sniffed. "Oh, dinner will be marvelous."

Mama paused outside the door to the kitchen. "Well?"

"Yes," I said finally.

"Good use? Or merely, well, you know. A peck on the cheek."

"Mama! It is hardly your place to ask," I said. My cheeks flamed bright red.

"Who else can ask? That is answer enough. Good boy," Mama said, and pushed open the door to the kitchen. "Let's steal a bite of dessert, shall we? Plum torte instead of plum pudding?"

I was glad Mama approved of Percy. After all, I suspected she had agreed to go on this Grand Tour in part as a matchmaking scheme. I followed Mama into the kitchen reluctantly. I wanted to be in the drawing room, not having a cooking lesson.

The cook and several servants darted everywhere. Pots clanged. Aromas filled the air, both savory and sweet. The cook noticed us and gestured to the staff. Everyone stopped their work at once.

"My lady?" She continued to stir something while she looked at us.

"What are these delicious smells?" Mama hovered at the edge of the kitchen.

A smile split the cook's face. "Come in." She waved her hands and the servants commenced working again. We squeezed into the middle of the kitchen.

The cook pointed down at the thick, brown liquid she stirred. "Gravy to go with the sauerbraten. The meat."

"What is that smell?" I asked. I thought it was heaven on earth.

"Bay leaves." The cook fished one out of the gravy. "My secret ingredient."

"Spaetzle over there." She pointed to a woman holding a metal grater over a pot of boiling water. Dough dropped from the grater into the water. "Tiny dumplings. Just wait. We will fry them in butter with onions and cheese."

"I thought I smelled onions." I moaned. "When can we eat? Oh, this is too divine."

"Oh! What is this?" Mama pointed to a fifteen-layer cake. Seven or eight delicate layers of yellow sponge cake stacked together, each separated by a thin layer of chocolate icing.

The cook beamed and put her arm around a small girl, not even as old as I was.

"Dobos torte. Annika is Hungarian." She beamed at the girl.

Mama eyed the torte.

I hoped we had stayed long enough. "We'd better leave, so we don't eat the desserts before our meal."

"Yes, *danke*," Mama said. "If I could take you home with me to England, I would."

The cook smiled and rushed back to stir the gravy again. I pulled Mama out of the kitchen and back through the maze of hallways.

I wondered which would be Percy's favorite dish. When we were nearly to the drawing room, I pinched my cheeks.

"Oh, they're already red, dear," Mama said. I could feel a full blush cover my cheeks.

I settled myself on a seat wide enough for two people and waited.

The Duxfords arrived with Mr. Felsted. The Harwiches arrived. Finally, John arrived with Percy. He immediately seated himself beside me. Papa began telling everyone about the art at the Albertina museum, and I could not concentrate on the conversation. Not that I wasn't interested in Albrecht Dürer's paintings, but Percy's leg kept bumping into mine every time he shifted on the seat.

We sat, intensely aware of each other, pretending to watch Papa, nodding every now and then when my father exploded emphatically about some point. Meanwhile, Percy's foot worked its way closer and closer to mine. He leaned back on one hand and crossed his ankle, finally adjusting his position on the seat so that no space existed between our legs. I forgot to breathe.

Percy's mouth quirked in a half-smile and he glanced over at me. I put my hand down on the seat. Percy placed his next to mine. His smallest finger covered mine and tangled them together. I arranged my skirt to hide our hands. He smiled again, while facing straight ahead and watching Papa expostulate on the wonders of the fine brush strokes of the painted hare.

I was reluctant to leave when the butler announced dinner was ready. We made our way through the meal, relishing the bitter tang of the red cabbage, a favorite dish of mine. It was the most delicious meal I had ever eaten. Bay leaf gravy on spaetzle, roasted beef, apples, carrots, and thinly sliced potatoes.

Mama had seated me to Percy's right. Since he ate with his left hand, Percy's right hand found my knee under the table. I startled and tried to cover my reaction by coughing and covering my mouth quickly with my napkin. I moved my left hand slowly below the tablecloth until I could tangle our fingers together.

Mama watched me from the far end of the table. I tried to take a bite with my fork, using just the one hand. Evidently, I carried it off well enough. She turned back to Mr. Duxford.

"The noodles are called spaetzle," Percy whispered to me.

I picked up my napkin and dabbed at the corners of my mouth. "They grate the dough into boiling water." Now I was glad Mama had dragged me to the kitchen. "Cook uses bay leaves in her gravy," I said. "Your cologne smells like gravy."

Percy choked. He put a napkin over his mouth and tried to cover a laugh. "It does not."

"It does."

He whispered behind his napkin. "It's called Bay Rum. Very expensive. Best in Paris."

"Well, the best men's cologne in Paris smells like bay leaves in Christmas gravy."

Percy put his napkin down. "What's for dessert?"

"But I like the smell. I like Christmas gravy."

He nudged my knee with his under the table. "Dessert."

"You're trying to change the subject."

"Yes," Percy said. "I want dessert." He held my eyes.

I could feel my cheeks blushing again. Really. I studied the napkin in my lap.

"It's Hungarian." I glanced back up.

"I'm listening," he said, a half-smile on his lips, still looking at me intently.

"Dobos torte," I said.

"Never heard of it," Percy said.

"Fifteen layers."

He raised an eyebrow at me. "And who will feed it to me?"

I opened my mouth, then shut it. The possibilities that came to mind were too distracting. Percy laughed loudly, and Mama looked our way again.

"Oh!" Mr. Duxford spoke across the table at Papa. "I have a missive for you, Lord and Lady Barrington. Brought it myself. Letter for you, too, Hauxton."

Percy turned back toward the other dinner guests. "Are the packets getting through, then? Despite the Crimean War?"

"Sure, sure, no trouble," Mr. Duxford said, and dug the thick envelopes out of his vest.

Mama tore open her letter and scanned it quickly. "I know it's terribly rude to open this during dinner. You must excuse me. I must see whether I am a grandmother. A girl! Oh, Thomas, she's healthy. Georgiana is healthy."

My ears perked up. "I have a niece?"

Mama tucked the letter away. "You do! Adeline, she's called."

"Will she be as musical as you, Eleanor?" Papa chuckled. "Looking forward to your concert tonight, eh, Mr. Felsted?"

"Oh, yes, soon." Mr. Felsted loaded a large bite onto his fork. He sat up taller. "Yes, I've got to leave soon. Miss Duxford, will you be accompanying me to the concert hall?"

"Can't even talk. How can she sing?" Papa asked.

"You can sing, can't you?" Mr. Felsted shifted in his chair.

Miss Duxford shook her head. Her voice croaked, then faded to a whisper. "It hurts to talk," she said, her voice scratchy and faint. "I do not think my voice would fill the concert hall."

Mrs. Harwich put her fork down. "Of course, my dear. You must not push yourself."

Mr. Felsted took another large bite of red cabbage and roast beef.

"Nonsense. Eleanor can sing it," Papa said. "Right, Felsted?"

Mr. Felsted gulped as he swallowed. "I'm not sure. Last minute changes."

Papa waved to the butler to clear the dinner dishes. "Better than cancelling. Of course she can."

Panic rose in my chest. Sing? In front of hundreds of people? What was my father thinking? It was one thing to sing with a few friends. It was quite another to perform in a concert hall.

"No, Papa, Mr. Felsted is right. Last minute changes," I said.

Percy let go of my hand under the table, and I glanced down. Had I done something wrong? I was frightened and needed his support right now.

A footman put a thin slice of the rich, chocolate torte in front of me. I stared down at my plate and pushed the cake around. The delicate layers fell apart. I cut a piece with my fork and thought of Percy, but he didn't even dart a gaze in my direction.

Rehearse alone with Mr. Felsted on Christmas Day instead of spending the afternoon with Percy? No. I could not do it. Would not.

"But Mrs. Harwich's school would be represented if you could sing, Lady Eleanor. You are the only one at her school with the same vocal range who has rehearsed the piece," Percy said.

I took a single bite of the cake. Percy knew I sang alone. Not in front of other people, unless forced to. I set the fork down as my stomach began to churn.

"There!" Papa said. "Excellent. Felsted, what do you need?"

Mr. Felsted looked at Papa. "Perhaps a private lesson this afternoon." He was clearly trying to extort more money. The man never gave up. It was how he survived, moving from city to city, living on his reputation.

"No," Percy and I said at the same time.

"I meant rehearsal," Mr. Felsted corrected himself. "If I were compensated for the extra time, Lord Barrington."

The vanilla layers of the Dobos torte tasted like sand in my mouth.

"I'll accompany you," Percy said. "Barrington and I can accompany you, right?"

John nodded. He watched Miss Harwich cut another bite of her cake.

"Right, right," Papa said. He wiped his mouth with a napkin and pushed away from the table. "It's decided."

I hadn't agreed. Papa, John, and Percy had decided for me in order to help Mrs. Harwich, but they would not have to stand alone on a stage and perform without any true rehearsals or experience. Miss Duxford had sung in operas and other concerts. I had sung in my parents' drawing room.

The rest of the company wished us Merry Christmas and left to prepare for the city-wide concert. Mr. Felsted agreed to meet me at John's apartments.

I pulled a cloak around myself. What had just happened? Here I was, rushing through Christmas dinner, walking through Vienna in the cold, and rehearsing on Christmas Day with a man who terrified me. Instead of spending time playing more parlor games or basking in the warm glow of a drawing room fire.

John rushed ahead of us as we made our way toward his apartments. Anger rose in me. "I did not want to sing," I said to Percy. Cold air nipped at my cheeks.

"Mrs. Harwich needs you," he said, keeping pace with me. He flexed his hands. "Really, Eleanor."

"What?" I asked. "You know why I don't want to sing with him."

Percy's pace grew faster. "Is that the only reason?"

I struggled to keep up. I put a hand on Percy's arm. "Slow down."

He stopped and faced me, a chill wind between us. "You don't want to sing in the concert. You never did."

"Yes. I told you that from the beginning."

"Even if it means the Harwiches' school closes."

John turned the corner ahead of us. We stood alone on the

street. How had all the good feeling between us evaporated so quickly?

I lowered my eyes and studied the grey snow on the street. "No, I do not wish for that to happen."

"You would hide yourself, Elle, when others need you," Percy said. He reached out and tilted my face up.

I met his gaze. "I can't do it. I can't sing with him. For him. In front of so many people," I said.

"Can you sing for me? For Mrs. Harwich? For your father, who believes in you, who has paid so much to a scoundrel?" Percy's eyes pleaded with me. "You are magnificent, and I want the world to see what I see."

I wanted to turn around. I wanted to walk home. I wanted to say no. I couldn't say anything. I felt frozen. Percy seemed close to declaring the feelings I had hoped he would, but not in a way I had ever dreamed. Not while we were arguing.

Percy shook his head. He put a hand on my face. His leather glove was even colder than the surrounding air. "I need a wife who doesn't pretend to be less than she really is. I'm going to be a diplomat. In the public eye all the time. I need your support. I want your support."

He said wife. Percy was thinking about marriage.

He searched my face. "I want it to be you. But if you can't do this...If you're going to conceal yourself and deny what you can do. I have to constantly act like I can do more than I am capable of. I have to fight for every opportunity. And you throw yours away. Let them see what you can do. Don't hide."

I started to slowly walk forward again, but I felt sick to my stomach. In the public eye. All the time. Percy still didn't know our family secrets. He would not want to be part of our family if he did. He would not want *me* to be a part of *his* family. I watched the cobblestones underfoot as we turned the corner toward their apartments.

It seemed so harsh and unfeeling for Percy to ask this of me. He knew my fears. He asked too much. *Why did he care more about the*

Harwiches than me? Would it always be like this? Was Percy's need to help others, to impress others, more important to him than anything else? Would I always be secondary?

I stopped again, just outside their door, and turned to face him. Maybe I needed to tell him all my concerns. Maybe I could trust him. Let him decide. Or maybe he already knew? Maybe John had confided in him? I hovered between decision and indecision, between anger and acquiescence.

Percy waited, rubbing his hands together in the cold. I had no answers for him. He plunged his hands into his pockets and looked surprised when he pulled the crumpled letter from Mr. Duxford out of his pocket.

"Go ahead and read it, if you'd like," I said. I needed more time to think. Or perhaps he wasn't trying to impress anyone. That wasn't fair to him. Percy was trying to help me face my fears. He had more confidence in me than I did. Was that enough to face an entire concert hall? He had done so much to help me face Mr. Felsted. He knew how much I worried, and he knew my strengths as a singer. Did I trust Percy? Did I trust myself? Could I do this?

Percy broke the seal and unfolded the missive. A black-edged paper fell out of the envelope and into his hands. That could only mean one thing. Someone in his family had died.

CHAPTER 23

Percy tried to tear the paper open with cold, clumsy fingers. He stripped his gloves off impatiently and threw them to the ground. He unfolded the letter and scanned the lines.

"My father! My brother! Both. Within days of each other." Percy's face paled. He slumped against the wall of the building. The letter fell from his hands to the street as his hands dangled loosely at his side.

A wave of pain shot me as though the family members were my own. My only concern was for Percy. He looked lost.

I leaned over to pick up his gloves and the paper. I took him by the elbow, opened the door to the building, and helped him up the stairs to the first floor. When we reached the door to their apartments, I pounded on the door.

Parker opened it.

"Get John, please. Now." I dropped Percy's gloves and pulled at the sleeves of his thick, wool overcoat. I dropped that on the floor, too.

I guided Percy into the drawing room and helped him onto a sofa. He crumpled, putting his hands on his knees. I put the letter down on his lap and sat beside him.

John rushed into the room. "What is it?" he asked. "Old man?"

"Both of them! Dead! Of the same illness," Percy said.

"Who's dead, Percy?" John knelt in front of him. "Tell me."

Percy waved the missive and shook his head.

"Not like this, John. You know that. I never wanted it this way."

John picked up the paper and scanned it. "No. *No.*" John paced around the room. "I'm so sorry."

"A month ago." Percy's voice was anguished. "My mother and sister have been alone all this time, and it will yet take me weeks to return."

"You're leaving?" I asked. "When?"

"This instant." Percy tried to stand.

John came over to him.

"Not this instant. We're all attending the concert tonight, and you can leave in the morning," John said. "You need to be with people, not alone."

"I'm the earl now. The earl." Percy's voice was strangled. He put his hand on his forehead and covered his eyes.

"I'm so sorry, Percy." All the feeling drained out of me. I felt hollow. I couldn't imagine if Papa and Matthew both died. I couldn't imagine losing either one of them. What had Percy lost? His father. His brother. His sense of security. His plans to travel. The Foreign Office connections he carefully cultivated throughout Europe. The arrangements for ambassador assignments. No trip to Italy next spring. No Roman ruins.

I reached out to comfort him but did not know what to do. I let my hand fall back into my lap.

"I must leave immediately. I have responsibilities now." Percy stayed on the couch. He seemed incapable of movement or thought.

Even if I had been angry with him, even if I thought he had been harsh or unfeeling, Percy had lost people he loved and was beside himself. It hurt to see him in pain. I wanted to ease his pain. I placed a hand on his shoulder.

"I must go pack." Percy seemed as if his thoughts were a mile away.

"No," John said. "Parker and I can pack. You can't leave until morning, anyway. You've lost half your family, and you don't like the other half. You're giving up Italy. Don't give up the concert, too. It's Christmas Day. Talk sense into him, Elle." John walked out of the drawing room and yelled for Parker.

I could hear John giving orders to staff members while I sat with Percy in silence. I leaned down, put my arm around him, and put my head on his shoulder.

Percy began to cry. His shoulders shook with sobs. I could feel the cries from his chest all the way through his back. Gradually, they subsided. I took his wrinkled handkerchief from his vest pocket and handed it to him.

Percy wiped his cheek and turned toward me with haunted eyes. "The worst part is that I resented them, Elle. I wanted a title. You know that. I wanted everything that came with being a peer." Percy sounded anguished. "But never at this price."

"It would have happened whether you wanted those things or not, Percy," I said. "You did not cause this."

I didn't know what else to say. I prayed silently. *How can I help Percy find peace? He needs to feel joy. He needs comfort. What should I do?*

"Will you come to the concert tonight?" I asked. "Music brings you so much comfort."

Percy slumped over, one elbow on his knee, and rubbed his hand over his eyes again. "I don't deserve it. I don't deserve peace or joy. My mother and sister are alone in England. On Christmas Day." And Percy's shoulders began to shake again.

I pulled Percy's chest onto my lap, then laid my arm on his back while he sobbed silently.

What will you sacrifice for him? A thought came into my mind. *He has lost everything. What can you give up?* A sense of peace washed over me.

I knew what to say. "You never wished their deaths, but did your father wish you to go on this Grand Tour?" I asked.

Percy didn't answer.

"Did your brother want you to go?"

Still nothing.

"Would they wish you to go to the concert or sit home alone?"

It was harsh, but it got his attention. Percy pushed his way up from my lap, turning toward me.

I could see the pain in his eyes. "I will sing the 'Ave Maria.'" I couldn't let him give this up. He'd given up too much. I could give up something, too. Anything. This was what love meant. Sacrifice. I knew what Percy needed.

Percy needed to be with people, and he needed the healing power of music. He should not be alone, and Christmas carols were the most peaceful, soul-filling sound on earth.

"And you could support the Harwiches by attending the concert," I said.

He wiped his eyes. "Of course. They need this success."

"You need this, Percy."

His eyes looked hollow and he sagged under the weight of grief and new responsibility. Percy needed to be alone with the overwhelming emotions, but I could not let him drown in them.

"You need to feel joy and hope more than anything right now. You need to be with people who care about you. I've got to prepare for this evening. Mr. Felsted and I will rehearse at the concert hall. I will be well enough with musicians all around and my fearsome maid to chaperone." I waited. "Will I see you tonight?"

No answer.

I tried to look into Percy's eyes. "Promise me you'll come tonight. I cannot leave you like this." My voice cracked.

Percy nudged my foot with his, but he did not look up. "Go. I'll be there. I could not let the Harwiches down."

It felt bittersweet. Percy had agreed to attend the concert, but only for Miss Harwich and her mother. And I would have to spend my Christmas afternoon with Mr. Felsted. But if Percy attended the concert, it was all worth it.

Perhaps it was unfair for me to ask him to worry about anyone else when he had a burden of his own grief, but I knew Percy. Aiding others would ease his pain. Giving service would comfort him. He would have hours and days and months to mourn, but I could not let him leave Vienna without saying goodbye to his friends or performing one last act of kindness.

I left instructions with Parker to send Mr. Felsted to the concert hall. I rushed home to change into one of my new dresses from Paris.

As Sibley and I walked toward the concert hall, peace washed over me again. I had made the right choice. Either Percy could sit home alone in a dark room, grieving and feeling lost, or he could attend a soul-lifting concert.

I would sing alone. In front of hundreds of people. And pray that no one remembered me. I was just one among many musical numbers.

Hopefully I would not embarrass Mrs. Harwich or myself.

But my heart felt shattered. Percy was leaving. I would not see him again for a year, or perhaps, ever again. Papa might not ever go back to London. Would Percy ever visit us at Barrington Hall? He would be busy with an estate of his own. Percy would attend the Season and want to be involved in Parliament's debates.

What would Percy think of me? Our last conversation was about how deeply I had disappointed him. How unsuitable I was as a wife. How I could never live the life he needed me to live.

Yet here I was. Singing in a concert. Like he had asked me to. What would Percy remember? Or would he forget me completely after he returned to England?

CHAPTER 24

Sibley and I dashed through the streets to the Academy of Sciences, where the concert hall was located.

Musicians rushed through the doors. We hurried through the halls, trying to find Mr. Felsted. Finally, I located him.

"Excuse me," I panted. "Did Parker tell you that we need to rehearse here?"

Mr. Felsted paused in the middle of pointing a violin player toward the stage. "One moment, Lady Eleanor." Mr. Felsted finished giving instructions and turned toward me.

He glowered at me. He pulled me aside and hissed, "What do you mean, changing things at the last minute?"

"I apologize for the change of location, which I know will cause you more distress during this busy time. Could we please rehearse 'Ave Maria,' as you wished Miss Duxford to sing it? So I may represent Mrs. Harwich's school well." I played with the tassel on my reticule as I waited for his answer.

Sibley hovered behind me.

Mr. Felsted stared at me. I had his full attention now. "I don't have time. I'm sure you sound fine."

"Again, I am so very sorry for the change of location." I kept my voice calm and maintained eye contact with him. I tried to summon every bit of courage and strength from deep inside myself. "But I have not rehearsed with the choir that will also sing behind me or the orchestra."

"Of course," Mr. Felsted replied. "I see you are determined."

"Thank you," I said. I took a deep breath. "Miss Duxford has improved so much under your tutelage, Mr. Felsted. I know you are an excellent musician and teacher."

Mr. Felsted grunted, but seemed appeased.

We stepped onto the stage and Sibley followed close behind. With so little time and so much noise, there wasn't much to be done, but I had rehearsed often enough with Miss Duxford at Mrs. Harwich's school that I knew the notes and dynamics. If Mr. Felsted got the credit for Mrs. Harwich's work, there was little I could do.

We practiced the song once with the choir and orchestra, and Mr. Felsted scurried off. Sibley went to wait in the box. I had insisted she sit in my place with my family tonight. I could not ask her to walk the darkening streets of Vienna alone on Christmas night.

I turned my head to take in the entire stage. It was the largest assembly of musicians and singers I had ever seen. I could hear violins tuning their instruments. A harpist plucked at the strings. Risers filled the stage. A low hum of conversation filled the air.

I could see the orchestra in front of us and an enormous hall filled with empty seats. Someone lowered the curtain. It was nearly time for the concert to begin.

I wondered if I could hide my fears and worries behind a veneer. Did the other singers feel as nervous as I did? My stomach filled with butterflies. I felt both excitement and dread. I didn't even know when to sing, where the "Ave Maria" came in the program, or if I would be able to open my mouth once I stood on the stage.

I moved backstage and found someone with a program. I scanned the rows of names. I would sing last.

There was a whoosh as the thick red curtain lifted. I scanned the theater. The rows of cushioned seats had all filled in.

I spotted my family and Percy among the rows and rows of boxes in the balconies.

Other musicians around me shifted in their spots, waiting for their turns. One long, clear note rang out from the lead violinist. Other instruments followed suit. A hush fell over the theater as the lights dimmed.

The city mayor came on stage to introduce Mr. Felsted and wish everyone a Merry Christmas. He welcomed the city. The entire city. And distinguished guests. *Who were they?* I blocked all thought and went over the song again and again, visualizing myself singing.

I had worked hard to learn how to pronounce all the lines. The song delighted me, since Sir Walter Scott's original poem, "The Lady of the Lake," was in English, written by a Scotsman, translated into German, and set to music by an Austrian composer.

Choirs entered and exited the stage. I watched as the list of songs grew shorter and shorter. Soon, it would be my turn.

Then a quartet sang "Still, Still, Still," and peace filled me. I prayed that Percy would feel the joy of Christmas and some measure of comfort in his grief. I prayed for calm, so I could sing for Mrs. Harwich. For Percy.

I heard my name. I heard "Ave Maria." I took a deep breath and walked onto the stage. Limelight illuminated the theater. It shone directly on me, so I could hardly see anything beyond the orchestra. Perfect.

Chills ran up my arms as the orchestra began playing and the first notes sounded in the air. I imagined I was at Mrs. Harwich's school. I imagined Miss Duxford and Miss Harwich singing next to me. I tried to imagine that I was not the only person standing in the middle of a very, very large stage. That I did not have to sing loud enough to be heard over an entire orchestra and choir.

I began to sing. I filled my chest and let the sound vibrate. Soon, everything flowed automatically. My mind floated, free of thought. I became the character in the song, praying to Mary in my distress.

I was Ellen, the lady of the lake, a loyal daughter, cast off from the king's court, wandering through harsh mountain terrain. I knew how Ellen must have felt, accompanying her exiled father to live in a hermit's cave, and poured my dramatic energy into the melody's supplication.

I had never felt so alive. My heart raced. I felt like a part of something, creating music with a live orchestra and the hum of the choir behind me. I wasn't alone at all, even in the center of the stage.

I actually liked singing in front of an audience. My voice reverberated through the concert hall, magnified, ethereal, and a thrill of exhilaration shot through me.

The song ended, and I gazed around me in wonder. Deafening applause rang out.

I felt like I could walk on air.

I glanced up through the darkness and wished I could see Percy looking at me. There was something deep in my soul that I couldn't define, but I felt it throughout my entire body. Sheer joy. Power surging through me as I hit the piercingly high notes. I had felt aware of everything, yet completely lost in the moment.

The air felt jubilant, as joyful as the music had been. It was a shining, bright spot in a dark and painful day.

I realized I would have given anything in the world for Percy to attend this concert and experience this moment with me. I understood, too, that perhaps my father wanted to do more than help Mrs. Harwich. Perhaps he paid unreasonable sums to Mr. Felsted for me to participate because he understood, as a painter and artist, that talents were meant to be exhibited and shared. Perhaps he would even be willing to return to London at the end of our Grand Tour.

I joined my family in the concert hall's grand lobby to return to our apartments. Across the crowded entrance, I saw Percy congratulating Mrs. Harwich.

Mama rushed over and took my hands. She beamed. Papa seemed speechless. He simply shook his head and stared.

John said, "Well done, Elle. I couldn't believe it was you up there."

Person after person came over to pump my father's hand and thank him for his patronage. Evidently Mr. Felsted had let several starving musicians know that Papa paid generously for lessons.

I waited restlessly, looking over the heads of the crowd for Percy, while greeting each person who came over to congratulate me.

Almost an hour later, the throngs had died down.

"Worth a Grand Tour just for that moment, eh?" Papa said. "Over a thousand seats, Eleanor."

I gasped. "Truly? I am glad I could not see past the limelight."

We maneuvered our way through the crowds of people.

Once we reached the relief of the cool night air, we began walking toward a hired carriage. I took a deep breath. The stars were beautiful tonight.

"Where is Percy?" I glanced around, shivering in the brisk breeze. I drew my cloak around myself.

"He is gone. Took his own carriage ages ago. Exhausted. It's been quite a day for him." John eyed me. "Said he needs to pack. He will be up all night."

A twinge of sadness tainted my joy.

John leaned his head closer to mine as we walked, so that Papa and Mama could not hear. "You are the only one who could have convinced him to come. Well done again, Elle."

"Nonsense. He listens to you. But I'm glad he came. He needed this," I said.

He would be buried in grief, but tonight he needed this brief moment of peace.

"Will I see him before he leaves?" I didn't know whether Percy wanted to see me. I didn't want to ask. It was my brother, though, and we had grown close during our time in Vienna.

"He leaves first thing." John squeezed my arm. "I'm sorry."

"Surely he will take his leave of us before he goes?" I asked.

"Percy insists on leaving at first light," John said.

I stopped.

It sunk in. Percy had told me that I wasn't enough. I had sung for him tonight, and it still did not suffice. Percy would not approve of me, no matter what I did. I had faced my fears for him.

He didn't even care enough to say farewell.

Hurt, anger, confusion, rejection hit me. How much pain could one person carry? It felt like more than I could hold. I could not will my feet to carry me forward. I had no strength to give. The cloak slid from my shoulders, but I didn't feel the winter wind.

John wrapped the wool around me and kept his arm around my shoulders. "Come on. I'll help you."

I thought of my embroidery. I had finally finished the seascape with the grey sky and covered a small cushion. Every time I saw it, I thought of him. Of crossing Calais. Of picking the exact shade of thread together. Of our hands touching.

I wanted that pillow as far away from me as possible. "Can I give you something for him? Perhaps he could use it on the hard coaches and train benches," I said.

"That's kind of you, Elle. I will make sure it is packed in his bags," John said. He guided me toward the carriage as I stumbled over the uneven cobblestones. "I am sorry."

❦

Percy left without saying farewell in person. John brought over a brief letter with heartfelt thanks to my parents and a line of farewell to me.

"Got to buy him a Michelangelo," Papa said. "Says he authorizes me to make his purchases, John. How do you like that? Me! For the estate at Shelford. Ha."

"Thanks for treating him like a son—better than his own mother could have. Oh, he is a dear. We will miss him in Italy." Mama clutched the paper. "My thanks to Lady Eleanor for the concert last night and the traveling pillow."

That was all.

John pulled me aside. "He just couldn't do it. The lights. The people. The noise. You were surrounded by a crowd, Elle. He had no chance of talking to you. You know that, right? He's completely done in with grief."

So was I.

CHAPTER 25

February 1855

Percy's departure made our own inevitable. We all wanted a change of scenery. Mama sent several trunks home to England. We bid farewell to Mrs. Harwich and Miss Harwich. Mama pressed an invitation on them to come with us, but they declined. Mrs. Harwich needed to see whether her school would revive after the attention she received from the concert.

Now that the concert had been such a success, Miss Duxford and her father were considering touring with Mr. Felsted around Europe. Mr. Duxford was due for new diplomatic post in Germany, which would accommodate Miss Duxford's burgeoning career as a singer.

The only things I regretted leaving behind, other than Miss Harwich and Miss Duxford, were the bakeries and our Austrian cook's rich tortes. Everything else reminded me of Percy.

John rode with us to Italy, since Percy was gone. Four fit perfectly in a carriage or train compartment. At first, I dreaded the arguments I knew would come without Percy to smooth things over. To my surprise, they never did. We made it to Florence without a raised voice. I could only attribute the truce in hostilities to the deaths of Percy's family members. Papa and John seemed eager to reconcile.

John also stayed with us. Papa rented a villa in the hills above town, near the Etruscan ruins in Fiesole. I had missed John so much while he was at Cambridge, and I delighted to have him with us.

Every time I saw a set of ruins, I thought of Percy. I didn't know how to separate traveling from memories of Percy.

I was miserable at first. If I had been afraid that no one would ever marry me before, now Percy had confirmed that fear. He found me completely unsuitable. And I was. We were completely wrong for each other. He wanted me to put myself forward, like he did, and I wanted to recede into the background. That would never work.

Instead, I threw myself into studying art, trying to fill my mind with something other than reminiscences and self-recrimination. Playing the piano reminded me too much of him.

The months passed quickly: sitting for portraits, learning to paint, visiting the towering marble statue of the David and the green and white *duomo* and baptistry in the center of town. I wandered over the Ponte Vecchio bridge with Mama to visit the goldsmiths and visited the Uffizi Gallery with Papa. Art was everywhere, and he was happier than I'd ever seen him.

Gradually, my mood lifted, too.

We studied the sculptures and frescoes of Michelangelo, but none were for sale. "For that, you must go to Rome," we heard over and over. So, at the end of May, we left to spend the summer in Rome.

I thought about Percy on the long ride from Florence to Rome. What was he doing? Had he grown used to estate management? I couldn't imagine him doing very well. He couldn't even keep track of his walking stick or eyeglasses. He immersed himself in singing and art and politics. John was the mathematician.

I hated spending time thinking about him. Percy had rejected me. He left without saying farewell. I needed to focus on what was in front of me. My family. Italy.

I didn't want to spend my time pining for someone who had no use for me. Thinking about Percy only knotted my stomach and gave me headaches. I relived our last argument and could not think well of myself when I did.

Was I truly hiding myself? Had I been fully honest with Percy? I did not like the answers, so I stopped thinking about the questions.

Yet, as we approached Rome, how could I not think about him? I knew how ardently he wished to see the city and its ancient sites. I wanted to memorize every detail to tell him when I returned. If he still wished to speak with me.

As I sketched, thoughts of Percy lingered in the back of my mind. Percy would love the Roman baths, covered in fields of newly grown wild grass. He would appreciate my commentary on the contrast of new plants growing on the ancient grounds in the early summer.

John did not. He snorted and asked whether I had finished yet because the fields of wildflowers and weeds made him sneeze when I trampled them.

When I visited the Coliseum with Papa, he took the time to sketch with me. I wondered if Percy had already seen too many portrayals of this building. He wouldn't need to see my scratches. I was only drawing for myself. No one else.

Summer turned into fall. Papa and I spent another long afternoon in the Roman Forum. Half-crumbled buildings towered over us, row upon row of buildings. Inscriptions carved in Latin covered stones. Towering trees grew between ruins. Sculpted archways drew me toward buildings I could never enter.

I tripped over some uneven stones along the path and wished Percy were there to catch me. I missed him. I wanted to share this with him. But would he ever see my sketches?

We searched for a place to set up our easels. Some older gentlemen and ladies beckoned to us and showed us a stable spot for our easels. We sat together with them in silence and sketched. A late summer wind blew through the plaza after we had drawn for a while. It tried to lift our pages and scattered Papa's pencil shavings. One by one, the other artists left until we were the last ones remaining.

"This is the end of our drawing," Papa sighed. "We have quite enough sketches. We must move on to oil paints."

I turned around, gazing over the landscape. So many ruins. I felt an urgency to capture them all. Percy needed to see these. "Just a few more hours. If it truly is our last afternoon, I'd like to get as much as I can."

Papa smiled at me. "Can I blame our late arrival on you, dearest?" he said and went back to sketching.

"Yes, dinner can burn," I said, trying to capture the warm afternoon light with my pastels. "But I must get the house of the Vestals finished."

"You are my favorite daughter," Papa murmured, engrossed in his own sketching.

"I am your only daughter." I tilted my head. I had difficulty capturing the intricacy of the columns and the effect of draped fabric on the statues. "Except for Matthew's wife."

"And she will be my favorite when we are back in England and I can hold my first granddaughter, who will then be my favorite." Papa stopped sketching to look around his easel at me. "But right now I am with you, and you will always be my dearest girl."

I turned my head away to hide the tears that unexpectedly pricked my eyes. He rarely spoke seriously or affectionately to me. Then again, I rarely spoke with him about the subjects that mattered to him, like the angle of the sun or the exact hue of an autumn sky.

We spent the late fall completing our rough sketches and then making oil paintings from them. We set up easels in one room of our rented apartments. Papa acquired oil paints and taught me how to mix colors. We stretched canvases ourselves. Our sketches hung around the room to inspire us. I tried to copy the ruins at the Roman Forum.

More than once, I ruined a dress with oil paints and Mama despaired about my wardrobe. Although I used an apron, I often ended up with oil paint on my sleeve and in my hair.

I finally understood why Papa sometimes came to dinner wearing his artist's smock instead of formal attire.

Even John painted with us, although he insisted on using water-colors like Turner.

"Watercolors wash out of clothes, Elle," John teased me. He pulled at something in my auburn hair. "And they don't change the color of your hair."

"I don't mind acquiring new dresses," I retorted. "And I think I look very well with blue and green curls."

Indeed, Mama seemed eager to visit Roman dressmakers and compare their fashions to the ones in Paris. We also found some excellent bonnets and caps to hide my hair when I painted.

John and Papa painted together often. They agreed to disagree on the subject of oil paints and watercolors as part of their newly won peace. John carefully organized his still life objects, arranging them along the shelves in neat rows until he required their use.

My sketches reminded me of Papa now more than Percy. I convinced myself that I did not care about Percy any longer, and I felt deeply loved by my family. When I looked at the Roman baths, I tried to think of John itching all over instead of Percy. When I looked at the Ponte Vecchio bridge, I thought of wandering among the tiny shops with Mama. When I looked at the Coliseum and the Forum, I thought of Papa patiently teaching me how to use oil paint.

I had the best October and November of my life, enjoying the warmth of Italy. John acquired several pieces of art that made my father sigh. Papa purchased several pieces of art to reestablish his place in Society and grace our picture gallery at home. I felt hopeful that perhaps we would truly return to London for an art exhibit.

It was nearly time to spend Christmas in Germany.

One day we received a note from the Stuarts in Paris. They had sent inquiries for us and found an art dealer with a Michelangelo for sale in Rome. But only one.

We all went with Papa down the cobblestone street to an unassuming door. Stray cats ran everywhere in the alleyway.

"This is the address?" Mama asked. Papa checked the slip of paper and nodded. We entered a light-filled shop. Paintings lined the walls and rested on easels. A stack of canvases lay against the wall in one corner. One wall held shelves filled with small marble busts.

We walked around a corner and through a corridor filled with life-sized statues on plinths into another room. A single round marble relief hung on one wall, covering it entirely. The Christ Child draped across his mother's lap, while an angel floated on one side, his hand cupping a goldfinch.

"Who is the angel?" I asked.

"It's John the Baptist," Papa said, "of course."

I didn't see how he knew that, but he had studied more art than I had.

"See the baptismal bowl next to him? Exquisite." He sighed.

The smooth white marble showed the marks of Michelangelo's chisel. The figures were rounded in places, with intricate folds and detailed curls for hair.

I leaned forward to study each curve, each mark of the chisel, each fold of fabric on the Virgin Mother's head, each finger of the Christ Child. One finger dug into his mother's arm, like a child's would. The baby looked so real, I could only think of home and wanted to hold my new niece. With a pang, I realized Adeline must be nearly a year old by now.

We all stood in silence. Even John.

"England needs this." Mama put her hand on my father's arm. "Our whole trip will be worth it for this."

Papa turned to the art dealer. "Can you ensure its safe delivery?"

"Of course, *signore*. What is the address?"

Papa hesitated. He leaned over the table to look at the packing slip and purchase agreement. He considered John for a long moment, glanced at me, then spoke. "Shelford, Cambridgeshire, United Kingdom."

Papa's voice was certain. Almost too loud.

Mama put her hand over her heart.

I was stunned. Papa was going to sacrifice his Michelangelo for Percy. His reason for the trip. His way of ensuring a return to Society.

"And the payment?" The art dealer handed my father the quill. He signed.

"I will have my bank send it to you." Papa approached the round marble relief. He stared, as if memorizing it.

"Fine thing for you to do, Father." John put his hand on Papa's back and considered the sculpture. "You'll be welcome at Shelford anytime."

Papa turned around reluctantly, as if the act created physical pain.

"Most beautiful sculpture I've seen. To own that…" Papa closed his eyes and took a deep breath. He let it out, then left the room quickly. Mama hurried after him.

John and I studied the Taddei Tondo. "I can't believe he would give this up for Percy." I whispered. I wanted to touch it, to trace every line with my fingers. I held my hand up, inches away from it, and followed the lines of the Christ Child's plump legs, the folds on his stomach and arms, and out to his left hand resting gently on his mother's lap.

"He didn't give it up for Shelford, Elle. He gave it up for you and for me." John left the room and I followed, trying to puzzle out what he meant.

CHAPTER 26

December 1855

The train rattled north toward Berlin. Papa slept in one seat. John slept in another. Mama and I read our copies of Alfred Tennyson's "Charge of the Light Brigade" and "Maud." The poet embraced by the Pre-Raphaelite art movement that Papa despised.

Papa stirred. Mama slipped her copy to me and I casually put both our books into my embroidery basket.

The squealing of brakes and sudden stop let us know we had arrived at another station. A couple and their son entered the open space and looked around for seats.

"Lord Barrington! Where have you been, my old friend?" A beautiful woman, barely younger than my mother, pushed herself between my parents. She waved to her husband. "They'll make room."

Startled and curious, I moved to make room for the small family. There were six seats in the area around us. The man lowered himself gingerly onto the bench beside me and John. The young boy scampered onto his lap.

"I have missed arguing with you. Why have you abandoned us?" The woman fixed her gaze on me. "Who are you?"

Mama took charge of introductions. "Mrs. Elizabeth Barrett Browning, Mr. Robert Browning. My daughter, Lady Eleanor. My younger son, Mr. Barrington." Mama's gaze shifted from us to the child on the man's lap. "And what is your son's name?"

"Ah. This is little Pen. Is your daughter not out yet?" Mrs. Browning asked. "But why are you in Italy with the rest of us outcasts?"

"You mean artists, dear," Mr. Browning corrected her.

"Same thing," she said, and turned on my mother. "Really, it is too cruel. The salons in London have been absolutely dreadful. So civil and polite. No one to contradict me. We're on our way home from London right now."

Papa finally found his voice. "Anne talked me into another Grand Tour. Been buying art for the Royal Academy, you see. And Barrington Hall."

Mrs. Browning laid a hand on Papa's arm. "Have you really? Will it be in the summer exhibition? I'll be going back for the publication of a poem next year. If I can face my dreadful father, surely you can face the summer heat and stench of the Thames."

Mr. Browning nudged his son aside to try to see my parents. "Really. We have missed you."

My father tried to face Mrs. Browning, but the seats were narrow and cramped. "I've enjoyed Europe. Might stay awhile."

My heart sank.

"Artists do flourish in our climate," Mrs. Browning said.

Pen began to squirm. Mr. Browning tried to hold onto him, but he slipped off his lap and began playing in the middle of the aisle.

"We just don't fit," Mrs. Browning said. "Let's find somewhere else. So, I'll see you next spring in London? Promise me, Lord Barrington. You cannot leave me alone another year." And she left without waiting for a response.

Pen ran after her.

Mr. Browning bowed to my father and mother. "She will hold you to your promise."

John and I exchanged a look. What promise?

"What's this talk of staying in Europe?" Mama asked. "I have a grandchild I intend to see on Easter Sunday next year. You have six more months, Thomas, and then I will return home. With or without you."

I felt an enormous surge of relief. If Mama had set her mind to returning home, then I would escape Miss Harwich's fate. Even if Papa wanted to stay in Italy forever, Mama and I could go back to Barrington in the spring.

Mama reached across, pulled her poetry book out of my embroidery basket, and began reading it in front of my father.

Papa's eyes traveled between the door of the train car where the Brownings had been, Mama, and the title of her poetry book. Tennyson. I felt a little sorry for him. So much. All at once.

I moved over to sit between Mama and Papa. I wedged myself between them and put my head on his shoulder. Papa leaned his head on mine.

"I have a letter from Percy," John said, and dug a tightly folded bit of paper from his vest pocket. "He asks about you, Father. I don't think the Taddei Tondo has arrived yet. Letter is old."

Papa nodded.

I played with the fabric of my skirt. "Did Percy ask about me?"

"Uh, no. Mostly just complains about bookkeeping." John folded the letter back into a square and tucked it away. "He's a bit of a wreck. Doesn't understand estate management at all. Woodford's taken him in hand."

I nodded. *Why doesn't he write to me in John's letters?* Nothing. I'd heard nothing in the year since he'd left. Just the snippets from John.

He must be indifferent to me. We will meet as casual acquaintances, if we ever see each other again. And that will be all. He has forgotten me, and I must forget him.

. . .

The train sped us north for days. We spent two weeks in Berlin, then moved on to Munich. The Harwiches wrote to say that the school was struggling once again. They had agreed to close the school and tour with Mr. Felsted, Miss Duxford, and a few other singers. Their schedule brought them to Munich for Christmas.

This time Miss Duxford, her father, and Mr. Felsted accompanied us to the Christmas market. I saw a man roasting chestnuts. I remembered Percy and shoved the thought aside.

Snow blanketed the spruce and pine trees of the nearby forests. We wandered through a lantern-lit path with displays of nativity scenes. Lamps hung on the mangers. Wise men held ornate painted gifts. Donkeys and oxen stood vigil over carved images of the Christ Child. Mama bought a complete set to send home and display next year.

The donkeys reminded me fleetingly of riding mules up the St. Bernard Pass with Percy, so I focused on the bright colors and intricate designs of the manger scene instead.

Mr. Felsted approached me with an artificial smile. "Would you sing with us tomorrow, Lady Eleanor? I've already spoken with your father, and he assures me he is eager to contribute to the concert fund."

I thought quickly. This was a remarkable opportunity for me, even if it was offered by Mr. Felsted. If Papa ever did allow me to have a Season, this performance would help set me apart in the crowded marriage mart. And I had enjoyed singing in Vienna. I did not want to miss something I enjoyed just to spite a horrid man.

"Thank you. Yes. I will need to rehearse," I said.

"Tomorrow afternoon before the performance. Miss Duxford and Miss Harwich can give you more details," he said, then moved forward to discuss the specifics of financial remuneration with my father.

I slowed down to walk with John and Miss Harwich. "How do you manage?" I asked her. "Traveling with him?"

Miss Harwich grimaced, then let her face assume a neutral

smile. "We do what we must. He is exceptionally talented and a skilled businessman."

"Mushroom," John muttered.

I swatted his arm. "We never use that word," I said. "You know that. Vulgar."

"The man is vulgar," John said.

Miss Harwich slipped on the snow. John quickly steadied her and offered her his elbow.

"You must return with me at Easter time," I said to Miss Harwich. "Now that the school is closed. I will return in a moment," I said, and sped up. I moved past Papa and Mr. Felsted.

Mama and Mrs. Harwich led the group. I sandwiched myself between them.

"We're nearly finished with the walk," Mama said to me.

"I want the Harwiches to join us at Barrington Hall when we return." The words rushed out of me.

Mama stopped walking. Papa and Mr. Felsted came to a halt. Behind them, John, Miss Harwich, Miss Duxford, and her father, all waited. Mr. Felsted stomped his feet and rubbed his hands together.

Other people came up along the path, stopping behind us.

Mama turned to her friend. "I told you, Catherine. It is time to come home."

Mrs. Harwich examined the growing queue behind her. "Is this the place to discuss it?"

Mama stood her ground. "No one remembers your husband's financial mismanagement. What do you and I care about gossip? You will be welcomed home as the latest bit of interesting news from Europe, I assure you."

Mrs. Harwich started walking again.

Mama refused to move. "I'm not leaving this spot until you agree."

"It's freezing," Mrs. Harwich said.

"I suggest you decide quickly," Papa said. He widened his

stance so that no one could pass him either. The crowd of people behind us grew larger.

"I can hardly afford it," Mrs. Harwich said.

"We can," Papa and Mama said at the same time.

"Now, if you're going to take my best singers away—" Mr. Felsted began.

Papa scoffed. "Come now. I've paid you enough to live on for years. Can we keep walking? It's cold."

Miss Harwich spoke up. "Mama. I would like to go back to England. I don't recall it."

Mrs. Harwich bowed her head in defeat. "Then, yes. Thank you, Anne, Lord Barrington. We should very much love to visit you in March." Mrs. Harwich pulled me forward with her. "Your parents have no concept of what the *ton* will truly think of me."

I had to agree. My parents' cavalier attitude about Mrs. Harwich's reputation was completely at odds with my father's own fears for himself. But I also did not know whether we would stay in Essex or go to London after Easter.

"Perhaps we will simply stay at Barrington Hall and never have to find out," I said.

CHAPTER 27

March 1856

We arrived home before Easter. A pang of unexpected joy burst inside when we rounded the lane and I first saw Barrington Hall. It was as familiar as my mother's face, but I hadn't seen it for nearly two years. It was like the warmth and welcome of an old friend.

Miss Harwich seemed overwhelmed by the size of our entry way. She stared around the enormous hall as if lost, until I dragged her upstairs to our bedchambers. I was exhausted and wanted to rest, but glad to be home finally.

After laying down and washing up, I wanted to meet my baby niece. I climbed back downstairs, stiff from weeks in carriages and rickety trains.

"Matthew!" I held my hands out to my brother. "Where is my little niece?"

"She's hardly a baby anymore."

"What do you mean?" I held the toys from the Christmas market in Vienna. Would she still like them?

"Adeline can walk and talk. Go see for yourself." Matthew took my arm. We crossed the entrance hall and went through the picture gallery.

"Crates have been arriving for months. I cannot wait to see what he bought." Matthew pointed to the Rubens. "Can we get rid of that one?"

I laughed. "Yes, please, donate that one first. You purchased it," I teased.

"I had no idea what I was doing. Woodford selected it. Truth be told, I think he was playing a joke on me," Matthew said.

Adeline sat in the middle of the drawing room floor. Tight, blond curls covered her head. Miss Harwich and John knelt across from each other on the floor, rolling the ball back and forth with Adeline. Adeline celebrated her successes by shoving the ball in her mouth most times.

She was everything delightful, and I laughed with her and the others. I couldn't wait to hold her and play with her and watch her smile.

John retrieved the ball, dried it with his handkerchief, and rolled it back to Miss Harwich. She was a natural with young children. She sang songs and made Adeline smile. John watched Miss Harwich with gleaming eyes.

I joined them on the floor and unrolled my bundle of toys from Vienna. I offered the pull-string toy to Adeline. She took it and pulled the string. The man's arms and legs flew out. Adeline laughed and pulled the string again. Her giggle touched something in my heart.

I had imagined showing these toys to a baby in my arms, but here was a small child who could walk and talk and play with the toys on her own. I realized how much I had missed while I was away. Nearly two years. All of Adeline's time as a baby. What else had changed?

And when would I see Percy? I knew he would spend the spring and summer in London for the Season. What would Papa do? Most peers left for London after Easter.

Mama invited the neighborhood over for Easter dinner. Lucy and Rachel arrived before the Chelmsfords.

Lucy pulled me aside. "I am betrothed."

I lowered my voice, so we would not be overheard. "What? Congratulations. To whom? Oh, this is wonderful. Did your father relent and let you marry George? You have enough money."

"Don't say his name," Lucy said.

"George?"

"Papa sent him to work in a mine before Christmas," Lucy said in a choked voice. "He thought the festivities might encourage us to take liberties. There are a lot of babies born in September."

"Shall I call him 'the groom' instead?" I asked.

Lucy's lower lip trembled. "Grooms marry brides."

"The stablehand?"

"Just call him 'him,'" Lucy said.

"Have you heard from him?" I asked.

She shook her head. "Men die in those mines. I can't think about him."

"But your Papa gives you anything you want," I said.

"He wants to join the aristocracy more," she said. "Your family, and Rachel's, are the only ones who truly accept us. The rest tolerate us because of you. He feels slighted everywhere he goes."

"Has it gotten worse?" I asked.

"You have no idea what it's been like with your family gone. Papa's desperate," Lucy said.

I took Lucy's hands. "I'm so sorry. When?"

"As soon as George left. The settlement took months to negotiate. I didn't believe it would really happen, but they signed the marriage contract last week. Papa will finally have a daughter with a title."

"Oh, Lucy," I pulled her in and hugged her tightly.

She wiped a single tear from her eye. "But of course, the whole neighborhood knows I admire Lord Chelmsford greatly and am vastly happy."

"You're engaged to Walter?" I asked. I had imagined it might happen while I was away in Europe, but I had never received any hint of it in a letter from Lucy or Rachel. I felt nothing but shock.

Lucy nodded. She seemed as surprised as me.

I took Lucy's face between my hands. "Hear me, Lucy Maldon. If the time ever comes that you need anything. If he is not what he seems. If you are desperate. I do not know. You will always have me as your friend."

Lucy's eyes filled with tears, and a few ran down her face. She wiped them hastily and pinched her cheeks.

"How do I look?" she asked.

"Beautiful, as always. Radiant and happy. Come meet my friend, Miss Harwich," I said. "Let's celebrate Easter with your fiancé."

Dinner was awkward after that. Lucy and Lord Chelmsford sat next to each other, but hardly spoke to one another. I looked down the table at them. Nothing. No pricks of regret. No jealousy or remorse. I was sorry for Lucy and sorry for Lord Chelmsford, but not sorry for myself. If I had to choose between a Grand Tour or staying to pursue a romance with Lord Chelmsford, I would choose the Grand Tour.

Thoughts of Percy surfaced. I remembered riding mules over the St. Bernard Pass and seeing the view of Italy from atop the mountain ridge together. I remembered the humble soup, bread, and cheese we ate and considered the lavish Easter meal in front of me. I preferred the rough, carved wooden bowls provided by the monks over these polished silver plates. And the company. I pushed the thoughts down and waited for the meal to end.

But all I could think about was when my father would decide to leave for London. If he did.

Papa began lecturing Lucy's father about our itinerary. "In

Switzerland they took the blasted carriage apart." Papa checked to see whether my mother had heard him. "Pardon my language."

"And what did you see of Italy, Lord Barrington?" Peter Chelmsford asked.

Mr. Maldon leaned back and folded his arms. "And how much did they charge you for the Rembrandt?"

"You went on a Grand Tour, too, Dunmore?" Lord Chelmsford asked.

Matthew peered at him across the table. "Indeed, with Woodford, after I finished at Cambridge. Peter, you're finishing this year, aren't you? Will you be leaving on yours soon?"

Peter glanced at his brother. "Walter and I discussed going together before our father died. Had it all planned out," Peter said. "I'm not sure now."

"What were the lodgings like at the embassy in Paris?" Lord Chelmsford asked.

I watched Lucy. She sat with her head down, playing with a napkin in her lap. Completely quiet. Lord Chelmsford's eyes were blazing, full of curiosity, as he and Peter continued to ask question after question.

Lord Chelmsford seemed restless, and I wondered the real reason why he got betrothed. He hardly seemed like a man in love. What would drive him to agree with Mr. Maldon's proposal? Why had he chosen Lucy for his wife?

I thought Percy might be in love with me, back in Vienna, only to have him tell me that I would be unsuitable as a wife. My bite of Easter ham stuck in my throat. I put down my fork.

Finally, my father finished with his travel stories. "But you have your own adventure, eh, Chelmsford," Papa said. "Marriage. When do they read the banns? Next Sunday? I was surprised not to hear them today, but it is Easter after all."

Lord Chelmsford tugged at his bowtie around his neck. "Ah, yes. Easter. Holy day."

Peter squirmed next to Lord Chelmsford.

I tried to catch Lucy's eye. She continued to stare at her hands.

"Truth is, we have not set a date just yet." Lord Chelmsford played with his knife. "Lucy will need to get her clothes, and it might take a while. I could not possibly rush her. I want her to have everything perfect on her wedding day."

"How considerate." Papa's dry tone told me that he thought the same thing as me. Lucy was resigned. She wasn't happy, but she wasn't the one slowing things down. But why wasn't Lord Chelmsford in any rush?

The guests left. Matthew and Georgiana went back to Dunmore with Adeline. I paced back and forth in the drawing room. Mama and Miss Harwich embroidered while Mrs. Harwich read a book. Finally, Papa and John joined us and settled onto sofas.

"What, Elle?" John barked. "Stop wearing a hole in the rug."

I had to deal carefully. How could I get Papa to agree to take us to London? *Percy knew how to handle my father. What would he do? Make Papa think it's his own idea?*

Joseph waited by the entrance to the drawing room. I walked over to him. My father needed to realize that no one would see the priceless paintings here.

"Have you uncrated the new paintings yet, Joseph?" I asked in a casual tone. Not too loud. Not too quiet.

"No, miss."

"How long have they been here?"

"A few months. Lord Dunmore and the servants have been most eager to see them," Joseph said.

"It will be an astonishing collection. The servants will enjoy the others from London, once Papa sends those as well."

"There's more?" Joseph said. "Will we be putting them upstairs?"

"Probably," I said.

"We could hang some in the corridors for you."

"Eleanor," Mama called. "What are you speaking of?"

Joseph gave me a small smile. He always understood me. He knew I was trying to bait my father. After all, he fenced with him every afternoon when we were home. He knew how to goad Papa better than I did.

"The paintings Papa bought for England. If he's not going to donate them after all, where will we hang them?"

Mama put down her embroidery.

"Now who says I'm not going to donate them?" Papa asked.

"If we're staying here after Easter," I said, "then I suppose Joseph and I will be the only ones to see the paintings. And the Harwiches. Or Mr. Maldon. Can I have the Lorrain in my bedchamber? You'll want the Dürer for yours."

"Nonsense," Papa said. "Didn't buy those paintings for the footmen. Sorry, Joseph."

Joseph bowed to Papa and resumed his post at the door.

"You're right. I suppose Sims will help you uncrate them," I said. "And the maids will clean the frames. I'm not sure where they'll all fit, though."

Papa stared at me.

"How many did you buy? Eleven? And the portraits we sat for?" I asked. "Does it make fifteen when they all arrive?"

He left the drawing room to count the number of paintings already hanging in our picture gallery. There wasn't room for the paintings. Papa had intended to donate several of them, after all. Joseph and I both knew it. He had carried most of them himself.

"If you want to go to London, just tell him," Mama said. She followed Papa.

I waited. Footsteps echoed on the spiral staircase. Evidently, he was checking the upstairs gallery as well.

Miss Harwich smiled at me. "I am content here in the country, but it would be a treat to see London."

Mrs. Harwich continued to read her book.

Finally, Papa returned. "Room for six. Maybe eight. I bought them for England, and I'll give them to England. Well, daughter, we're going to London."

CHAPTER 28

I thought my heart might stop beating. "I'll have a Season?"

"Promised the Brownings I'd be there to argue with them," Papa said. "Of course we'll go."

"Really, Papa? Mama?"

"We will begin packing tomorrow," Mama said. "Now that your father has finally decided."

I ran to a sofa and grabbed Miss Harwich's hands. I pulled her up. "We're going!"

"Yes, yes," Miss Harwich said softly.

I twirled her around.

"Really, Eleanor," Mama said.

"I haven't been to London in four years. Five years? How long has it been? And there are so many places to visit. Oh, Mama." I ran over to her and hugged her around the neck. Now I would have a Season. Visit the Italian Opera, Almack's, everywhere I had never been. See Percy, if he wished to see me. The thought stung. Seeing a cold and indifferent Percy would hurt. But I had forgotten him. At least twelve times. There were other people to meet and so many new experiences to be had.

"Now, our dresses from Paris are dated. And the ones from

Italy. We'll need new ones for all of us," Mama said. "Do not object, Catherine. You know I am determined."

Mrs. Harwich said, "Thank you," and bowed her head to hide her emotion. She and her daughter were as opposite from Mama and me as could be. While I was twirling again and pretending to waltz, Miss Harwich was settling herself back on the sofa.

"John, join me at billiards?" Papa asked. His grin split his face. "When they start talking about how much this is going to cost, I leave the room."

"All our clothes cost less than one Rembrandt," Mama yelled after them. She clapped her hands. "Thank you for making up his mind, Eleanor. He's been dithering for days."

As soon as we put up our door knocker and settled into our town house, we received an invitation from the duke's mother for a musicale the following evening. The Season was underway. We had already missed a week. That was time enough for three couples to get engaged. I hadn't even ordered calling cards yet.

John had found apartments next door to Percy. I hoped that meant I would see Percy more often and wondered how things would be between us. A year was such a long time, and I did not know how he felt.

Miss Harwich and I traded compliments as our carriage rolled along the cobblestone street toward His Grace's town house. My mother and Mrs. Harwich listened indulgently. Papa had stayed home.

"But you will be a Diamond of the First Water, Lady Eleanor," Miss Harwich assured me.

"Oh, I have not set my sights so high. But please, call me Eleanor," I said. "We are going to be together for the Season."

"And you must call me Charlotte," she said.

"You will be far and away the most stunning singer at the musicale," I said. "I wonder what they are like. I've never been to any of these events."

While we worried and wondered together, the carriage made its way to our destination. We held up our skirts as we climbed the stone steps to enter one of the grandest town houses in London. I caught my breath at the sheer size and magnificence of the grey stone façade.

People crowded the entrance and lined the hallways leading to a large music room. A piano rested on a small, raised stage surrounded by glass windows that reminded me of the Crystal Palace. I could see extensive gardens behind it.

The view was charming. Roses and flowers set a backdrop for the performers. A light summer breeze blew in through the open windows.

A tall man approached us. He had dark chestnut hair, swept forward, and brilliant blue eyes that radiated warmth and kindness. "Lady Barrington. It has been an age. Dunmore has written to tell me all about your tour. I am delighted to hear it has been a success. How are you?" He took my mother's hand.

"May I introduce you to my dear friend, Mrs. Harwich? Her daughter, Miss Harwich? And perhaps you remember Lady Eleanor? She was younger last time you saw her," Mama said.

"At your service." His Grace took Charlotte's hand and bowed over it, then took my hand and did the same. His coat stretched across his broad shoulders as he bowed.

My hand tingled where he held it.

"You have grown up, Lady Eleanor," he said.

I could see Percy approaching out of the corner of my eye. My heart began to race. "Indeed, Your Grace, it has been many years since I last saw you," I said.

Percy joined the duke. I hadn't seen him in over a year. I wanted to stare, to drink in the sight of him, but the duke was talking to me.

Woodford barely flicked his eyes sideways toward Percy. "May I introduce Lord Shelford? He is my nearest neighbor and an old friend."

"*Shelford.*" The thought hit me unexpectedly. *He's not Percy. He's an earl.*

"We are acquainted," I said. I waited for Percy to say something. He bowed. So proper. No lopsided grin or mischievous sparkle in his eyes. I hardly recognized him.

His Grace held my hand still. "Of course. Dunmore has told me about your tour, too, Lady Eleanor. A concert in Munich. Quite impressive."

"Munich?" Percy asked.

"Yes, a Christmas concert," I said. "But how did you know?"

"Your brother is a regular correspondent and keeps me apprised of everything I deem important." His Grace let go of my hand but continued to maintain eye contact. "And I deemed your Grand Tour important."

I fought a blush. I could see Percy watching me. Why didn't he say anything?

"Let me introduce you to my mother. Miss Harwich?" The duke held out an elbow to each of us. He waited to lead us away.

I tried to catch Percy's eye, to say something to him. Anything. I wanted to greet him, but he turned away. A young girl had come to talk to him. A very beautiful and very young girl. He was deep in conversation. I couldn't interrupt him. I tried to wait to see if he would finish the conversation quickly.

The girl seemed to talk without drawing breath. On and on. How was she old enough to be at a musicale? He watched the girl intently. As if he were avoiding my gaze.

Finally, I could delay no longer. I took the duke's arm and left to meet his mother. Her Grace looked nothing like I imagined. A short, thin, wisp of a woman.

"Mother, I bring you two additions for your program tonight." His Grace spoke with undeniable authority, but kindness. "Miss Harwich from Vienna. Her mother, Mrs. Harwich, the preeminent musician, of course. And Lady Eleanor Barrington. You remember."

What should she remember? What had he said? *A duke? Take notice of me?* I was new in London. We had barely unpacked and only been there one day. Why would he care? I felt overwhelmed and hoped I could live up to his expectations. I didn't know much about the social circles, only that we associated with the same members of my father's political party. Other than that, I had no idea who had social influence and who did not. *But a duke?*

"Yes," Lady Woodford spoke in a breathless voice. "We must have both of you perform. His Grace has told me so much." Lady Woodford sounded as though she never got enough air. I wondered if she ever sang herself.

His Grace held out his elbows to us and escorted us to the front row of chairs.

A stunning young woman perched on a chair. Diminutive, curvy, and blonde, she couldn't have been older than fourteen or fifteen. Her skin glowed and her emerald eyes sparkled.

Percy sat beside the girl. Their heads were bent together.

I felt a pang of jealousy.

I glanced down the row. Most of the other girls were younger than me. Sixteen. Seventeen. Charlotte and I were both nearly twenty. I began to fiddle with the seam of fabric on my skirt.

The girl reached a hand back to touch her hair. "Guy!" she said. "Did you bring any friends?"

"Octavia," the duke replied. "What are you doing here? She's not out yet, Shelford?"

"Couldn't shake her off," Percy said, "My mother insists on bringing her to some events."

She was Percy's sister. I sagged a little in my chair, then caught myself and straightened. I should have seen the resemblance. The fair hair, the piercing green eyes. The air of nonchalance and a total disregard for rules. Of course she was related to him.

"I should greet your mother. How is she holding up? Where is she?" His Grace waited for Percy to lead the way.

Percy moved off toward a corner of the spacious room without saying anything to me.

Percy had left without even acknowledging me. After a year apart.

I had expected that he might no longer have feelings, but I assumed we would at least be passing acquaintances. I never dreamed Percy would ignore me, or not even introduce me to his sister.

I watched Percy as he left, noticing the snug fit of his jacket, the cut of his trousers, an elegant new walking cane, and the style of his hair. Someone had taken him to get a new wardrobe. He had a new hairstyle, too, a cut that accentuated the curls, making his hair look almost respectable. I remembered the feel of my hands in his soft hair and shook myself.

Would he be different now that he was an earl? Would his behavior change as drastically as Lord Chelmsford's had? Would he become insufferable, too?

Several girls noticed him move around the room. Their mothers inspected him carefully, too. Percy would be the catch of the Season.

But so would the Duke of Woodford. The two of them walking together drew almost every eye in the room. I considered the duke. He must have lost his father, too, if he was also a peer. A wave of sympathy rushed over me. He seemed so kind, so compassionate, so knowledgeable. So tall.

The program commenced. Percy's mother, Lady Shelford, was evidently a member of Her Grace's musical society. She sang a piece, and I began to understand why Percy worried that I would screech on high notes. I wanted to catch his eye and grin at him while his mother sang, but I was seated on the front row. And Percy was ignoring me.

It was Charlotte's turn to perform. The applause was steady before she began. She looked beautiful, poised as always. Her dress hung just right, her skirt flaring out to showcase a tiny waist. She seemed like an angel with a halo of dark hair pulled back into a chignon.

And then it was my turn. I prepared myself. I could do this. I had sung in front of hundreds of people. What was fifty?

When I surveyed the audience, I saw John seated next to Percy and His Grace. Without thinking, my gaze fell on Percy. His face was impassive. I had expected compassion. Help. He was my anchor when I was afraid. But now his face was a blank. I couldn't read any emotion. He had learned how to play by Society's rules, and I did not like the new version of him. The earl.

His Grace watched me with interest. John winked at me and I relaxed a little. I would look at them instead.

I began to sing, and the familiar feeling of losing myself in the music took over once the song began. Worries fled and, instead, I became the country girl wandering through her meadow in springtime.

After the program of songs finished, Charlotte and I found ourselves surrounded by young men with glasses of lemonade. The duke never left our side. Lady Octavia hovered around us, trying to get the duke to introduce her to his friends.

He managed to turn away at just the right angle to ignore her. She would maneuver into a new position, and he would shift his position to block her view.

It distracted me from the men introducing themselves, but I caught His Grace's eye. Every time he shifted to block Lady Octavia, he would smile at me. It became our game for the rest of the evening.

At one point, His Grace leaned over and whispered to me, "Fifteen years old. I'm not introducing her to men who are ten years older than her. Let her try."

I loved the flash of challenge in his eyes. His Grace and I talked with our heads close together, laughing.

I noticed Percy glance at me from his knot of admirers. Mamas with young daughters surrounded him. Percy spoke attentively with each one.

I didn't think he had even tried to come over to speak with me. "Perhaps Percy does not mind fifteen-year-old debutantes," I whispered back to His Grace.

He glanced over at Percy and laughed. "I shall have to teach him how to evade them." Percy raised an eyebrow at us.

Charlotte and I were a success, far beyond anything I had ever hoped or imagined.

Now we just had to survive our first ball in two days, and the duke had already spoken for my first dance.

But Percy had not even spoken to me.

CHAPTER 29

April 1856

Sibley tugged my chestnut hair into tidy ringlets and affixed brilliant roses. The blush pink flowers matched the pattern of my ballgown and highlighted the auburn color in my curls.

I had her snug the corset tighter and slip the ballgown over my head. Lace fell in rows down the shoulders and over the puffed sleeves. The white and pink printed silk-satin dress was covered in rows of tiny rosettes and ruffles at the bottom. I felt like a garden.

I wondered at my situation. Was this a dream? Would my father change his mind and leave halfway through the Season, like he had four years ago? *I need to make the most of this while I can. Before people remember too much about Papa or ask why we left on Grand Tour in such a rush.* Papa's impulsive nature might seem eccentric to some or a touch too close to insanity to others.

And what about the duke? I had always hoped to marry a peer of the realm, someone who could protect my family from accusations if my father ever acted as wildly as his brother had. We had nearly lost our home and income when my uncle died in a reckless accident. Some suspected my grief-stricken uncle of causing the accident himself.

And then my father had fled London after the publication of a satirical cartoon that mocked him. He'd hidden away in Essex for two years before we left on our Grand Tour. I imagined that would set off rumors of instability and insanity running in our family. I hadn't heard any whispers yet, but I worried all the same.

I needed someone who could vote in the House of Lords, if an issue ever came before them. If someone accused my father of insanity and tried to strip his title and lands away from him. I never imagined someone with as much social and political power as the Duke of Woodford.

But you love Percy, a voice inside my head said. *Do I still? Does it matter?*

Because he certainly did not care about me. He felt as unconcerned as I had suspected. He did not even feel strongly enough to make the effort to greet me after an absence of a year. Instead, he had paid astute attentions to every eligible heiress and debutante.

We were, indeed, merely casual acquaintances now. Just like he had thrown himself into every diplomatic event when he aspired to become an ambassador, now I would have to watch Percy attend to every jealous mother and socially connected patroness at social events.

No. Better to allow the attentions of a socially connected duke who also cared enough to ask Matthew about me. I had learned that my heart was not to be trusted. A marriage of convenience would be prudent and much less painful.

❦

"Are you nervous?" I asked Charlotte as we waited to enter. I fidgeted with my gloves and tugged at my gown.

"You worry a lot, don't you?" Charlotte moved forward as the line of people progressed. "You did fine with the dancing instructor this week. It is not that different from Vienna."

"But the men are." I gulped. Charlotte and I had attended a New Year's Eve ball together and danced mostly with men as old as my father.

Singing was one thing. I had learned how to perform and pushed myself to face my fears. But I could rehearse for musicales and concerts. Making idle conversation? Holding hands? My cheeks burned at the thought.

"Then pretend they are *Herr* Wabnitz," Charlotte said.

We moved forward again. My stomach felt queasy. I was not sure I wanted to be a Diamond. Our success at the musicale made me feel I had to live up to expectations tonight.

"And talk about their children and wife?" I tugged at my ball gown again. "That will not work here."

Mama put my arm down from behind me. "Leave your dress alone, Eleanor."

"I am not ready for this," I said.

Charlotte took my arm and threaded hers through it. "We are in this together."

Charlotte and I entered at the same time with my parents behind us. Mrs. Harwich entered after them. I scanned the ballroom. It was a sea of colors and faces and movement. Musicians tuned up in the corner. The sound soothed my nerves.

Almack's looked entirely different from the ballroom in Vienna. The tall ceilings allowed room for a curved observation balcony on an upper level. Crown molding covered the upper levels of the walls. I wanted to study the intricate designs. Were they Roman? Or Greek laurels? Where was my sketch book?

Mama nudged me. "Start walking."

We made our way across the room. I tried not to notice how much my new slippers pinched. My walk was a little unsteady. Charlotte glided.

We reached a spot where we could stand along the edge of the dancers. The musicians signaled they were ready for the first song.

Lord Romford appeared. Although nearly the same height as Charlotte and me, he had an attractive, muscular build and rich, brown eyes. I thought of roasted chestnuts at the Christmas market in Vienna. Charlotte and I looked at each other and smiled. He bowed to Charlotte and held out his hand. They left, and I was alone.

The Duke of Woodford came over. His evening attire fit him well. The long coattails hanging behind him made his height more pronounced. His auburn curls were swept forward. "May I?" He held out his hand.

I took a deep breath, smiled, and entered the fray. The duke danced well. He put me at ease quickly and, thankfully, the dance did not require too much conversation.

Colonel Loughton followed him, then Mr. Kempton.

Hours later, well after the supper dance, I sat on a sofa. I had danced every dance. Mr. Kempton and Colonel Loughton stood nearby, talking to me about their philosophical society for medicine. My feet were sore, and my throat felt parched. Balls were exhausting.

I had only seen Charlotte, John, and Percy in passing as we moved through the dance patterns.

I was grateful to sit and talk instead of dance. Mr. Kempton was describing the new surgical technique he was researching.

"Rather rough subject for a ballroom," Colonel Loughton said. "Perhaps Lady Eleanor would prefer something else."

"Like the weather? No, no. I am committing everything to memory to tell my friend Rachel in Essex when I return," I said.

I heard the musicians preparing for another dance.

Percy's deep voice cut across the colonel and Mr. Kempton. "May I have this dance?"

Colonel Loughton and Mr. Kempton moved aside.

Percy blinked when he saw me.

"Percy?" I was so surprised I spoke without thinking. And my feet hurt.

Percy stared. "You look stunning this evening."

"Thank you."

Colonel Loughton and Mr. Kempton were watching him. "Good to see you, Shelford," Colonel Loughton said. "Excellent sparring yesterday."

Percy nodded and held out his hand to me.

I knew I should accept and join him right away. It was the gracious thing to do. But this was Percy, my old friend. I could be honest with him. "The dance has nearly begun. Would you not rather talk with us? The ball is nearly over, and my slippers are worn out." I lifted up my skirts so that just a little bit of my slippers showed. There was a tiny hole on the bottom of my new shoes. "My feet hurt."

"Eleanor," Percy's hoarse voice choked out. He took a deep breath. "Those ankles." He tugged at his jacket sleeves. "Keep them covered."

Colonel Loughton and Mr. Kempton smirked at one another, leaned against the wall, and folded their arms.

"Are you turning me down, Lady Eleanor?" Percy's voice was recovered now. Formal. He dropped his hand. "You do not wish to dance with me?" As if we hardly knew each other. As though I would give him the cut.

He stood, stiff and inflexible, waiting for my reply.

I sighed. How could he think that? My feet were merely tired. It was so easy for me to forget that he had changed while I had not. "Of course not, Percy. I mean, Lord Shelford."

I offered him my gloved fingers and winced as he drew me up from the chair. He placed my hand on his sleeve.

"Excuse us." Percy led me away toward the roped-off dancing area.

The feel of his arm beneath my hand was achingly familiar. I could not reconcile this distant, dignified man with the warm, informal one I had loved in Vienna.

We waited side by side. Percy took my left hand in front of him, then placed his right hand on the small of my back, pulling me toward him. Heat spread throughout me.

We began marching forward, four counts, then swung toward each other, one arm over our head. We stared into each other's eyes. This was nothing like a fast-paced Viennese waltz with men my father's age.

The timing was slow, the movement intimate. And Percy was not my father's white-haired friends. Around and around. Then marching forward again with Percy's hand on my back. Finally, he spoke.

"How are you this evening?"

"Well," I said. I could hardly breathe. "Although my feet are sore."

Percy turned his head to gaze at me. "And your family?"

We twirled in a tight circle, just the two of us, eyes locked, as if no one else existed in the whole world. Time seemed to stop, as it had once before when I was with him.

"They are well," I managed to reply.

Percy pulled me beneath the circle of his arm and back around to his side. "And Dunmore? How is your niece?" Percy asked. His face flickered in the glow, his eyes deepening in the shadows cast by the candlelight.

Soft light filtered down from tiered chandeliers. Emotions swirled inside me as we moved together. How could he look at me like this and talk to me of such superficial things?

I sighed. "Adeline is well."

We walked side by side.

"And how are your estates?" I asked.

His face was an inch away. "They are well." His fingers on my back pressed me closer until I could see the gold streaks in his emerald eyes. "I am sorry your feet ache. Thank you for dancing with me regardless."

I yearned for an emotional closeness to match this intimacy, but the dance drew us apart. We moved through another turn. "I understood from John that you were allowing him to assist you with some bookkeeping. As a favor to him. Even though you have the estates well in hand. Because he enjoys mathematics so much."

For one moment, Percy's face split into a grin. A true smile. The Percy I remembered. He even laughed. "Yes, the books are a disaster, if I'm honest. Barrington is a brick."

But then we were moving away again. We formed into a promenade. By the time we held hands and walked side by side again, Percy's face had slipped back into a formal mask.

Disappointment washed over me. I wanted the real Percy back. The one I knew. Not this new one, the earl.

Gradually we became aware that the music had ended. I realized I had been holding my breath. At least, that's why I told myself I had felt dizzy. That, and all the spinning.

Other couples around us were moving off the dance floor. The space was nearly deserted. Percy held on to my hands, not moving.

Then he led me off the floor and back to the colonel and Mr. Kempton. Several mothers hovered nearby with their daughters, trying to catch his attention.

"Thank you for the dance." Percy bowed over my hand as he let go.

"Of course, Percy," I said.

An emotion flitted across his face momentarily and was gone. What was it? I could not tell, but I needed to remember to call him Lord Shelford in front of others.

The duke approached the sofa where I sat. "You managed to keep Octavia at home, old man." He clapped Percy on the shoulder.

"No small feat, I assure you." Percy scrubbed a hand over his face. "My mother encourages her nonsense."

I stifled a yawn.

"Not used to Town hours yet? May I sit with you?" The duke settled next to me on the small sofa without waiting for an answer. "I wondered if you might be amenable to a carriage ride tomorrow afternoon," His Grace spoke quietly, gazing into my eyes.

I could hear Mr. Kempton describing a new school for nurses in Germany while Colonel Loughton plied him with questions. Percy leaned casually next to Mr. Kempton but seemed to be watching me.

"I have so many questions about you." The duke glanced down at our hands, nearly touching, and back up at me. "And I would like to know your friend, Miss Harwich, better, if she would accompany us."

The musicians tuned their instruments.

His Grace held out his hand. "We began the night together. Shall we end it as well?"

I felt a thrill of excitement. Two dances with the duke in one evening. And a carriage ride the next day.

I put my left hand on the duke's arm and began to leave.

Something brushed the hand resting on my skirt and almost tugged at my dress, holding me back for the smallest moment. I turned.

Percy's hand.

"I thought your feet hurt," Percy muttered, his eyes averted. He turned back toward the colonel's conversation, and I moved toward the roped-off dance area.

My excitement dissipated as I walked with the duke.

It was hard to forget the feel of Percy's hand brushing mine. Like he hadn't wanted me to leave. Like perhaps he still cared.

His Grace held out his hands as the dance began. His brilliant smile and kind eyes invited me to get swept away. I caught my breath. I waited for the same kind of feeling I had with Percy.

But this was not a waltz.

And this was not Percy.

The duke led me over to my father afterward to line up and wait for our carriage.

Papa immediately began to discuss politics. "Stanhope's going to try for a National Portrait Gallery again this year. Been telling him not to include Turner." His voice was too loud. People around us giggled and whispered. "Got to get on the project and make sure it's done right. How are you voting?"

Oh no. *It's starting already*, I thought. *Why does he argue and draw attention to himself everywhere we go? I've got to get married quickly before he embarrasses himself so much that no one will have me.*

But the duke didn't mind. In fact, he agreed with my father.

We waited and they talked. Percy lingered casually ahead of us in line. I knew he could hear Papa and the duke. Everyone could.

But Percy didn't turn around. He didn't join us in line. Instead, he made polite conversation with the well-connected patroness near him. And her sister. And her aunt. And he had everyone laughing.

I strained to hear their conversation instead of Papa's and the duke's.

Was Percy ashamed to be seen with my father? He knew us well enough to suspect how unstable Papa was. He also knew how vocal and argumentative he was. Percy was doing everything he could to let me know he did not want to acknowledge our connection.

Finally, the patroness got into her carriage and it left.

Percy assisted his mother into his carriage. Just as he stepped up himself, he turned toward the line and looked at me.

He knew exactly where I was. He had known the entire time, I was sure.

Our eyes met. I felt a yearning for the old closeness instead of this new formality. This snub.

Percy hesitated on the stair of his carriage. He gave me a long, serious look, then tipped his hat. He ducked inside his carriage and was gone.

CHAPTER 30

I woke up to the smell of hyacinths in my bedchamber. Sibley had arranged a large vase of flowers on my dressing table.

When I went down to breakfast, Charlotte was already in the dining room with a small pile of cards.

"Those are yours." She gestured toward another stack of paper. "And you were worried?"

"Who are they from?" I picked up the slips. "The colonel. Mr. Kempton."

"Lord Romford." Charlotte grinned. "The largest bouquet is from the Duke of Woodford. For you. I received some as well. Do you have a note from him?"

I flipped through my cards. "Yes, here it is. Oh, my. His hand-writing is beautiful."

We went to examine the vases of blooms. Small pansies, yellow marguerites, daisies.

"Charming!" Charlotte fingered the stem of a delicate violet. She picked it up and twirled it. "Shall we put our flowers in our dressing rooms?"

"Indeed! Sibley already has. And the drawing room and hallway," I said. An enormous display of cheerful lilies spilled over the sides. "These are from His Grace?"

"Yes," Charlotte said.

"Are any of these from Percy or John?" I asked Charlotte.

She shook her head.

I couldn't help feeling disappointed, both for myself and for Charlotte.

I had not seen who else Charlotte had danced with. Last night was a whirl. But I hoped she had danced with John.

The drawing room overflowed with visitors the entire afternoon. The colonel and Mr. Kempton arrived first, with Lord Romford, and stayed their allotted time.

Near the end of our at-home hours, Percy and John came with the duke. They sat silently while the duke told us about their ride with the Four in Hand club that morning, their fencing lessons with Angelo in St. James Street, and their shooting practice at Purdey's in Oxford Street.

The duke entertained Charlotte with another story while I sipped my tea.

Percy held his teacup but did not drink. He did not take any cake. How many other at-homes had he attended already today? Had they spent the time at other debutantes' homes?

My eyes locked with Percy. He stared back at me. I couldn't read the look.

I felt an ache, a yearning. Why was he so distant? He wasn't a younger son who had to have a profession. He was a peer. Yet he sat silent, haughty, and indifferent, now that he was Lord Shelford. He wasn't a diplomat or ambassador who needed a sociable wife. There were no obstacles. Just his lack of regard for me.

Or was that still his concern? That the wife of an earl needed to be socially proficient? Move in the highest circles? Help him pass bills in Parliament? Hold salons and help him meet the right people?

But here was the duke, fully accepting of my quiet nature and intent in his pursuit of me.

After the duke took his leave, Mama exclaimed, "Oh, girls! You are beyond anything. How many proposals shall I tell Thomas to prepare for?"

John and Percy both looked alarmed.

"Has Father received any offers yet? It hasn't even been a week," John said.

"Oh, I don't think it will take much more than that," Mama said.

Mrs. Harwich sat calmly but seemed pleased.

"With whom are you going riding? What is next? Tell me everything." Mama patted the cushion next to her.

"The duke. Later this afternoon," Charlotte said, glancing over at John.

Percy searched my face. "Both of you?"

I nodded.

"Good day." Percy bowed to the room and left.

I watched him go and ached for the closeness we had in Vienna. I hated this formality and distance between us. I hated that I still missed him. After a year. More than a year. After I had tried so hard to forget. Was he jealous? He didn't try to talk to me himself, so it seemed unlikely. But why else would he leave?

Perhaps I would go watch my father paint.

"Woodford is a good man," John said grudgingly. "Always liked him. Good head for numbers. Good day, Mother, Mrs. Harwich, Miss Harwich, Elle." John leaned over to kiss Mama on the cheek. When he straightened up, John glanced at Charlotte.

Charlotte returned his gaze and flushed. "I am fatigued." Charlotte rose to make her escape upstairs.

"I'm going to look for Papa." I followed Charlotte from the

room. I needed to find someone who loved me unconditionally right now.

But John followed us into the entryway. "Miss Harwich."

She stopped.

John wrung his hands. "I did not get a chance to speak with you."

"You did not try." Charlotte waited at the base of the stairs. "I am sorry, Mr. Barrington, but I am tired." She disappeared upstairs.

I remembered Percy's assessment of John's romantic skill. He wasn't wrong. John was completely bungling things with Charlotte.

"Get your things. Please, Elle. I need you," John begged. "Will you walk with me?"

He practically dragged me out the door.

"Where are we going?" I had hardly put my bonnet on before John began walking rapidly.

"Slow down!" I tried to catch my breath. "Let us act dignified, if we must rush."

"Yes, you are a Diamond now. Never know who's watching," John said.

"That is not fair." I stopped walking.

John bumped into me. "Sorry. Keep going." He pushed me.

"What is the rush?"

John was ahead of me again.

I pulled his arm. "What is wrong? Do you have a destination?" I asked.

"No," John said. "I just need movement right now." John ran a hand through his hair. "We can walk to my town house."

"Let us take a long route, then," I said. "No need to go directly there. I do not leave on my carriage ride for another hour."

We wandered the streets for a while until we were nearly to his home.

"Tell you what, Elle." John pointed to a large town house. "Can we stop at Shelford's instead? He lives next door."

CHAPTER 31

Without waiting for an answer, John climbed the steps. He knocked before I realized what he was doing.

"I can't call on a gentleman," I yelled up the steps.

"So, call on his sister," John said. "Quickly."

A butler answered.

"Jones. May I?" John disappeared inside.

The butler considered me, standing alone in the middle of the sidewalk. "My lady?"

I trudged up the steps and entered the town house. What else could I do but hope no one saw me?

We entered an enormous marble foyer. Large alabaster statues filled the entryway, next to a circular staircase beneath a chandelier. I caught my breath. The statues reminded me of Schönbrunn and of Rome. It was exactly what I would have expected in a home belonging to Percy. What I would have wanted in a home of my own.

I walked over to the far corner and began to examine the first one. "Exquisite," I murmured, reminding myself of Papa.

"Barrington?" Percy's voice startled me.

I turned around, feeling guilty. I had been about to touch the folds of fabric and trace the lines on the statue.

Percy marched through the entryway. He looked completely disheveled. His jacket was off, and his untucked shirt opened at the collar. His tie lay abandoned on the floor.

The sight made my pulse race. I had never seen him like this before.

John marched over to him. "This can't go on. May I unburden myself? I am in agony."

"Of course." Percy gestured toward the drawing room, hesitated, then said, "The library."

They began walking down the hallway when Percy noticed me over in the corner.

He stopped. "Eleanor."

"They're beautiful." I felt embarrassed to be found lurking in his entryway. "I wanted to see them up close."

Percy stared at me. "I did not realize you were here."

"I am here." I wasn't sure how he felt about my presence. Did he want me to leave? Was he angry?

John glanced between us. "She caused this predicament, Shelford, and perhaps she can help. You do not mind, do you? I could not speak of it at my mother's home."

Percy shook his head. "No, no, of course." He looked around. "Jones! Jones! Get me a coat." He blinked, then readjusted his glasses. "Apologies for my appearance."

He ran a hand through his hair. That made it even more tousled and attractive, but certainly less orderly.

John said, "It's only Elle. She's seen me walking around the halls, old man. Keep the jacket off, I say."

Percy pointed down a hallway, and I hesitated, not sure where the library was.

"The statues—" I began.

"They are replicas from Schönbrunn," he said.

He began walking down the corridor. I couldn't help glancing over at his open shirt and remembering how it felt to put my hand on his chest. I brushed the thought aside.

"You bought replicas of replicas? Aren't the statues in Schönbrunn based on ancient statues?"

Percy grinned. "Yes, the absurdity of that did appeal to me."

He fiddled with the front of his shirt. "And I remembered how well you liked them."

He couldn't get it closed and fastened the buttons in the wrong holes.

Percy shrugged into a jacket with his butler's help, tugging at his rumpled shirt sleeves and fiddling with the ends.

"Sir." Jones cleared his throat.

He stared at him, not comprehending. Jones moved forward, pulling up the collar points on Percy's shirt. He redid the mismatched buttons while Percy shifted his weight from side to side.

"Thank you, Jones," Percy said, tugging at his collar as we started walking down the hall again.

I loved to see Percy discomposed. Not well-dressed or refined. Finally. I smiled at Jones. A half-smile appeared on his face. He picked up the discarded bow tie and shook his head at me. I stifled a laugh. This was the real Percy. I walked a little lighter toward the library.

We entered a beautiful, light room with grey damask wallpaper. Groupings of light blue chairs and sofas filled the room. My embroidered pillow rested on a well-worn chair by the fireplace. His favorite chair. He'd kept the pillow, all this time.

A watercolor painting hung above the fireplace. A Turner. The same Turner which inspired my needlework. Grey clouds swirled around a tiny dot of blue in the sky. White-capped waves washed against the deck of a ship. Women lined the pier as men set off in over-full boats into the storm.

How did Percy know it was my favorite painting? Could he

recognize it from the pillow? Or was it a coincidence? Did he buy it because we had landed at Calais on our way from Dover?

"Calais Pier," I breathed. "How did you acquire it?"

"Woodford helped me arrange the purchase. I am grateful."

I put my hand over my heart. "It's beautiful. Just like I remembered."

Percy sat in a chair by the fireplace and gestured to us to sit down. John settled into a chair across from him, which left me on a small sofa next to Percy's chair. Heat from the fire warmed me and I studied the painting. So much motion and color.

Percy handed me a grey blanket for my lap. I snuggled into it. He still knew what I was thinking before I even spoke. I'd barely shivered, and he'd given me a blanket. I didn't even think he was watching me, yet he anticipated my needs before I asked for anything.

Did he buy the painting because of me? Or simply because he liked it?

"They are too popular," John began. "I can't take it. I can't get near Miss Harwich. She will have a dozen marriage proposals in a week, and so will Eleanor. And I won't approve of any of them."

He left his chair and started pacing. "Except Woodford. Man is a paragon."

"He is," Percy admitted reluctantly. "Like a brother to me."

"It has only been a few days, and I hate the Season already. This has to end." John slammed his hand on the fireplace mantle.

"Sit down," Percy said.

John reluctantly returned to his chair.

"How can I help?" Percy's voice was calm.

He loved projects. He had tried to help the Harwiches when their school was on the brink of financial disaster. He was a compassionate man who could not turn down the chance to help someone in need.

But I did not want to think about his good qualities when he was indifferent to me. I pulled the blanket tighter around myself.

My brother loved Charlotte. That was a better subject to dwell on.

"I don't know," John said, tapping his leg with his hand. "I have calculated again and again. I can't start a stable without a loan. No matter how much better my relationship, I could not ask my father for money. He would own me. You know how that would feel. I don't have a home for a bride. How can I propose? How can I ever compete?" John looked at Percy. "You know my pain. I am a younger son. Why would Miss Harwich choose me?"

Percy nodded, deep in thought. "You need a supplement to your income? Enough to support a family and a larger home?"

"How can I bring a wife back to my bachelor apartment?" John's voice sounded anguished. "Elle, you know Miss Harwich. Would she favor my suit? Whom does she favor?"

John's direct question startled me.

"We have not discussed any suitors," I said.

Percy darted a gaze sideways at me.

"Well, please do." John stood again. "If I don't have a chance, this is pointless. I will go home to Barrington. I cannot watch this."

"And leave me?" Percy went over to John. "No, I am in Parliament all summer. Don't make me do this alone."

John placed a hand above the fireplace and studied the flames. "You heard Woodford talk about taking up that post in Paris. He wants to marry this Season, as soon as possible. Find a wife who speaks French fluently."

Percy and John turned toward me.

Woodford wanted to marry so soon? And move to Paris? My feelings of drowsy contentment fled. I could not settle comfortably on the sofa anymore. The blanket fell to the floor and I rearranged myself.

"He's been paying attentions to Eleanor and Miss Harwich both, and I cannot tell which he favors. They've both lived in Europe. They're both perfect for him. I must act before he does. What if he proposes to Miss Harwich before I do?" John asked. "Or does he favor Eleanor? Could we ask him outright?"

Percy considered John. He would not meet my eyes.

I swallowed. Did they really talk like this with the duke when they went driving and shooting? While fencing and boxing? Just casually decide my future?

"I must marry Miss Harwich, but I cannot if Woodford proposes first," John said. "I saw those ridiculous lilies. Did Lord Romford send those flowers, Elle? Or Woodford?"

"Woodford sent the lilies," I said.

"For Miss Harwich or you?" John asked.

Percy began twisting his signet ring. "For Elle." He peered at me. "Am I right?"

I nodded. "John, you cannot expect Charlotte to know how you feel. She's right. You haven't tried. You've hung back and ignored her. You don't speak to her when you visit," I said, looking askance at Percy. He had done the same to me, but I did not know how he felt.

"He danced with her at the ball," Percy said.

"After dancing with several other girls," I said. "She was not his first choice. Lord Romford asked for her first dance. And sent a bouquet of violets."

"I knew it," John muttered. He picked up the fire iron and poked at the coals in the hearth.

"He showed her attentions in Vienna," Percy said. "Marked attentions."

"And then left without bidding her farewell," I said.

"I saw her in Munich," John said.

"But he kissed her in Vienna," Percy said, still playing with his signet ring.

I picked the blanket up from the floor and pulled it tightly around me. "And has done nothing since then."

"I don't remember telling you about that," John said.

"What could he have done?" Percy asked.

"He could have enquired after her when he wrote to her family," I said, "instead of ignoring her for more than a year." It still stung. Asking John every time a letter came.

"But you were the one writing, not me," John said, turning around.

"But he still cares for her," Percy said, gesturing to John.

"Then he should take some action," I said, sitting up straight, "and not sit back while all the other men of London woo her." The blanket fell to the floor again.

"What if she no longer cares for him?" Percy asked. "Other men pursue her, and she does not send them away."

"Why should she change her affections if he has not changed his?" I wrapped my arms around my waist.

Percy scrutinized my face. He folded his arms across his chest. "How can he know for certain how she feels?"

"If he truly cares, he will pursue her and take a risk, whether or not he knows that she returns his affection," I said. "Otherwise, someone else will."

Percy's voice rose. "Why should he take all the risks when she gives him no encouragement?"

My voice rose in response. "Perhaps he once told her that she would never be the kind of wife he wanted to have."

Percy gaped at me. "No. No. Perhaps he said she would be the best wife he could imagine." His voice cracked on the last word.

John leaned back on the fireplace mantle, watching us back and forth.

Percy strode across the room to me, talking as he approached. His voice was louder, more strident. "Perhaps he spent a year in the expectation that they would marry as soon as she arrived home. Perhaps she gave him no sign of encouragement when she saw him."

"None of that happened," John said. "Except the lack of encouragement part."

I sank back into the sofa, my feet curled beneath me. I drew the blanket up over me. "Then we are back to where we started. He is waiting for her, and she is waiting for him. They are in limbo."

Percy stared down at me.

I rested my head on the edge of the sofa and studied Percy. I could read so many emotions in his eyes. Sincerity. He was as confused and hurt as I was. I spoke quietly. "He may have said things that made her think he would not want an alliance with her."

He put his hands down on the arms of the furniture and leaned over me. He peered intently into my eyes. "Perhaps he does not remember everything he said." He lowered himself onto the seat.

I swiveled my head to watch him. He did not break eye contact with me.

"Perhaps he said things he did not mean." Percy searched my face. "Perhaps he was wrong. And is tired of waiting."

I hoped it were true. I snuggled deeper into the blanket and against the arm of the sofa. "How is she to know which of those things he meant and which he did not?"

John poked the fire again. "Just who are we talking about right now, Elle?" he said gently.

Percy crossed over to the hearth. "Give me time, Barrington. Perhaps I can speak to my steward about retiring. Trust me?" He shook hands with John and put his arm around his shoulder.

"Like a brother." John pulled Percy into a hug and patted him on the back.

John came around and nudged my legs with his boot. "Time to leave now." He tore the blanket off me. "You have a carriage ride with the duke in half an hour."

That was the last thing I wanted to do right now, and I didn't want John to remind Percy, either.

"He has been impossible all afternoon," I told Percy as John dragged me to my feet. "If this is what love looks like—"

I stopped as I considered Percy.

He and John were mirror images. Disheveled hair, rumpled shirts, dark circles beneath their eyes.

Percy seemed to be feeling John's pain.

Or his own pain. He loves me. Percy still loves me. He's holding back, too, for some stupid reason. Did he really think he proposed to me in Vienna, when I thought he rejected me?

I crossed the room toward Percy. How could I show him I cared?

I laid my hand on Percy's arm and gazed deep into his eyes. "Thank you for caring for John."

Percy returned my gaze. "Will you help him woo Miss Harwich?" he asked.

"Of course," I said.

The look in Percy's eyes intensified. "If he wants to show her that he still cares?" He put a hand on top of mine.

"I'm certain Charlotte reciprocates his affection."

"Now you're certain?" John asked. "I thought you didn't talk about this with her."

"The opera tonight?" Percy asked. His hand caressed mine.

"Certainly."

He smiled broadly. "For Miss Harwich."

"For John," I said.

Things were about to change between Percy and me.

CHAPTER 32

Percy and John sent a footman over with bouquets that clearly must have been the last flowers of the day. They were small bunches, and a little dry, but Charlotte seemed delighted. Percy sent me wild roses and red carnations, and John sent apple blossoms and honeysuckle to Charlotte. I quickly replaced the flowers in my room with Percy's and smelled them over and over while I dressed for the opera.

Streetlights flickered as we approached the imposing building. We entered between marble pillars and waited in the lobby for Percy and John. I tried to peek inside the main theater. I had never been to the Royal Italian Opera before.

An ornate crystal chandelier hung from the ceiling. Row upon row of balconies filled the space. Scalloped edging and crown molding decorated the walls and ceilings.

I checked to see what was playing tonight. *La Bohème.* Had Percy known that when he invited us?

A swarm of young men surrounded Charlotte and me. I wondered whether I should send Colonel Loughton and Mr. Kempton away, but how could I do that politely? So, I tried to be less talkative than usual and let Charlotte entertain Lord Romford. Hopefully, Percy would notice when he arrived.

John and Percy approached from one side of the entrance while His Grace and his mother arrived on the other side. Lady Octavia and her mother trailed along with the Woodfords. I was in the middle.

"Lord Barrington, I simply had to speak to you." Lady Shelford's voice carried. I wondered if she wanted to be heard by Lord Romford and the other men. "Lord Shelford tells me we must invite you over for dinner on Friday."

My parents exchanged glances. Mama gave an imperceptible nod. Lady Shelford had the audacity to wink at me.

"We would be delighted," Papa accepted.

"Mrs. Harwich, you and Miss Harwich must come. I won't hear no. We can discuss our musical society plans."

"Thank you, Lady Shelford," Mrs. Harwich said.

Lady Shelford moved next to me. She regarded Charlotte expectantly. Charlotte moved out of her way.

Lord Romford and the other men left to find their own seats.

Lady Shelford adopted a whisper. "Shelford insisted I arrange this exclusive little dinner. Clever girl. I saw through the ruse immediately. To pretend to be tired of the crush of the Season already. Turning down invitations. Only associating with the duke and my son. As a former Diamond myself, I must tell you, this will only enhance your reputation. All those men," she waved her fan behind her, "will think better of you because of your exclusivity."

Lady Shelford rapped me on the arm as she spoke to emphasize her words. "Clever, clever girl. Shelford would do well to go along with your schemes. It should help him, too." She glanced behind her at the retreating men. "Have we been introduced, dear?" She held her hand out to me.

I wasn't sure what I was supposed to do with it. I grasped it lightly and let go. "You must include the Brownings. We had a prior engagement with them, I believe."

"The Brownings! Even better!" she said. "Oh, you are a blue-stocking and a Diamond? What are your intellectual pursuits? We must talk." She paused. "No wonder you are all the rage this week."

She wandered back to stand with the duke's mother before I could answer any of her questions. Lady Shelford was a force of nature. I felt like a windstorm had swept by.

She clearly misunderstood Percy's intentions. He was trying to help John carve out a little time with Charlotte, away from other suitors. Nothing more.

Percy smiled at me and John grinned. What had I just agreed to do? How exclusive was I going to be?

The Duke of Woodford came over to me. "Scared away the competition, Shelford? Many thanks." The duke bowed toward Percy. "You are invaluable, old man." His Grace smiled at me.

Percy returned the bow.

"What was this I heard from Shelford?" He considered John. "You thinking to hire out as a secretary?"

John put a finger to his lips and jerked his head back toward Papa. "Maybe. Unless I take orders."

"Hire him as your steward," His Grace said. He looked between John and Percy. "Unless you want your vicar telling you when to rotate your crops. The two of you are inseparable. You're going to hire him for one thing or another. It may as well be what he's good at."

"But my steward—" Percy began.

"Is ancient and useless," the duke said. "We both know that. Retire him."

Percy stiffened. Clearly, the duke was used to giving advice and having it taken without any argument.

The duke surveyed the group. "I'm at a loss to understand why I accompanied your mother and sister to the opera tonight, Shelford, if you were coming, too."

"Thank you for doing that," Percy said. "Mother will send an invitation around for dinner first thing."

"Well then," the duke said and took my hand. "I will anticipate my time with you, Lady Eleanor." He maintained eye contact as he bowed over my hand. He glanced at Charlotte, standing with John, and nodded his head to her.

So, he was still undecided between the two of us? I needed to find a third option for him.

Percy stepped back as the duke passed him.

As soon as Woodford was gone, Percy led me into the box. He fit himself into the seat beside me. The chairs at the front were small and his knee pressed against mine. I could hear the musicians tuning their instruments.

"That did not go as planned," Percy grumbled.

I drew a deep breath. "Perhaps you and I can distract His Grace at dinner."

He stared into my eyes. "That was exactly what I was worried about." He held my gaze until the musicians began to play in earnest.

I tried to focus on the stage. "Are you staying here?" I whispered.

I glanced behind me. John and Charlotte had settled into the middle row.

Percy's nearness made it hard to concentrate on the opera or anything else. The front row seats were narrow and small. His legs barely fit.

"Do you want me to leave?" His breath was warm in my ear.

I turned my head to respond. The theater was dark. His face was inches from my own. Percy's emerald green eyes went to my lips.

I hitched a breath. "No," I whispered. I lowered my voice. "So John can sit by Charlotte."

I let my hand drop slowly, brushing his leg as I placed it in my lap. *What am I doing?*

Percy heaved a deep breath as he leaned over to whisper, "For Barrington and Miss Harwich." His cheek brushed mine for a moment as he moved his head slightly.

I felt the slight roughness of the stubble tickling my face.

Percy straightened in his chair, the perfect model of decorum for once, but left his arm resting discretely on his leg.

The opera began. As Act One drew to a close, Mimì and Rodolfo began to sing a duet. A love song. The same duet Percy and I sang together two years ago. The one he bought in Paris. The one he spent weeks practicing so he could sing it with me once more.

He shifted so his entire leg pressed against mine, not just his knee.

He remembered, too.

My heart beat faster. The fingers of Percy's hand splayed across his knee, as if in invitation. I moved my hand out of my lap and onto my knee. Our fingers lay beside each other.

Percy studied the stage, but his littlest finger reached over and stroked my finger with his. I took a sharp breath. He smiled.

I struggled inside. I wanted this more than anything. I knew I still cared for Percy, but I could not bear another rejection, like I'd had in Vienna, or a hollow flirtation, like I saw him practice with every girl at every social event. Letting him deeper into my heart meant it would be all the harder to remove him.

What if Percy meant something more, like he had hinted? What if he still loved me? I hooked my little finger over his. He covered my hand instantly.

Mimì and Rodolfo continued to sing "O Soave Fanciulla" and I enjoyed the warm comfort of our intertwined fingers. The familiarity. The rightness of it. At last. The music rose to a peak, and my heart swelled with the song. I knew every note, and Percy did, too.

He had brought me here, to this opera, to share this moment. A memory of Percy holding me under the mistletoe and whispering "Amore mio" swam in front of me, and hope flared.

As Act One ended, John leaned down from the row behind us. "Can't see over you, old man."

Percy squeezed my hand before letting go. I missed the warmth of his leg and hand immediately.

He turned around. "Barrington?" Percy looked back at him and Charlotte.

"Hate to ask, really do. Believe me." The pain in John's voice was real. "Can you trade seats with Miss Harwich? She can't see a thing."

Percy brushed my leg with his hand as he moved past me into the middle row. I closed my eyes and threaded my hands together in my lap to keep from reaching out to him.

I spent the rest of the opera thinking about Percy. My heart told me he was sincere. This was Percy. Unpredictable. Sometimes he went to great lengths to plan elaborate schemes, and other times he jumped in with no forethought. If he loved me still, as I loved him, what would he do next? And what could I do to encourage him?

CHAPTER 33

Fog hovered near the ground as our carriage worked its way toward Percy's town house, making it hard to distinguish when evening fell. Lights glowed in the windows of shops and buildings. Trees cast odd shadows in the mist as we progressed through the streets. Cobblestones rattled beneath our carriage until we reached our destination.

Tall, stone steps led to the main entrance. Percy waited at the top. We gratefully climbed out of the carriage and into a slight mist.

"Come in. It's damp tonight." Percy gestured toward the front doors where Jones and footmen stood.

I entered and looked around. The entryway soared up to a balcony I had not noticed before. An ornate circular staircase led to the first floor. Immaculate marble floors lined the hallways. I wanted to go examine each statue in detail, since I had not been able to before.

A hand touched the small of my back and I startled. Percy leaned close to me. My heart started pounding.

"We're dripping." He dropped his hand and pointed down to a puddle of water at our feet.

I glanced down.

"The marble gets slippery when it drizzles outside," Percy said, taking my arm to help me over the slippery floor. Jones waited nearby with footmen to dry the marble entrance.

He ushered us into the drawing room where Lady Shelford rested on a sofa. His sister waited near a small chess table nearby. "May I introduce my sister, Lady Octavia?"

"Delighted." She gave a half-curtsey.

Lady Octavia had fair hair, but it was as curly as Percy's. Her skin was porcelain smooth, like her mother's, and her green eyes danced with mischief. She knocked two chess pieces against each other in her hand.

"You invited Guy." Lady Octavia twirled one chess piece and set it down. "Excellent. We never finished that last game of chess."

"Really, Octavia," the duke said. "Without even a greeting?"

She curtseyed again. "Welcome. You left for Parliament halfway through our game."

Lady Shelford held her hand out to the duke's mother. "Join us. I will let His Grace and Octavia settle things on their own."

"How dare the weighty affairs of state interfere with your entertainment," the duke said.

Lady Octavia smiled an adorable grin at him. She could be quite charming, like Percy. Or a force of nature, like her mother. I liked her immensely already.

"One game, Octavia, even if I win. That is all," His Grace said firmly. "There are other guests tonight." I couldn't tell whether he was setting the boundary for himself or her.

She smiled and restored a game in progress, setting aside some pieces. "Then let us finish the game from last night."

"I don't recall having lost both my bishop and my pawn," Woodford objected. "You were winning. Let us start fresh."

"Would anyone like to see the pictures Lord Barrington purchased for me in Italy? I have them uncrated now. We have a few minutes before the Brownings arrive," Percy said.

"Perhaps we can postpone the game," His Grace suggested.

"Because you were losing." Lady Octavia sat up straighter.

"Nonsense." His Grace examined the chess board. "I've made an excellent move. I believe I now have the upper hand."

"If you resign the game and declare me the winner." Lady Octavia raised her eyebrow at the duke.

"Very well, Shelford, go without me. I can see them another time." His Grace looked at Lady Octavia. "I am not losing to Octavia under any circumstance. I am certainly not resigning."

Lady Octavia grinned. She moved another chess piece. They ignored us as we moved away toward the picture gallery. Perhaps I would have found a third option for the duke, if only she were not fifteen years old.

Papa gazed like a man transfixed at the Rembrandt, the Holbein, and the Carpaccio. "They are exquisite. But where is the Taddei Tondo?"

"I have not uncrated it," Percy said. "I wanted to wait until you arrived home. Perhaps tomorrow?"

My father put his hand on Percy's back. "Thank you."

I said to Percy, "I made some sketches in Italy. Papa and I painted a great deal."

We left his picture gallery and began to walk down to dinner.

"Did you really? Are they any good?" He grinned. "I should like to inspect them sometime." He lowered his voice and inclined his head toward me. "Closely."

He walked beside me all the way down the stairs and through the hallways to the drawing room. I could smell his cologne and feel his arm brush against mine.

I did not know how I was going to manage dinner with Percy and the duke at the same table. Hopefully, his mother had seated His Grace next to Lady Octavia.

The newspapers had been full of the treaty of Paris and the end of the Crimean War for weeks. Now they turned back toward gossip and news of the Parliamentary session. Lord Stanhope's push for a National Portrait Gallery, and my father's passionate efforts in his behalf, were a topic on everyone's lips.

I had looked forward to the dinner at Percy's home as a safe respite from the talk of the *ton*. I should have known better. Mrs. Browning was seated near my father and Lady Shelford, and her husband sat next to my mother and Percy. John engaged Charlotte in conversation. Lady Octavia monopolized His Grace, to my relief and his annoyance.

That gave my parents plenty of opportunity to argue with the Brownings. Mrs. Harwich and the duke's mother watched the discussion quietly without interjecting themselves. I played with the napkin in my lap, hardly noticing what I ate.

I kept thinking, *If this is a test, then I am failing. Percy loves dinners like these, and I'm too nervous to open my mouth.*

Not that I minded arguing privately. But having Percy at one end of the table and the duke at my side had paralyzed me. If I spoke with one, I would alienate the other. I could show no preference when they were both present. Clearly, I favored Percy, but it would not be wise to alert the duke to my preference.

I was not prepared to show my feelings openly. That wouldn't help John. If the duke knew how I felt about Percy, he would switch all his attentions to my friend. John couldn't hope to compete with the duke.

Besides, I had always preferred to be discreet.

Nevertheless, I felt my eyes drawn toward Percy's end of the table. Was he glancing at me? He had that uncanny, falcon-like ability to focus on two things at once. He could give Mrs. Browning his full attention, or so it seemed, yet every time I glanced at him, his lips quirked in a smile. He knew I was watching him.

I hid a smile behind my napkin.

Eventually, Lady Octavia paused for breath, and the duke turned to talk to me.

Before he could speak, however, Percy caught his mother's eye.

"Ladies, are we ready to retire to the drawing room?" Lady Shelford asked.

The duke rose and offered me his arm to escort me out of the room. At least Percy knew that I cared for him and that I was merely trying to keep the duke away from Charlotte.

After the men joined us in the drawing room, Mama asked Mrs. Browning, "Will you read one of your poems for us?"

"Oh, I hear my own voice so often. I love to hear others read my works instead, or that of another poet."

"I have *Poems* and *Sonnets from the Portuguese*," Percy said. "Got them in Paris. In the poetry section." He raised an eyebrow at me.

Why that should make me want to blush, I wasn't sure. But it did. It also raised an alarm in my mind.

"Then I shall send you *Aurora Leigh*, as soon as it is published," Mrs. Browning said.

"How about sonnet forty-three?" Mr. Browning said. "My favorite. I never tire of it."

Percy grinned. "Barrington, perhaps you would like to read it with me." He took up a well-worn book from a side table and opened it to a page with a bookmark.

Now I was truly worried.

He folded his arms, leaned against a wall, and sighed dramatically.

Mrs. Browning applauded. "Well begun."

We all laughed.

Percy pushed off the wall. He cleared his throat, peered at me intensely, and began, "How do I love thee? Let me count the ways."

Oh. That sonnet. That was number forty-three. So much for subtlety or subterfuge.

He handed the book to John.

A deep flush crept up my neck and onto my cheeks. Out of the corner of my eye, I could see the duke studying me.

John's deep bass voice boomed across the room. "I love thee to the depth and breadth and height my soul can reach, when feeling out of sight for the ends of being and ideal grace."

He handed the book back to Percy.

I glanced at Charlotte. A light blush formed on her cheeks, too. Well, the duke would also figure out how John felt about Charlotte.

Percy's voice grew soft, but still carried through the room. His eyes were directed at me as he read. "I love thee to the level of every day's most quiet need, by sun and candlelight."

Now Papa and Mama were staring at me. I felt certain. Still, I felt the same burning from my cheeks move into my chest and expand.

"I love thee freely, as men strive for right; I love thee purely, as they turn from praise," John said.

Percy held the book but recited the poem from memory. "I love thee with the passion put to use in my old grief, and with my childhood's faith."

Were the Brownings looking at me, too, now?

John took the book out of Percy's hands and read from the pages, "I love thee with a love I seemed to lose with my lost saints. I love thee with the breath, smiles, tears, of all my life!"

I did not turn my eyes toward Charlotte. I was sure she would be bright red. Everyone in the room knew toward whom the poem was directed by now.

Percy pushed the book away and recited without looking at it. His voice grew serious, slow, and deep. His gaze had never left my face. "And, if God choose, I shall but love thee better after death."

Warmth filled me entirely. The certainty of Percy's love. The breadth of it—we had loved each other for a year. Maybe two. The depth—he knew my fears and weaknesses, my strengths, and loved all of me. The heights, the passion, the breath, smiles, tears. I wanted to be alone with Percy right now.

Polite applause broke out and reality came crashing back.

I should have known. Percy would not do anything in small measure. If he decided he was going to show me his feelings, he would show the whole world.

Part of me felt elated. Percy loved me. Still. Despite everything. Deeply.

The other part of me felt mortified. This should have been a private matter. I would have dearly loved to have shown Percy my appreciation in private.

But what would the duke do now that Percy and John had shown their intentions? Would he back away or consider it a challenge? Would I now have a second, more ardent suitor to contend with, or would the duke withdraw entirely?

CHAPTER 34

"Oh, bravo!" Mrs. Browning cried. "You captured the feeling precisely. You young men are such romantics. Tell me, how did you like the opera last night? I saw you there, did I not? Let me pose a dilemma to you." She motioned to my father. "You, too, old friend."

"I am already opposed," he said.

"No, you must choose a side, and then I will be opposed," Mrs. Browning said. "Tell me, was the young lover right to give up Mimì so the wealthy viscount could care for her? Or should he have stayed with her in her sickness and decline? What is true love?"

"Of course, he should have given her up, so she could have enough money for medicine," Papa said right away. "Puccini had it right."

"Not at all. In sickness and health. Richer or poorer. 'Til death parted them," John said. "Rodolfo was a scoundrel to send her away."

"And you, my young romantic?" Mrs. Browning asked.

Percy hesitated. "I agree with Lord Barrington this time. They weren't married. He made no vows. Selfless love and sacrifice are far more romantic than clinging to her for his own needs."

I couldn't help but wonder if Percy would act the same way

himself. He was a hopeless romantic, but I had to agree with John. If a man loved a woman, he should fight for her and stand by her at all costs. Not give her up for some ridiculous notion of self-sacrifice that would make them both miserable.

"Ah," Mrs. Browning said. "Then I shall have to argue Rodolfo's case with young Mr. Barrington to even out our numbers. Two and two. But would you say that spoken vows are the only bonds that connect true love? Shall we begin with that point?"

Across the room, my father gesticulated, and Mrs. Browning shook her head violently.

I was relieved to have the attention drawn away from me and the poetry reading and toward something else. I would have to thank Mrs. Browning privately.

"Have they known each other long?" the duke asked me.

"Yes. They are old friends," I said. "Or rather, sparring partners."

"It is well that your father and I agree on so many points, then," His Grace said. "He has a fierce intellect. I cannot understand why so many are opposed to the establishment of a National Portrait Gallery. The National Gallery is overflowing."

"Will the bill pass?"

"We are uncertain. It requires a great deal of effort still." The duke smiled at me. "But never tell me you are a bluestocking."

"Would that surprise you? Knowing my family and Matthew? And those with whom we associate?"

His Grace leaned in. "I confess, it is one of the things I like most about you. Your wit."

Oh, dear. The duke did not seem in the least deterred by Percy's obvious interest in me. In fact, he seemed to like a challenge.

But I still knew who I preferred. Even if he had no sense of propriety at times.

I tried to keep my tone casual and friendly, but not too encouraging. "And my family? Is that one of the things you like the most or the least?" I gestured toward my father, whose raised voice we could hear from where we sat.

The duke shifted to sit closer to me. "Your family is one thing I like the most," the duke said. "I count my association with your parents and Dunmore as a blessing. Regardless of what the papers say."

My heart sank, and I felt chills. "What do the newspapers say?"

"Did your father not see the cartoon today?"

Oh no. No. Not the cartoon again. "The old cartoon? Or a new satire?" I asked.

His Grace glanced around the room. I did as well. No newspapers.

He lowered his voice. "Your father did not read *The Art-Journal* or *The Illustrated London News* yet? Barrington? Shelford?"

I shook my head. "They've been uncrating and hanging paintings, I believe."

"It is the old cartoon from four years ago. Reprinted. Some feel his defense of the new portrait gallery is a touch fanatical. A bit zealous," His Grace said. "Needless to say, Stanhope and I find him invaluable. We do not agree."

"Your Grace, this will cause him great distress," I said. I could feel all the energy draining from me. I looked across the room to Papa, so happy right now.

The duke put his hand over mine. His touch startled me.

"I am sorry if this news causes you distress." He studied me. "Are you well?"

"It would be best if we leave," I said. "I must see the papers. Thank you for alerting me."

The duke escorted me to the center of the room. Percy watched us walking toward him, staring pointedly at the duke's hand covering mine.

"Lady Eleanor is unwell. We need to retire for the evening," His Grace said to Lady Shelford. "Thank you for your hospitality."

"I will escort her," Percy said. He held out his elbow. "And call for the carriage."

"Yes, of course," the duke said, and let go of my hand. It was Percy's home, and he was the host.

I rested my hand on Percy's arm. We walked into the entrance hall.

As soon as we were out of sight of the drawing room, Percy threaded my arm through his and covered my hand. "What's really going on?" he asked in a low voice. "You are pale."

"The cartoon. Someone reprinted it," I said. "I'm scared. What will Papa do this time? Last time, he left London the next day. He went into hiding for years. What if he does it again?"

Percy stopped walking. "Jones! The carriages! Get the footmen. Our guests have an urgent need to leave." He turned back to me and said quietly, "Don't go."

"I have no choice, if Papa returns to Barrington," I said. "What if he goes to Italy?"

He searched my eyes. "You have to understand something, Eleanor." He paused, then cupped my face gently with his hand. "Will he really sever all ties with Society? Again?"

I heard voices in the hallway. Papa and Mama. The others. I couldn't let them find us like this, as much as I craved the comfort he offered.

I pulled away. "I don't know."

Percy looked at the empty place, at the space where I had been. He gazed at me earnestly. "Understand that I mean your family no harm," he said.

"Of course not," I said, confused. I drew on my cloak and pulled the hood over my head. "Why would I think that?"

Percy's brow was furrowed. I wasn't sure if he had heard me.

The carriages arrived and my family descended the slippery marble steps to the street. I settled myself in the middle seat as we left for our town house. I turned around to watch through the back window. I could see Percy standing on the top step as we left in the thickening fog.

At home, I pulled Mama aside as we stripped off our gloves and cloaks. "The newspapers have reprinted the cartoon."

"The cartoon," Mama said.

"Yes. Today."

"No," she said. She stumbled into the drawing room. "Ring for tea."

Mama and I waited in silence. Charlotte and John were somewhere upstairs saying goodnight, and Mrs. Harwich had already gone to bed.

"Get your father," Mama finally said. "Find the papers."

"Now? Before bed? Can it wait?" I asked.

"Now," she said.

Papa's response was worse than the first time the cartoon was printed. He pointed at the paper. "They reprinted the editorial, too!" The cartoon showed a tall, thin man, who clearly resembled my father, standing over a deep grave. He had devil horns and a pitchfork. He shouted into the grave, "Bury the paintings with him!" and shook a fist at the coffin. It had the date, February 1852, just a few months after J. M. W. Turner had died.

"I will be the butt of every joke. The bill will never pass. We're leaving." Papa crushed the paper and threw it into the fireplace. He strode out of the room and pounded up the stairs.

I could hear him yelling at his valet to begin packing.

Mama stared into the fire. "He tries so hard. He means so well. He cares so much. Who would do such a thing? Mock such a fine man?" She moved slowly out the door. "I'm so sorry, dear. I know this meant a lot to you."

John passed Mama on the stairs and came into the drawing room. "I heard yelling. What happened?"

"They reprinted the cartoon. Papa is leaving. We are all leaving," I said. I didn't know when I would see Percy again, or whether he would want to see me. Rumors would fly about my father after he dropped everything and left abruptly. Again. If only he would stay and face the gossips.

John sat next to me. He took my hands. "Oh, Elle, this is my fault."

"It's not your fault. Papa is passionate and people do not understand him. I do not understand him."

John's expression was pained. "Yes, it is my fault. You see, Percy and I drew that cartoon."

CHAPTER 35

"Shelford and I drew it as a joke at Cambridge for the college newspaper. I never imagined someone would publish it in London. We didn't have the heart to tell Father," John said.

"Percy did this? Who wrote the editorial?" I asked.

"He drew the cartoon, and I wrote the editorial," John said. "We were stupid. I'm sorry. I've tried to mend things with Father this last year."

Papa stood in the doorway. "You did this?"

John hung his head. "I'm so sorry."

"Get out!" Papa said.

John shuffled from the room.

I walked in a stupor up to my own bedchamber. *What will I do now? We'll leave for home and never return to London. I'll never see Percy again. And I never want to see him again.*

But I did not know how my heart would ever mend.

Papa left early the next morning on his own. He stayed up all night packing and took the first available train. Mama, Mrs. Harwich,

Charlotte, and I packed quickly and left in the afternoon. The servants had instructions to close down the town house and ship everything to Barrington Hall. It would take them days, and we could not wait that long.

We were a subdued group. We traveled home in an afternoon. Matthew sent word to the duke the next day. He arrived the following day to stay nearby at Dunmore.

Everyone in London knew that the duke had dropped everything, left Parliament while in session, to come show support for my father. And, of course, they whispered about the attention he showed to me. People made bets. The gossip columns speculated about when an announcement of our engagement would be made.

My mother and I still read the newspapers, even if my father did not. It was mortifying to see the gossip about our courtship, then have to eat dinner with His Grace. I could scarcely look him in the face.

At least his attention seemed completely removed from Charlotte now.

To make things worse, John showed up a few days later with Percy. At first, I feared they would ask to stay at Barrington, but Matthew offered to house them at Dunmore as well.

Percy and John came over the next afternoon and asked if Charlotte and I would walk with them. I wanted to say no. But I thought of Charlotte and my promise to help John. We fetched our shawls and returned.

"Where is His Grace?" I asked.

"Riding. With Matthew," John said. He offered his elbow to Charlotte.

They led the way in front and quickly outpaced us. I was in no mood for a brisk walk. He was the last person in the world I wanted to see or spend time with right now.

Percy found a small bench enclosed by a vine-covered trellis. He gestured to it. He dug in his pocket for a handkerchief to wipe the dust but couldn't find one.

"It's in your other pocket," I said, annoyed with myself at the tug of fondness I felt for him. He could never find his handkerchief. Or glasses. Or pocket watch.

Percy searched his vest pockets and found a wrinkled square of cloth. "Ah. May I speak with you? Will you sit with me a moment? Please, Eleanor. I know you're angry." He wiped the bench to clear a spot.

I glared at him. "You have no idea how I feel right now."

Percy reared back. "You promised you would help your brother with Miss Harwich."

"What does this have to do with Charlotte?"

"We are giving Barrington time to be alone with her," he said. "He's even more panicked, now that you've been here with Woodford while we've been in London."

I blew out a breath. "Of course. Let us give them time."

Percy settled beside me. "I'm sorry." He tried to take my hand.

I kept my hands clenched together in my lap. "Do you have any idea what I've been through? For four years?"

"No," he said.

"My father lost all confidence. My mother lost friends. Matthew and Georgiana rushed their wedding. I thought I would never have a Season or a suitor. I'm nearly twenty, Percy. Twenty. And how will I ever marry, hidden away here with a father that refuses to even attend a dinner party? What if he moves my family to Italy and never returns?"

I hiccupped. I did not want to cry in front of him. I did not want to talk about marriage with him. I struggled to fight the tears.

"But there's more. When my uncle lost his wife in childbirth, he went mad with grief. He stopped caring for tenants or managing the estate. He drove himself to death one day, riding recklessly, and they nearly confiscated the estate because of his insanity. What if my father goes mad, too? What if Matthew and Georgiana lose their inheritance? What if they turn me and Mama and Adeline out of our homes?"

I began to cry in earnest. "Because of your cartoon. What if Papa loses everything? What if I lose everything, too?"

Percy leaned forward, putting his hand on his knee. His jaw was tense as he rested his forehead in his hand. When my tears subsided, he handed me his dusty handkerchief. "I'm sorry," he said. He threw his hands in the air. "I was an idiot. I've berated myself time and time again."

He scrubbed a hand over his face. "But that doesn't help."

Percy pried my hands open and took them. "Eleanor, there's nothing to worry about. Your father isn't mad. No one will come after your home."

I jerked my hands out of his and wiped my tears with my hand instead of his handkerchief. "They nearly declared my uncle's death a suicide at the inquest. They would have taken the estate from my father and seized all our property."

Percy's eyebrows drew together. He shifted closer to face me. "I'm sorry. We are all worried about the pain this caused him. But there is nothing insane about your father. Anyone who knows him will tell you he is passionate and strong-willed. He would never harm himself or anyone near him."

"But what if his grief pushes him further into darkness, like his brother?"

Percy tried to take my hands again, but I would not let him. His voice was deep and low. "Eleanor, please." He ran a hand through his hair. "I cannot see you this way. Not when it is my fault."

"I cannot stop hurting to ease your conscience," I said. "I am going to live the rest of my life at Barrington Hall, and, if I am lucky, we will have an occasional dinner party with the Maldons. After traveling in Europe and having a taste of London, it is not a pleasant prospect."

Percy focused intently on me. "Unless you marry," he said. His arms were straight, his hands gripping the edges of the bench on which we sat, as if he barely restrained himself.

"Who would want to align themselves with my family now? After this scandal? I am terrified of what will happen when I go out of fashion or when Papa embarrasses himself beyond recovery.

Again. I live one step away from the edge of a cliff all the time, and only I can keep my family from ruin if I marry well."

He swatted at the branch of an overhanging vine. "Woodford seems willing."

The pain was too much. Hearing Percy tell me to marry someone else.

"John and Charlotte have had enough time. Let's find them. It's chilly." I left the bench and began walking into another part of the garden to look for my brother.

Percy followed me. "What if I were willing?" he said. "If I don't want to step aside for him?" He grabbed my hand and turned me toward him. In an instant, his lips were on mine. He crushed me to him, holding me tight, hungry. He pulled me closer, urgent.

I was too surprised to react.

Percy stopped kissing me. Shock must have registered on my face, because he recoiled, a deeply pained look on his face. "I'm sorry. I've thought of no one but you for this last year. But I see. Your father would never approve of me."

He swatted again at the vine and this time it bounced back and lashed a cut across his cheek. Percy swore and strode back to the house.

I was stunned. I went back and collapsed on the bench. I needed Percy to listen to me. To hear my anger. To hear my fears. He had. And he had tried to allay my concerns, as he always did for me.

But I needed time to think. To wonder if he could be right. I wasn't ready for a proposal. I wasn't sure how I felt about Percy right now. He was like the ocean. Boisterous or calm. Now was not the time that I needed the spontaneous side of him. I needed his quiet strength today.

I ran a finger across my lips where Percy had kissed me and wished I had not been so slow to react. I drew my shawl around me and wondered at the emerging flowers in the garden.

Percy wants to marry me. Is he right? Would Papa ever approve of the match? Could he ever forgive Percy? Could I?

CHAPTER 36

Mama invited the Dunmore household over for dinner. It was tense. Finally, the men left to go play billiards after the meal. I didn't imagine things were any less strained in the billiard room than they had been in the dining room.

What had Mama imagined would happen? Papa would forget his grievances, and all would be well? Hardly. Even the women were tense.

Mama, Mrs. Harwich, Charlotte, Georgiana, and I waited in the drawing room on separate sofas. I could hear the clicking of a new clock we'd purchased in Switzerland.

All I could think about was Percy. And Papa. Percy and my father were together right now. With the duke. Maybe I could go to bed early tonight.

John stepped inside and asked, "Mrs. Harwich, could you spare a moment?"

She set aside her book and left the room.

I moved over to Charlotte. "How are you getting along with John?" I asked.

"He's been much more attentive here than in London," she said.

"I did think, in Vienna, that he cared for me." She stopped and twisted her hands together in her lap.

"My mother put up the mistletoe," I said. "It's quite all right to speak freely in our household."

Mama coughed. Or choked on a laugh. It was hard to tell which.

"But then he was so distant," Charlotte said.

"John has always had to share," Mama said. "Being a younger son. He hates to come in second place. With all those other men around, he had no idea what to do. I hope that leaving London has at least helped you, Miss Harwich."

"The only good thing to come of it," I said.

Mama plumped a pillow. "Nonsense. Thomas is fine. Merely brooding for a bit. He'll recover."

"Uncle never recovered," I said.

"Love and grief are very different from embarrassment and shame," Mama said.

Mrs. Harwich returned to the drawing room. We all stared at her.

"Well, Catherine?" Mama said.

Mrs. Harwich sat and picked up her book. "Your son is a fine man, Anne."

"That is all?" Mama said. She glanced at Charlotte. "What did you speak of?"

But just then the men returned from playing billiards. Matthew joined Georgiana. John settled himself next to Charlotte.

I sat in a secluded corner of the drawing room, as far away from other conversations as possible. I had a lot on my mind. I had expected Percy to try to talk to me again. Or hoped. But he sat on the opposite side of the room, as far away from Papa as possible. I picked up a pillow and hugged it, then realized I was not alone. Now was not the time to feel sorry for myself. I put it down and straightened on the sofa.

The duke strode across the room to join me. He walked with purpose. I picked the pillow up again and played with it in my lap.

John and Charlotte were engrossed in their quiet conversation.

We sat so far away from everyone else that our conversation would not easily be overheard.

His Grace shifted to move closer to me. "Lady Eleanor. For the last few weeks, I have enjoyed getting to know you."

Panic rose in me. *Was he going to propose? Here? Right now?*

The duke leaned in, his eyes intent on my face. "Let me assure you of my regard."

"Thank you," I said.

"I have a serious question for you."

Oh no. He was going to propose. He must have spoken to Papa.

"When Matthew and I were riding today, I thought I saw two people in the Barrington gardens," His Grace said.

"Yes, Charlotte and I went walking, as well as Percy and John," I said.

The duke gave me his most piercing gaze. "It was not Miss Harwich you were with."

I hesitated. "No. Our paths diverged at one point."

"I thought, and Matthew did agree, that a man seemed to force himself upon a woman at one point."

"Oh." He had seen Percy kissing me. I picked at the threads on the pillow.

"I told Matthew that I would take care of this. I did not want you married to anyone against your will or under a cloud of scandal." The duke paused. "Perhaps I have an interest of my own."

I could not meet his eyes. I put down the pillow. I smoothed the fabric of my skirt and studied my lap.

"Did Percy force himself on you, Lady Eleanor? Shall I call him out? He and I are close. I can speak freely with him."

I looked up.

The duke's face was dangerous. "He will not insult you."

I stared across the room at Percy. An angry red gash marked his face where the vine had sliced his cheek. I felt such complex emotions and had barely begun to unravel the threads to understand my own feelings.

How should I respond? Everything His Grace had said was

true, and yet, how honest could I be? Would the duke harm Percy?

"Thank you for your solicitousness. I was surprised by his actions, but not vexed. Neither did I welcome it. I would not have you reprimand him."

The duke leaned back and considered me. "It sounds like your feelings are complicated," he said. "Although I suspected something of this nature from Shelford, I was not aware of the depth of feelings until I saw his actions today."

"You are an imposing figure, Your Grace. I believe no one contradicts you," I said and smiled.

"Do you return his sentiments?"

"I hardly know. We are not on the best of terms at present," I said.

"Understandably."

"Have you ever experienced this?" I asked. It was bold of me to ask. I knew it. But we were being so honest with one another. And I did suspect...

The silence stretched for a moment.

"A confusion of feelings?" I asked.

Finally, he spoke. "Yes. I, too, have complicated feelings for someone."

"Will you tell me about her?" I asked.

The duke hesitated. "It seems impolite to speak of it with you."

"Please. I am not offended."

He rested his elbow on his knee and put his fist to his mouth. After a minute, he sat up and said, "I resent her but cannot escape the draw I feel when she is present. When she enters the room, I try to ignore her, but I find myself following her every movement. She is in every way unsuitable. She irritates me no end."

I smiled. "I do feel equal parts attraction and irritation toward Percy."

The duke shook his head and grimaced. "We understand one another. How long has this...complication...between you and Percy existed?"

I glanced at Percy. "We traveled through Europe together."

"Of yes, of course," His Grace said. "Naturally. Why did he never tell me?"

"I assume it is complicated," I said. "As you said, you took care of his estates and family. He is indebted to you. He probably thinks he is being noble and selfless because you can provide better for me than he can."

"Sounds like Shelford. Life's not an opera. However, he owes me nothing. I care for those I love." He paused. "I admit, I have never felt toward you the way I feel toward...her. I have tried to believe I could court you, but my heart tells me now I would be unhappy with anything less than a love match," the duke said.

"And I feel toward you like I do toward Matthew or John. A different kind of appreciation and affection. More brotherly," I said. "Will you tell Percy that you have no intentions toward me?"

"I think he would rather hear that from you, now that we are in perfect accord. He may be eavesdropping anyway."

We both looked across the room. Percy watched us intently.

"It's odd, isn't it? We should be an ideal match," His Grace said.

I studied the duke's features. "Yes. I feel absolutely nothing. Even though, I may say, you are extremely handsome."

The duke smiled. "And you are lovely in every regard. But it is true, there is no sense when it comes to love," the duke said. His face was earnest, as it so often was. "I shall have to amend the proposal I was considering." He laughed and took my hands. "Lady Eleanor, will you do me the honor of calling me Guy? Of adopting me as elder brother, even though you have two others? I promise to protect you and watch out for you, to be there for you when the *ton* is fickle. To help your father in Parliament and Society and help your brother, since Percy seems unable to retire his father's steward. I would be honored to have you as my sister."

A shadow moved across the room toward us.

"Of course, yes, Guy," I answered. "That would be my honor, too. You must call me by my Christian name, as well."

The shadow loomed over my shoulder.

"Then perhaps I should speak with your father," Guy said as he stood up, "and talk to your brother about working as my personal secretary."

Percy hovered on the edge of my vision as Guy walked away. He came around to the edge of the sofa, almost close enough to touch, and stared at me. "He wants to hire Barrington away from me."

"Guy is a good man," I said. "Please, sit with me."

Percy remained where he was. Clearly, he had been eavesdropping.

He was completely overreacting. If he didn't want Guy to hire John, then he should retire his steward and hire John himself. Even if his steward reminded him of his father. Percy's sentimentality sometimes endeared him to me, but not right now.

"He's like a brother to you. Your estates neighbor one another. John will often be nearby." I patted the sofa. "Please, Percy. I want to talk to you."

He stiffened. "Why?"

I'd had time to think since Percy's kiss in the garden, and I knew my own heart. Only a love match would do for me, and I loved Percy. Even if he made mistakes. Even if he drew a thoughtless cartoon years ago. I knew he regretted it.

I could forgive him. Mama already had. Percy and John were here, trying to redeem themselves in Papa's eyes. If Percy was willing to marry me, knowing everything about my family that he did, then I was eager to say yes. And I wanted to tell him. If he would just sit down.

I reached for Percy's hand, but he didn't move. Not toward me. Not away from me. Just frozen. I let my hand drop.

How could I make him understand that the duke meant him no harm by hiring my brother? "Guy is trying to protect me and my family," I said. "You know the kind of man he is. He's helping John. Now, will you please sit down? I really want to talk to you. It's important."

Percy's face paled. "Good night, Lady Eleanor," he said, and exited the room.

CHAPTER 37

May 1856

True to his word, Guy exerted his influence on my father. "Parliament needs you. The bill won't pass without your involvement. Stanhope's counting on you. So am I. And you must see your donated paintings at the opening of the summer exhibition tomorrow."

And no one said "No" to the Duke of Woodford. So, we left again the following day for London. The servants hadn't finished closing up our town house before we returned to it.

Papa was as enthusiastic now as he had been despairing the day before. The bill must pass. Only he could help. Guy had truly convinced him that my father's strident opinions were valued and necessary in Parliament. I was grateful.

But I wondered about Percy. He left at first light, without a note. It felt too much like Vienna, and I worried about him all day.

Even though my own heart was heavy, I tried to keep my conversation light for my friend. "I'm getting rather good at packing and unpacking," I told Charlotte. "Is this what it was like to travel on tour with Mr. Felsted?"

Charlotte laughed. She seemed in good spirits. John had whispered with Charlotte all evening. I suspect he might have taken another long walk with her, if Percy and John had not left for London first thing in the morning.

The rest of us, including Matthew and Georgiana, took the train.

It had a Jenny Lind steam engine. Adorable. Tiny, elegant, yet powerful, like the Crampton locomotive we took in France. Which reminded me of Percy.

"Why would they want to ride?" I asked Matthew. "The train is so much easier."

"Shelford needed the exercise," Matthew said, exchanging a look with Guy. "And you know how John is about horses right now."

"Is he going to start a stable?" I asked.

"He might," Guy said. "I'll keep him busy in London, though."

Mama pulled me into the emptiest section of the passenger car. "We need a mother-daughter conversation," she said, "And this train ride might be long enough."

She slid beside me on the bench. I was trapped.

"First of all, you and the duke seemed quite comfortable last night. You spoke for a long time. And gave him leave to hold your hand. We all noticed."

"Yes," I watched the landscape moving by slowly outside the window. Smoke from the train billowed back. I would have to change as soon as we reached London.

"And now you're calling him by his Christian name," she said.

"Yes."

"Eleanor. Tell me everything. You know I love gossip."

I smiled. "We are not engaged. He has feelings of a…complicated nature for someone else, and we agreed that we both prefer to find a love match."

"Ridiculous," Mama said. She waved her hand.

The train jerked forward and began moving. It picked up speed.

"You have a love match," I said.

"Yes, but you're perfect for each other," Mama replied.

"Nevertheless. We both feel… He feels…"

"Ha!" Mama said. "I knew it."

The train rattled along. I was not going to give her any more information than I had to.

"It's Shelford, isn't it?"

"He is a scoundrel," I said.

"But you love him."

"Papa and Percy could never get along. How could I marry Percy?"

"Pish," Mama said. "Your father loves to argue. He needs Shelford to contradict him. Otherwise, he'd never know his own mind. Like vinaigrette. Or salad dressing."

"Percy is not salad dressing."

Mama fussed with her dress. "I do wish you would spend more time with Cook. Oil and vinegar don't combine. They repel each other yet form the most delicious salad dressing when shaken up. Then add a little spice. It's why I married your father."

"Because he repels you?"

"Because he was spicy," Mama said. "Even as a vicar."

I wished she would end this discussion. Some things I did not want to hear.

"So what is Shelford?" she asked. "And what is His Grace?"

I tried to think in terms my mother understood. "Guy is steady and reliable. Like boiled potatoes. The same every time."

Mama nodded. "Or dry toast."

"Percy is Christmas gravy," I said. I refused to explain that one to her. I leaned my head against the rattling edge of the train's window and thought about him for the rest of the ride into London.

I had refused the Duke of Woodford. The kind of marriage I had dreamed about for years. I hadn't so much refused him as talked him out of it before he could propose. Reminded him of another option.

So here I was again. No obstacles. I just had to wait for Percy to come to his senses and propose. Again.

Because Percy hadn't understood my conversation with the duke. If his reaction in the drawing room were any indication, Percy thought I was engaged. And he was unlikely to propose to a woman he thought was engaged to the man he respected most in the world.

We reached our town house in time to refresh ourselves, have a light tea, and change into something formal for dinner. We settled into the drawing room as we waited. Cook had not expected to serve a full meal tonight. Papa opened his newspapers to pass the time. He had begun to read them again after our arrival in town.

"What the devil?" he exclaimed.

My heart sank. Not another cartoon. This would be the death of him. Of me. Of our family. We would take the morning train tomorrow back to Barrington Hall and never return to London. It was a minor miracle we had come today.

"Look at this." Papa shook the newspaper toward us. "Can you believe it?"

I recognized the style of drawing instantly. Another satirical cartoon. The caption read, "England's Art Savior." Papa was drawn with a halo over his head.

Oh no.

Paintings surrounded my father. Portraits. The exact ones he had purchased and donated. No one knew that except our family.

Below the cartoon, another editorial ran. "Lord Barrington generously donated several pieces of art to Lord Stanhope's summer exhibition in an effort to underscore the need for a portrait gallery. The importance of the Old Masters cannot be overstated. So, too, the importance of the bill before Parliament this year cannot be overlooked..." and the article went on in fervent praise of my father and urged passage of the bill.

Papa had tears in his eyes. "Same author. Same illustrator."

We all knew who they were. Percy and John.

CHAPTER 38

I couldn't ascertain Percy's feelings if he went into hiding. John came over the next day to help Papa and Guy oversee the sealing of crates and transfer of art from our town house to the National Gallery. Percy did not.

All was forgiven. My father was in high spirits and working hard. Yet, Percy stayed away.

My worries of the day before multiplied. Percy was avoiding me, and I didn't know why. I had several guesses. Some made me angry, others made me frustrated. Others gave me hope. But I sat in the library obsessing over reasons and listening to boots stomp endlessly up and down the stairs until I wanted to throw my book at the wall. Finally, I went to watch my father at work upstairs.

The summer art exhibition opened that evening. Lord Stanhope wanted to use the event to create momentum for the passage of the bill before Parliament.

"They'll see how crowded it is," Papa panted, as he nailed another crate shut. He didn't trust anyone to do the work but himself. "Must pass the bill. That cartoon created momentum. Brilliant, boys. Absolutely brilliant."

My father hovered over the men each time they lifted a crate into a waiting carriage. He intended to walk beside the carriages later as they made their way to the National Gallery.

I pulled John aside. "Did Guy speak to you about working for him?"

He wiped his brow. "Yes. Generous terms."

"Did you accept?"

"Yes," John said. "Grateful, too. Means I can marry."

"What about your stables?" I asked.

"I'll be in London," he said. "Working with the Foreign Office, mainly. No stables. Look, Elle, why so many questions?"

I gestured to a sofa. "Can you rest for a moment? Can Papa spare you?"

John shrugged.

"I'm worried that Percy may be upset if you work for Guy instead of him."

"He can't retire his steward. You know that," John said. "Shelford's too sentimental."

"Will you ask? Tell him Guy's offered you a position and see how he responds," I said.

"You want me to work for Shelford instead of the Duke of Woodford?" John shook his head.

"I know he may not pay as much, but you'd be in the country. You might have more time, the chance to breed stallions," I said. "And you and Percy are never apart."

"Has to happen sometime. That's what marriage means," John said. "I've got to get back to Father. He's a maniac."

I walked to the door with John and put a hand on his arm. I tried to put every bit of the urgency I felt into my voice. "Please. Will you do this for me? Will you ask Percy? He may change his mind about retiring his steward."

"I'll ask him, but Miss Harwich is my concern now, not Shelford. His Grace has given me a rare chance and I don't mean to turn it down. Can't wait around much longer, or Romford will propose."

"Where is Percy? Is he helping at the National Gallery?" I asked.

"Something like that," John said. "Father needs me."

I paced and paced. How long would it take John to find Percy? When would he leave? He'd have to help my father finish sealing and loading the crates first. Finally, I went down to the kitchen to find my mother.

"How do you make vinaigrette?" I asked her.

Mama rushed over and hugged me. "Did you and Shelford quarrel? Thomas and I have quite forgiven him. Cook? Cook? Where is the lettuce?"

So, I learned how to mix oil and vinegar and add spices. Mama, Mrs. Harwich, Charlotte, and I had a lovely salad for a light luncheon.

⚜

Late that afternoon, I could hear heavy footsteps on the stairs.

"Elle! Elle! Where are you?"

I put down my book and left the library. "John? Over here."

He ran and picked me up. He twirled me around. "You were right." He set me down. "Come on." He dragged me into the library, checked to ensure we were alone, and slammed the door.

"You spoke with Percy?" I asked.

"Offered me a job on the spot. Said he'd match wages. He can't afford that. I said I'd tell him what he can afford. But I can live in the country, close to him, and he's fine if I breed horses. Interested in them, too, actually."

I clapped my hands, just like Mama. "And Charlotte? Does he know you mean to propose? Do you have somewhere to live?"

"Worked it all out," John said. "He was eager to help."

"He always is," I said, feeling a rush of pride.

"This won't be awkward for you? Having me at the estate next to Shelford?" he asked.

I felt a surge of hope. Had Percy told him that he intended to propose to me as well? Did John think I would mind having him live nearby? Or having my brother work for my husband?

"No," I said. "I couldn't be happier for you. Have you talked with Mrs. Harwich yet?"

"Day ago. But she said I had to wait to talk to Miss Harwich until I had an income to support her."

"Why are we still talking? She's in the drawing room," I said.

John tore open the doors and bounded down the stairs. I followed after him. I could see him hesitate at the entrance to the drawing room. Mama and Mrs. Harwich glanced up from their embroidery. Charlotte lowered her book.

"Son," Mama said, "your boots are filthy."

He ran into the room and knelt in front of Charlotte. She gasped.

"Charlotte. May I call you Charlotte? Elle calls you Charlotte, so I think of you as Charlotte, but you've never given me leave to call you Charlotte. But you may call me John. Please call me John. But may I call you Charlotte?" John paused.

Charlotte closed her book without marking the place. "Yes." Her head was tilted to one side in the shy manner that she had, but she held his gaze.

Mama and I exchanged a look of glee. We were both restraining ourselves, and it was difficult. Mrs. Harwich set down her embroidery hoop gently. My mother simply dropped hers into her basket.

"Shelford hired me as his steward. I'll be in Cambridgeshire after the Season and maybe sooner, and there's an empty estate, and he needs someone to look after it. Hired me. I could use a wife. Dash it." He turned toward Mrs. Harwich. "I have an income now. I mean, enough income. A larger income. Enough for a wife. And horses."

Mrs. Harwich nodded.

Charlotte took his hands. "Yes, John." She beamed at him.

John gazed at Charlotte with an earnest expression. "Will you marry me?"

Mrs. Harwich smothered a grin.

"I believe she already answered you," Mama said. "Twice. Now, go take a walk. Without a chaperone. You're engaged."

John stood up, looking dazed at his own good fortune.

Mama and I laughed. She began to shoo the rest of us out of the drawing room. "A long walk. Somewhere with tall trees and bushes." Mama winked at Charlotte, who blushed. "And hold hands. At the least."

I climbed the stairs, running my hand along the smooth banister. John and Charlotte were engaged, finally. I wandered back to the library, grabbed a book, and flopped inelegantly into a chair.

I had been right. Percy had been concerned about John working for the Duke of Woodford instead of himself. Now that the issue was resolved, would he be at ease? Would he understand the message I was sending through John?

I tried to read for several minutes. I set my unread book aside.

Surely, he would understand. If I were engaged to Guy, I would not have sent John over to work for him. Percy must understand. He must know that I was not engaged.

Maybe John had told him. Maybe he asked John.

I curled deep into the chair and thought about Percy.

Perhaps he was right about my father. I had been so young when Uncle died, and everything seemed so frightening. Although he was eccentric, Papa was not insane. No one had tried to take the estate. He had recovered quickly this time. More quickly than ever.

Perhaps Papa needed people. Perhaps hiding away was the real cause of his melancholy for those two years we had stayed in Essex. Perhaps Percy understood my father better than I did, because he was so much like him.

Percy.

I wanted to be engaged, too. I wanted to take long, unchaperoned walks through Hyde Park when it was not a fashionable hour.

I sighed and stared at the clock. Nearly time for dinner.

Why hadn't Percy come over with John? Was he too busy,

preparing for the exhibit? Or was he upset with me? After all, I had not answered him in the garden. Why should he risk a second proposal? And he had almost asked me to marry him in Vienna. He thought he had. So, would it be his second or his third attempt at asking for my hand? Would a man offer three times?

I had not really spoken to him since that afternoon in the gardens. Since he offered himself. He had avoided me, refused to speak to me in the drawing room, and then he'd left for London the next morning. If Percy could love deeply, then he could hurt deeply.

I never wanted to hurt him again. But I needed him to at least talk to me.

I went upstairs to pick a dress. I wanted to look unforgettable when Percy came to his senses.

CHAPTER 39

I rode with my parents to the exhibit. John hired a carriage to escort the Harwiches.

Lord Stanhope had arranged for the National Gallery to host the Royal Academy's summer exhibit this year.

We entered under a set of archways. Tall marble columns decorated light blue walls. Corinthian columns. Just like the folly in Schönbrunn. I couldn't wait to see if I'd have a chance to tell Percy or whether he would tell me first.

The domed ceiling reminded me of the embassy in Paris with its medallions and ornate rosette designs. The geometric pattern below the ceiling intrigued me. Where was it from? I wanted to sketch it. And the mosaics on the floors. I drank it all in.

Stairs led in several directions. Percy loitered alone to one side, waiting for the exhibition to open. While Her Grace and Lady Shelford spoke, Lady Octavia chattered without drawing breath, and Guy pretended not to listen. He fixed his gaze on a point over Lady Octavia's head, but I could see him glancing down at her and then looking away again.

In contrast, John tilted his head down toward Charlotte, never taking his eyes off her. He laughed loudly at everything she said.

Percy seemed to lean on his walking stick at a precarious angle. I felt a thrill at the sight of him. He had no handkerchief at all, and his watchchain hung without a watch on it. I felt a surge of love. This was Percy. Unpredictable. Distractable. Irascible. Devoted. Compassionate. Hopefully, mine.

I left my family and went over to him. I wore a periwinkle silk dress with a light lace overlay on the sleeves and shoulders. I had matching light blue ribbons in my auburn hair and earrings of tiny tasseled pearls. I'd selected a gold shawl with an indistinct paisley pattern embroidered into it. The corset pulled in at the waist and flared out at the hips to create an elegant silhouette. I'd made sure to wear a bracelet of roped pearls that matched my earrings on one arm. I wanted everything perfect tonight.

A gleaming Roman locket lay just in the hollow of my neck. I wore a matching golden bracelet on the other arm.

He stared at my evening gown. "Why do you wear those things? I can see your shoulders. And your neck. And—a lot more."

"Nonsense. That's why the lace is there," I said. I had dressed so carefully, just for him. I'd spent the last two days thinking about the moment when I would see him. Hoping every minute that he'd walk through the door of my parents' town house. This was not the reaction I wanted. Hoped for. Expected.

Percy swallowed. He began to spin the signet ring on his smallest finger. "I like your day dresses better. The ones that go up to your neck."

"I haven't shown you my necklace yet." I leaned forward so he could see the markings on it. "I believe it's a Roman Cross. But I'm not sure about the markings. I've wanted to ask you."

"Eleanor," Percy said in a hoarse voice. He wobbled unevenly as he tried to back away from me. "Please don't."

I wasn't sure what to make of his reaction. He wanted to get away from me for some reason, but I didn't know which one.

"I'm sorry," I said. "I thought of you when I found it in Florence."

He stopped and leaned again on his walking stick.

"What happened to your leg?" I asked.

He hesitated. "Fell off my horse."

"I'm so sorry. Did she spook?" I tried to peek at his leg. I couldn't ascertain anything through the fabric of his suit. "How badly injured are you?'

"Not bad," Percy said.

"When did you fall?" I asked.

"On the way to London."

"Oh." When he rode like a madman, or so John had said. They'd had to stop and exchange horses halfway.

We heard voices echoing around us. I glanced around the entrance hall. "I'm eager to see the exhibit."

He scowled at me.

"Percy, what is wrong?" I asked.

"Lord Shelford," he said.

I took a step backward. "Pardon?"

Percy limped toward the main stairs and the roped-off entrance of the exhibit. "I said, Lady Eleanor, call me Lord Shelford."

I didn't understand Percy's cold behavior. I had sent John to make sure he knew I was not engaged, but he apparently didn't realize the truth. Or he did, but he was angry with me for another reason. There were so many possibilities. Regardless, I did not intend to let him walk away from me. Not now. Not again.

I grabbed at the first thought that came to mind and took Percy's arm to stop him. "Lord Shelford, did you hear my brother is recently engaged? A few hours ago."

He threw my hand off his arm. "Yes," he said.

I felt an almost physical pain at Percy's rejection. "I guess they don't need our help anymore." I tried to smile.

"They never did, Lady Eleanor," he said. He turned away from me, moving slowly toward the stairs again. The sound of his walking stick on the marble floor reverberated throughout the entrance.

A cold draft blew across my shoulders as someone opened the doors of the gallery. I pulled my shawl around myself with one hand. I grabbed Percy's arm with the other. I swung him toward me. "No, Percy. I did not ask you to call me Lady Eleanor."

He wobbled and nearly fell. His emerald green eyes lit with anger. "Look, Elle, you cannot call him 'Guy' and call me 'Percy.'"

I reared back in shock and let go of his arm. "Why does it matter what I call him?"

Percy began hobbling up the stairs toward the entrance again. Trying to get away from me. He clenched his jaw. "Because I will not have a married woman call me by my Christian name."

I almost sagged with relief. He was angry because he didn't understand. At least, I hoped that was the only reason. I spoke to his back as he walked away from me. "I'm not married. I'm not getting married. Guy and I are not engaged."

Percy stopped abruptly, turning toward me. His walking stick slid out from under him, and he started to collapse. He scrambled to find his balance. "Truly?"

I put an arm under his shoulder. "Truly."

"In that case." He looked at me for a long moment, then slid his arm around my waist. "I could use some help walking."

A footman retrieved Percy's walking stick and handed it to me. We made slow progress toward the entrance. One stair at a time. He leaned heavily on me. I loved the feel of his hand around my waist. Once again, here I was, in a completely inappropriate position, barely on the edge of social decency, in an increasingly crowded art gallery foyer. Because of Percy. It felt like coming home.

"Why the hand holding, heads together, staring into each other's eyes, sitting close together on the couch?" Percy demanded. "It was torture! You said, 'Yes,' Eleanor. I heard you. You said it was an honor. He went to speak with your father. He tried to hire your brother away from me. You had me fooled."

Percy's leg really must have been injured. Or his head.

We made slow progress.

Of course, he might have been enjoying the situation, too. It reminded me of the day we met in the ballroom.

"If you had eavesdropped on the entire conversation, instead of merely the end—" I began.

Percy interrupted. "I'm listening now." He stared at me intently. "Tell me everything." His hand at my waist once again pulled me toward him as he lost his balance.

Our cheeks were nearly touching. Percy. Always living on the edge of propriety. "He asked me to be his sister, as it were. We agreed that we...well, we agreed that I...this is very awkward." I stopped to help him up a stair.

"Go on," Percy said. His eyes held a mixture of caution and hopefulness. "I like it when you're awkward."

We stumbled onto the landing.

I turned my head toward him and stopped. We were at the roped-off entrance. I peered into his eyes. "We agreed that once one knows what love is like, one cannot settle for anything less than a love match."

Percy teetered on his unstable leg. Again. It was probably a ruse to get me to move closer to him. It worked.

"And do you know what love is like?" Percy searched my face intently.

I nodded. This was indeed awkward. Although we were early, there were still several people in the gallery entrance hall.

I looked at Percy's disheveled hair, his bent glasses, the rumpled vest. The vulnerability and yearning in his eyes that echoed the feelings in my own heart. "I have known for a very long time," I said. "Years."

A gleam entered Percy's eyes. Confidence, and a hint of mischief.

Percy smiled at the gentleman holding the rope. "Lord Stanhope, may I show Lady Eleanor the Taddei Tondo? Before the crowds come."

"Of course, my boy." Lord Stanhope undid the rope. "Anything for you."

Percy quickened his pace.

"What did you do?" I asked as we made our way through an

ornate set of wooden doors and into a large exhibit room. I could see a large crate in the middle. "You didn't."

"I did."

"If we weren't in full view of my family, I would hug you," I said. "Thank you. My father actually cried when he saw the new cartoon and read John's editorial in favor of the portrait gallery."

Percy tried to walk even faster. It didn't work. His cane slipped again. He tapped the floor with it. "I think I can manage to find a place where we are not in full view of your family." He winked at me. "Come on."

Step by step we worked our way toward the middle of the room. Percy's hand at my waist had slipped a little lower so it slid closer to my hip. Scandalously close.

Papa's donated portraits and paintings from Europe were displayed all around. In the center stood the Taddei Tondo, still in the crate, shining brilliantly white.

"It's stunning," I said. I examined it closely. A small plaque read, "A gift to the Royal Academy from Lord Barrington." A tear spilled onto my cheek, and I brushed it away. "Where's a potted palm?"

"Even better." Percy led me by the hand as he limped around the tall crate.

When we moved behind it, the crate blocked our view of the hallway and entrance to the gallery entirely. He grinned and waited.

I threw my arms around Percy's neck. He responded by crushing me tightly, his hands pressing me into him.

I pulled away enough to whisper, "Thank you. For my father. My family. Myself."

Percy. We understood, needed, loved each other. Oh, I had missed him. His compassion and kindness. His exuberance and ready laugh. Knowing he trusted me and that I could trust him to keep my secrets. Being able to share my worries and have Percy anticipate my fears. Knowing I could comfort him and that he would always protect me. Having him push me to be my best instead of hiding my talent. Scheming together to help John and Charlotte. This was love. And we were about to look even more disheveled.

Our faces were close. Close enough to gaze into each other's eyes. Nearly lip to lip. I didn't mind that he was nearly the same height.

Percy held me with a firm grip. Clearly, he had no intention of letting go.

If he had, he would have fallen to the ground because of his injured leg. Still, his eyes darted to my lips. I felt my pulse quicken.

Percy pulled me toward him with the eagerness of a starving man at Christmas dinner.

I put one hand on his chest. "I can smell your gravy cologne," I murmured.

"Bay Rum. Very dignified."

I could feel his heart beating as quickly as my own.

"I'm very sorry about the cartoon," he whispered.

"They're going to let other people in," I said, working my fingers into his hair.

Percy cupped my face with one hand. "But you need to know that I have also loved you for a very, very long time."

"I can hear footsteps."

He traced my lips with his finger. "I have so many romantic things planned that I was going to say if I ever got the chance. Again. I memorized more poems."

"Later. Kiss me, Percy."

He closed the gap in an instant, covering my lips with his own. I returned the pressure. I trailed my fingers down his neck. Percy deepened the kiss, running his hands down my back, bringing me closer to him. I wanted to melt in his arms. I ran my fingers through the soft curls in his hair. The kiss gentled, and he softened his hold. He slowly broke away.

"Will you marry me, Elle? This is not the romantic way I imagined it, but I cannot wait. Please." Percy covered the hand on his chest with his own. "I found fault with you in Vienna. I imposed myself on you in the gardens and then sulked for days."

I traced the shadow of a scar on his cheek where the vine had lashed him. "You are terrible at proposals, Percy."

"But I'm asking you now. A love match. I will cater to your whims. Far more than either of our fathers ever has. Just say 'Yes' to me. Not Woodford."

"I think you're jealous," I said. "For no reason."

"Yes. Yes, I am. Wildly," he said. His eyes blazed. "I nearly broke my neck riding here when I thought you were engaged to the duke. Your father is not insane. He's eccentric and will be in and out of fashion like the sun sets and rises. And I don't care. But I understand why your uncle went mad with grief when his wife died. I thought I lost you, and that it was my own fault." His voice was thick with emotion.

I covered Percy's hand with my own. "Yes, Percy. If you're going to break your neck, or your leg, or any body parts, for me, then yes. I will marry you."

Percy brought my hand to his lips and kissed the palm slowly. He moved to the wrist. "Do you know why I love the Taddei Tondo?" he asked.

"Mmm? No," I said, too distracted to wonder.

"Because the crate is so large," he said. He traced the edge of my jaw and down to my Roman necklace. He lifted it up and examined it carefully.

The touch of his hands on bare skin sent shivers through me. I closed my eyes.

"I lied to you," Percy said. "I prefer your evening gowns to your day dresses. If you're not engaged to Woodford." He leaned down to kiss me again.

"I'm engaged to you," I said, barely able to breathe.

Percy rested his forehead against mine. "Then let's get married. Soon."

I could hear voices moving along the hallway. Soon my parents and others would arrive at the Taddei Tondo. "We should wait until your leg is healed, so you can walk down the aisle."

Percy slipped his arm around my waist, snugged me into his side, and pressed a tender kiss to my lips. "Oh no, I like things just the way they are." He held me, and we wobbled a little because of his unstable leg.

Percy put his hand behind my head, drawing me closer into his embrace. I rested against his chest, and he held me gently.

"I have more poems memorized, *amore mio.*"

I turned my face up until our lips were an inch apart. "No more poetry in public, Percy. But I will sing duets with you anytime."

Percy grinned. He kissed me again and again until we heard the voices come in the exhibit room. I was a little out of breath as we slowly moved back around the crate to greet my parents.

EPILOGUE

Mid-May 1856

Lucy held the invitation in her hand. Eleanor wrote so beautifully. August first. Eleanor's wedding would be August first. That was almost three months away. Surely Lucy would be married before then.

She hadn't even sent out invitations. She had been betrothed for months before Eleanor, but Walter was such a dear. He wanted everything perfect for her. And perfect meant waiting for him to select the right paper, which he still hadn't done.

Perhaps Lucy would show him Eleanor's invitation. If it was good enough for an earl, it should be good enough for a viscount. Walter hated comparisons like that. She would have to be careful. No, she would not show him the invitation. Perhaps he received his own and was already thinking about it.

Lucy glanced at the next letter. She recognized Walter's writing. He probably wrote to say that he had selected a paper. Lucy unsealed the letter, unfolded it, and began reading.

Dear Miss Maldon,

Talk of Grand Tours will not leave my head. I cannot marry without having traveled on my own. Surely, you want this for me. My father's death prevented me from having a complete Grand Tour, but I can travel for six months without causing a great hardship to the estate.

My brother, Peter, will accompany me. He finishes at Cambridge this year and we've always planned to travel together. We leave immediately.

I want to spare you the pain of parting, so I will already be gone when you read this.

Walter, Lord Chelmsford

Lucy stormed across the hall to the library. "Papa!"

He was not there. She fought the rising panic. She'd already lost George. She could not lose her chance at marriage.

She yelled again. "Papa!" She marched through the corridor to his study. "Papa!"

She walked around the entire ground floor.

"Where is he, Finch?" Lucy asked. She tried to maintain a calm demeanor.

"I believe he is visiting Lord Barrington to view his art."

Lucy drew on her gloves and hat. "I need a carriage now, Finch. If you please."

She tapped her foot. The panic crept higher and higher.

"Lucy?" Her aunt wandered into the entryway. "What is amiss, dear heart?"

Lucy studied her aunt. Aunt Ellen liked to gossip.

"Nothing. Just a missive for Papa. I will return in a few hours."

Aunt Ellen beamed at Lucy and went back to her morning room. The footmen stared at Lucy. They liked to gossip, too. Best to take a maid with her.

She went outside to the front steps. Finally, a carriage pulled up. Lucy realized she was alone and hurried inside.

"And where is my maid?" Lucy looked around.

A small, young girl rushed forward. "Here, miss."

Lucy whirled without speaking and went outside. She ran down the steps and into the carriage. She tapped her fingers on the door while she waited for her maid to follow. The maid seemed to climb the steps more slowly than usual. "Can you hurry, please. Thank you, Jane."

The carriage began to move. Lucy held the crushed letter in her hand. She smoothed it out, folded it, and put it into her reticule. Everything was settled. The marriage contract signed. This couldn't be happening.

Lucy rode in silence until the carriage arrived at Barrington Hall. She scrambled down the steps, then caught herself. She moved serenely toward the front door, climbing the steps graciously.

Once inside and announced, Lucy peered into the drawing room. Happy couples. Lord Dunmore and his wife talked with their heads close together. They always seemed so happy. They preferred each other's company to anyone else's during every dinner party.

Eleanor and Lord Shelford stood scandalously close as they perused a set of fashion plates. Eleanor gazed up at him.

Lucy watched Lord Shelford put down the paper and stare back at Eleanor.

Lucy pulled her shawl around herself. Walter never looked at her like that. He hardly noticed her at all.

John Barrington sat on a sofa with his betrothed, Miss Harwich. They held hands and Miss Harwich had her arm threaded through John's.

"Please join us!" Eleanor called, catching Lucy's eye. "We are making plans for the wedding. You can help decide which dress to order." Eleanor held out her hands.

Lucy pasted on a smile. How long could she pretend? Until she

264 LISA H. CATMULL

knew Walter's abandonment was certain. "Oh, yes! May I see the pictures?"

"That is our cue to leave, gentlemen," John said. He got to his feet reluctantly.

Lord Shelford pulled Eleanor into a quick hug.

Lucy turned her head away. "Could you please tell my father I am here?" Lucy said sweetly. She would count the minutes until she could leave.

"Come, Lucy, what kind of dress will you order? Where will you have it fitted? Are you coming back up to London with us? We will be there until the wedding."

"I have not decided on a dress. Show me what you like." Not enough lace, Lucy thought, as she considered Eleanor's selections. Miss Harwich's were even simpler. Much worse.

Adeline ran into the room.

"Escaped, have you?" Lady Dunmore scooped her up. "We must have a new dress for her, too."

"Will you have bridesmaids?" Lucy asked.

"Oh, we have not decided. Percy's sister is too old, but Adeline is too young."

"Fifteen is not too old to be a bridesmaid," Lucy said.

"Will you have bridesmaids?" Eleanor asked.

She thought of her own family. No sisters. Walter had no sisters. Rachel definitely would not wear anything Lucy would want her to wear.

"Probably not," Lucy said.

"Does Lord Chelmsford have a ring for you?" Eleanor examined her hands.

"No, he wants to pick out the perfect ring himself in London."

Miss Harwich examined the fashion plates. "John does not even care whether I have a ring. He only wants the banns read. He says waiting until August is the hardest thing to do."

And Walter had run away to prolong their wedding date. Lucy's stomach knotted.

"Serving the traditional cake is the hardest thing Percy has agreed to do. We both would rather have an Austrian torte. That is true cake," Eleanor said.

Miss Harwich nodded.

Lucy wondered what it tasted like or how it differed. Why did Eleanor always know more than her? She felt so inadequate.

Mercifully, Lucy's father arrived at the door of the drawing room. "Were you looking for me, sweets?"

"Papa, yes, we do need you at home. I am sorry, Eleanor, but I must leave all of you to your preparations."

Eleanor studied her carefully. "Please, come back as soon as you can, Lucy. I do not see you often enough. Shall I walk with you to the entrance hall?"

"No, I am well," Lucy lied.

She made it inside the carriage and watched the footman close the door. "Chelmsford left England this morning, Papa. Without me."

"Oh, sweets. But I already paid him the settlement," her father said.

"Well, he is gone. With his brother. For six months."

"Then he will be back. Why the distress?" Mr. Maldon asked.

"How am I supposed to get married with him in Europe?"

"So you wait." Papa scratched his nose. "You are still a viscountess in the end."

"You do not understand." Lucy turned away and stared out the window. "What if he does not come back?"

⊗⋇⊗

Lucy sat in St. George's church with her father, Rachel, and her aunt. August first. At least the banns had been read in London, as Eleanor and her betrothed had spent the rest of the Season there.

By now, everyone knew she'd been abandoned by Lord Chelmsford. He had sent another letter in June saying that he would stay through the summer and fall and return in the spring. That would make a full year that he'd been gone. She was betrothed and could not break the betrothal without ruining her reputation, so she had to accept the postponement.

The humiliation had subsided somewhat. Lucy did not believe he would return until he made a complete tour of Europe. Probably two years, like the Barringtons.

It hurt to attend Eleanor's wedding, but with so few guests invited, Lucy wanted to come. She and Rachel sat with Eleanor's family, and the Duke of Woodford sat with Lord Shelford's family. She loved Eleanor, but this was exquisite pain.

Mr. Maldon had insisted on coming to London before the wedding to see Lord Barrington's paintings at the Royal Academy's summer exhibit. Her father had listed off the names of the artists— Titian, van Dyck, Raphael, Botticelli, Bellini. Lucy tried to concentrate on the unusual names to distract herself from the overwhelming emotion she felt. She needed to focus on something wholly unrelated to marriage. Titian. Botticelli. Bellini.

But the names reminded her of Italy. Of Europe. Of Walter.

Music began to play, and Lucy turned her head. Lord Barrington marched down the aisle with one bride on each arm. Here was something to distract her. Nothing to do with Walter. She could focus on the gown.

Eleanor's dress sparkled in the sunlight streaming through the church windows. Golden spangles shimmered along the ornate flowers worked in silver thread along the hem. Delicate rows of lace points covered the sleeves. The bodice dazzled with a golden tulle overlay.

Neither Eleanor nor Miss Harwich seemed to understand how large the current fashion trend would allow sleeves to puff. They could have easily layered more rows of lace, and there were hardly any tassels along the hem. At least Eleanor had flowers on her gown and in her hair.

What kind of gown would she have worn? Lucy lost all interest in studying the fashion.

Miss Harwich walked on the other side, and Lucy didn't try to see her gown. Not enough lace, perhaps. She favored the simpler white that Queen Victoria brought into style.

Lucy tried to fill her deep longing with images of her own wedding gown. How would she design it? Where would she go when Walter returned next year? How much would fashion change between now and then? Would he return? She pushed the thought aside.

John and Lord Shelford waited at the front, dressed in long coat-tails with paisley vests and dark trousers. Silk neckties covered perfectly starched collars.

Walter would look well in his wedding attire. Should he wear white trousers instead of black? Which would be the style next year? His dark hair would go well with a dark suit. Perhaps even better than the stablehand might have.

But she had promised herself never to think of George again. Never to feel sorry for herself. George was gone, and there was nothing she could do.

She would love and cherish Walter, since that was who Papa had chosen for her. She would embrace her position in the upper class and make Papa proud. He gave her everything she ever asked for. She could give him this one thing. If Walter would return.

Even from where she sat, Lucy could see the men holding their brides' hands tenderly. She could see John Barrington's foot tapping. He had always been impatient, even as a child when they played. Funny. She knew John and Matthew better than she knew Walter in a lot of ways, since she'd spent so much time with Eleanor and so little time at Chelmsford Hall.

After the rings were placed on the brides' fingers, Lucy took a deep sigh of relief. It was over. She watched the couples signing the wedding registry, hands on each other's backs. She studied her own bare hands. When would she wear a ring?

Now, just the wedding breakfast and they could leave. Of course, Eleanor could not have a simple breakfast. Lucy had heard of having an orchestra play at a wedding breakfast, but Eleanor engaged a complete choir orchestra, planned by Lord Shelford and Mrs. Harwich, playing for a larger, but still very elite, audience. There was no way Lucy could ever compete with that, regardless of her father's wealth.

But then the music began. Something changed inside Lucy as the melody played. Worry melted away, and something strong filled her. Determination. Walter would not make a fool of her. She would find a way to marry him. Soon.

Eleanor came to say goodbye before they left for their wedding trip. Fall and winter in Italy to complete Lord Shelford's Grand Tour. John Barrington and his new wife would manage the estates while Lady Shelford ran the household and renovated the dowager's cottage.

"Rachel, have you met Colonel Loughton and Mr. Kempton yet? You must hear about their upcoming trip. Loughton, where are you?" Eleanor glanced over her shoulder.

Lord Shelford and two men approached their table.

"Miss Maldon, Miss Wickford, my friend, the colonel, recently returned from the Crimea, and his friend, Mr. Kempton."

The men bowed. They were surprisingly young to have so much experience.

"They've been telling me about their involvement with a nursing school in Germany," Eleanor said.

"Fund raising, more like," Lord Shelford said. "For Miss Nightingale. You're quite the advocates."

"Oh!" Rachel said. "Are you acquainted with her?"

"Yes. Miss Nightingale needs more than funds, Shelford, though I thank you for your contribution," Mr. Kempton said.

Lord Shelford nodded.

"What we lack are women," Colonel Loughton said.

Everyone laughed.

"Truly," Mr. Kempton said. "We have to go to Germany to find women willing to train as nurses. And that won't help us here in London."

"You need Rachel," Eleanor said. "Come with us to Germany.

We could see you that far, on our way to Italy, and leave you at the school."

Rachel twisted her reticule in her lap. "I could never leave my mother."

"Great idea," Lord Shelford said. "Come with us as far as Germany. We'll stop in Mainz with the colonel and Mr. Kempton."

"Mainz?" Lucy asked. "That's where Walter wrote from."

Everyone turned their heads.

Lucy addressed herself to Mr. Kempton. "If you need women, I'll go." She turned in her seat. "Rachel, you've always wanted to learn more about medicine. Let's go together."

Rachel stared at her.

Lucy smiled at her father. "Papa? Walter is somewhere around there."

"He didn't give you his direction?" Lord Shelford asked.

Lucy shook her head.

Lord Shelford folded his arms. "And he calls himself a gentleman."

"Papa? Please?" Lucy asked. She was beginning to feel desperate as the truth sunk in. Walter didn't want her to find him. This might be harder than she imagined.

"Of course, sweet. Buy me a van Dyck and a Rubens. Perhaps a Rembrandt, if you can get to Italy. Mrs. Wickford? Can you spare Rachel?" Mr. Maldon asked.

"This is a wonderful idea, Lucy. You'd be a natural at nursing. Do consider it, Rachel," Eleanor said.

Mrs. Wickford smiled at Rachel. "I will be well enough at home, dear. I have plenty of friends to look after me."

Lord Shelford addressed himself to the colonel. "If you would be so kind as to give us your direction? I would like to see your training school."

"Of course." Colonel Loughton eyed Lucy and Rachel with interest.

Mr. Kempton dug through his pockets. "I believe I have my card here somewhere." He handed his card to Lord Shelford. "We can be reached at the address below."

Rachel let out a deep breath. "We already packed our trunks to come to London. We may as well continue on to Germany. I can't let Lucy have an adventure without me."

Lucy took her hands. "Thank you, Rachel!"

Lord Shelford came over to stand behind Eleanor. He put his hand on her back. Lucy felt even more determined. She wanted that kind of love. She wanted a besotted husband.

She needed to find Walter and convince him to keep his end of the bargain and marry her. She would find a way to make him fall in love with her. She would have a marriage of convenience for her father and a love match for herself.

Europe seemed like a good place to fall in love. She played nervously with her gown in her lap. Lucy's heart ached at the show of devotion between the couple.

Eleanor turned toward her husband. "Percy?"

"Am I already giving in to one of your schemes?" Lord Shelford gazed down at Eleanor.

"Perhaps we could extend our stay in Germany by just a week or two?" She smiled up at him.

"Of course. I am honor bound to indulge my bride's every wish." Lord Shelford studied Lucy and Rachel. "Are you serious about this? It's a real commitment. Attending nursing school in a foreign language. Do either of you speak German?"

"Anything," Lucy said. "I'll do whatever is needed."

"I can translate for you," Colonel Loughton said. "My sister is coming as well, so I'd already planned to translate for her."

Lord Shelford nodded. "Then I'll send word to my contacts in Frankfurt. Adjust our schedule."

"And find him," Eleanor added. "The no-account scoundrel who abandoned my dear friend."

Lucy felt hollow. Why would she even want to marry a man who ran away from her? But she had a signed contract. Papa had already paid Walter. Love could come later. In Italy perhaps. An extended honeymoon like Eleanor.

Lord Shelford grinned and bowed. "Please, Miss Maldon and Miss Wickford, will you accompany us on our wedding trip? It wouldn't be a Grand Tour unless someone invited themselves along at the last minute."

ALSO BY LISA H. CATMULL

Each book can be enjoyed as a stand-alone novel, or you can enjoy them as part of the Victorian Grand Tour Series.

An Engaged Grand Tour, Book 2 of the Victorian Grand Tour Series

She's engaged to his brother, but he can't help falling in love with her anyway.

Mining heiress Lucy Maldon is determined to track down her fiancé and make him fall in love with her, even if it means chasing him across the Continent.

Walter, Lord Chelmsford, has no intention of being found.

Peter Chelmsford lives in his brother's shadow. When his older brother decides to go on Grand Tour and leave his bride-to-be behind, Peter accompanies him. While Walter pursues other interests, it's up to Peter to keep his childhood friend safe from his brother.

But can Lucy ever forgive him for stealing her heart and breaking it at the same time?

A Disorderly Grand Tour, Book 3 of the Victorian Grand Tour Series

She's sworn she'll never marry him. He's sworn to change her mind.

Rachel Wickford has vowed to devote her life to nursing, like her heroine, Florence Nightingale. She'd rather avoid the heartache of love, but it's hard to evade the man who's already head over heels for her.

Colonel Curtis Loughton needs experienced nurses to help start Miss Nightingale's training program in London, but he needs a wife even more. He's willing's to wage war to win his true love's hand in marriage, but he's never encountered opposition like this before. It will take all his ingenuity and grit to prove his love is constant.

In a battle of wits, with a determined campaign on one side and underhanded insubordination on the other, can anyone claim victory, or will their hearts be the casualties?

An Attempted Engagement, Book 4 of the Victorian Grand Tour Series

Only one thing stands between Alice Loughton and the man of her dreams: her brother.

Frederick Kempton calls her his "little mouse." She's been shy and quiet ever since he met her at age three. But when timid Alice Loughton decides it's time to marry, there's only one man for her. The one man who doesn't frighten her. The only man she can talk to without wanting to run and hide. Her brother's hired secretary and closest friend.

But her brother knows Frederick Kempton too well, and he's not about to give his consent for a courtship, not when plenty of other men are pursuing Alice, too. And so obedient Alice, who has never broken a rule in her life, is forced to take drastic measures.

And she's dragged Freddie along with her. Can he walk the fine line between loyalty to his oldest friend and a chance to woo the woman he's secretly loved?

A swoony story of hidden messages, love letters, and stolen kisses

ABOUT THE AUTHOR

Lisa went with her family on BYU Study Abroad to Vienna when she was twelve years old. The college students voted her "Most Likely To Return Without Her Parents," and she did.

As an undergraduate at Dartmouth, she lived in Mainz, Germany, for three months, then lived in England during part of her senior year of college.

She's lived in seven states, four countries, and moved almost forty times. Lisa enjoys traveling, but her favorite journeys are in books.

She taught English and History for seven years before quitting to pursue screenwriting. None of her screenplays hit the theaters, but she met her future husband the day she moved to Los Angeles.

After leaving L.A., she decided to write books instead of movies. Lisa lives in Utah with her husband and two rambunctious children.

SOCIAL HIERARCHY IN THE
VICTORIAN ERA 1837-1901

Titles can be confusing because there are three ways to address people: (1) the way one addressed an envelope to them and the way someone announces their name formally, (2) the way one addressed a letter to them, and (3) the way one speaks to them. The graphics on the following pages illustrate the way one would address someone in speech.

I used examples to demonstrate. Victoria and Albert London are the hypothetical people. The title name are also London for our purposes, although the family name and title would not usually be the same.

Notes on the children of the aristocracy

Daughters of a duke, marquess, or earl are called Lady and their first name (Lady Victoria)

Daughters of a viscount or baron are called Miss, but not called Lady (Miss Victoria)

Younger sons of a duke or a marquess are called Lord and their FirstName, but they don't hold a title (Lord Albert)

Younger sons of an earl, viscount, or baron without titles are called Mr. (Mr. London)

Peerage and Titles Explained

Peers are the dukes, marquesses, earls, viscounts, and barons. They are the nobility and the title holders. They sit in the House of Lords.

A duke is called the Duke of a Place, like the Duke of London. Marquesses, earls, viscounts, and barons are always called Lord LastName, like Lord London. They are never called Baron Title or Baron LastName. It is the House of Lords, not the House of Marquesses, Earls, Viscounts, and Barons.

A baronet or knight is called Sir FirstName, like Sir Albert. His wife is called Lady LastName, like Lady London. The female equivalent of a knight is called a dame, and her husband is called Mr. LastName, like Mr. London.

Peers sat in the House of Lords and often attended Parliament. It often began January thirty-first and ended August twelfth, although it ended on July 29, 1856, the year this story takes place. Eleanor and Percy got married on August 1, 1856, after the Season ended for that year.

Although some families were in town in February, most Peers brought their families back after Easter. Parties, balls, excursions, and art exhibits were in full swing during May, June, and July.

Baronets and knights are not Peers and do not sit in the House of Lords.

Men often referred to other men by their title or last name only, like London, instead of Lord London or Albert.

Men and women did not usually call each other by their first name or given name. It was a sign of increasing intimacy or appropriate for childhood friends who had grown up together, like Lucy, Rachel, Eleanor, Walter, and Peter. Women might call each other by their first names once they became friends, like Alice, Rachel, and Lucy.

The oldest daughter was Miss LastName, like Miss London. Her younger sisters were Miss FirstName LastName, like Miss Victoria London and Miss Elizabeth London.

A nobleman often held more than one title. A duke might also be a marquess and an earl. An earl might also be a viscount. The oldest son or heir would be allowed to use the lesser title.

The *ton* was the Upper Crust that socialized in London. It was comprised of royalty, aristocracy, and members of the gentry. Some wealthy business owners or bankers were included as well.

Servants had a hierarchy of precedence, too. In the lower classes, some servants were called by their last names and others were called by their first names. The housekeeper and cook were called "Mrs." whether or not they were married.

And then there were the clergy. Oh, this is as complicated as everything else! It needs another page to explain…Here are some highlights. There are three forms of address for clergy as well.

For example, clergymen were never called "reverend" as their form of address, just as a title. The Reverend Albert London or the Reverend Deacon Albert London would be the formal address on an envelope, but in conversation or to his face he would be simply be called Deacon London or Mr. London, never Reverend London.

The archbishops and bishops sat in the House of Lords.

An archbishop was called "Your Grace" or "Archbishop."

Bishops, diocesan bishops, or suffragan bishops were called "My Lord" or "Bishop."

A Canon, Prebendar, or Archdeacon was called only by their title.

Other clergy in the Church of England were called "Mr." or by their position: vicar, rector, curate, chaplain, or dean. Someone might say, "Come on in, Vicar. It's good to see you, Mr. London," and be talking to the same person. He was the vicar, but he was also Mr. London. He was not Vicar London.

The illustrations on the following pages have the titles on the top and the names by which they were addressed on the bottom or to the side. Remember, this is the way one would talk to them in speech, not the way one would address an envelope. You would not use a formal title like "Earl" in conversation, like "Good day, Earl London," but would instead say, "Good day, Lord London."

Social Hierarchy in the Victorian Era
1837-1901

Presented in descending order of precedence (rank)

Royalty

Aristocracy

Duke	Duchess
His Grace	Her Grace

Marquess/Marquis	Marchioness
Lord London	Lady London

Earl	Countess
Lord London	Lady London

Viscount	Viscountess
Lord London	Lady London

Baron	Baroness
Lord London	Lady London

- The Duke and Duchess are never called Lord and Lady.
- For Lords and Ladies: the last name is taken from their title, not their family name.

Gentry

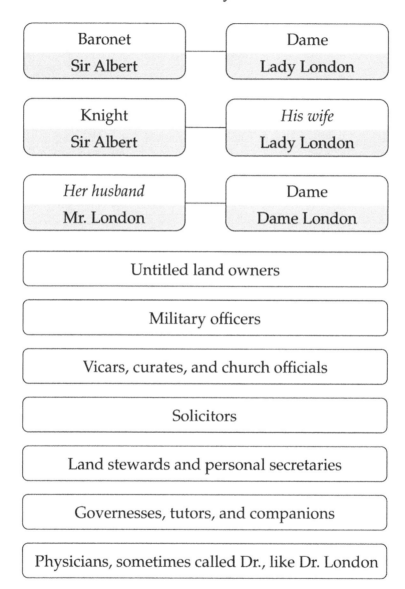

Baronet	Dame
Sir Albert	Lady London

Knight	*His wife*
Sir Albert	Lady London

Her husband	Dame
Mr. London	Dame London

Untitled land owners

Military officers

Vicars, curates, and church officials

Solicitors

Land stewards and personal secretaries

Governesses, tutors, and companions

Physicians, sometimes called Dr., like Dr. London

- Members of the gentry are called Mr. or Mrs./Miss unless specified otherwise
- Some men held more than one title. A man with a military rank might also be a knight or a baronet.

Middle/Merchant Class

Doctors, surgeons

Wealthy business owners, bankers

- The Upper Class usually called them by their last name only

---

Lower Class/Working Class

Housekeeper - Mrs. London

Cook - Mrs. London or Cook

Valet, butler - London

Lady's maid/abigail - Miss London or London

Coachman - Albert Coachman

Farm workers, tenants - London

- The housekeeper and butler were equals. The valet and lady's maid were equals.

Servants - Victoria or Albert

The poor - Victoria or Albert

Factory and shop workers - Victoria or Albert